13 ✗ 3/07 ✓ 3/07

BLOOD ON
THE WOOD

BLOOD ON
THE WOOD

GILLIAN LINSCOTT

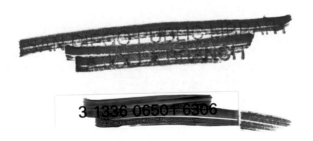

 St. Martin's Minotaur ✿ New York

www.minotaurbooks.com

Library of Congress Cataloging-in-Publication Data

Linscott, Gillian.
    Blood on the wood / Gillian Linscott.—1st St. Martin's Minotaur ed.
        p. cm.
    ISBN 0-312-33148-7
    EAN 978-0312-33148-1
    1. Bray, Nell (Fictitious character)—Fiction. 2. Women detectives—
England—Fiction. 3. Painting—Forgeries—Fiction. 4. Suffragists—
Fiction. 5. England—Fiction. I. Title.

    PR6062.I54B57 2004
    823'.914—dc22   2003069721

First published in Great Britain by Virago

First St. Martin's Minotaur Edition: May 2004

10 9 8 7 6 5 4 3 2 1

To Jane Jakeman,
who chose a picture for Nell to steal.

The Dolefull Dance and Song of Death

Can you dance *The Shaking of the Sheets,*
A dance that ev'ry one must do?

Sixteenth-century ballad

Introduction

THE INSPECTOR LEANED FORWARD, PAINFULLY POLITE. The constable prodded at a dead butterfly with the end of his pencil, not looking at us. It must have been dead for some days on the scratched table in this stuffy little room because its wing crumbled to dust as soon as the pencil touched it.

'What I don't entirely understand . . .' the inspector said. He paused. 'What I'm not entirely clear on, Miss Bray, was how you happened to find the body.'

'I opened the cabinet in the studio and it was there.'

Big black oak cabinet with the carvings of the murdered lady and the hanging man – not that I could see them in the dark, of course, but I could feel them in memory, knobbly and sharp under the fingers. Which wasn't relevant to what the police wanted. The butterfly had been a tortoiseshell, I think, or possibly a peacock. Hard to tell from the bright fragments that the constable was now stirring with his pencil. I looked up and met the inspector's eyes dishwater grey.

'So how did you come to be in the studio in the middle of the night?'

A long silence while I tried to think of a way out. Unsuccessfully.

He prompted me, 'Did Mr Venn know you were in his house?'

'No.'

'So you weren't staying as a guest?'

'No. I'm down in the field with the rest of the camp.'

A little wince at that, as if somebody had slid a dirty plate into the dishwater. The presence of a camp of young socialists was another complication he could have done without.

'So would you be kind enough to tell us what you were doing in Mr Venn's house in the middle of the night?'

I took a deep breath, not seeing any useful alternative to the truth.

'I was there to steal a picture.'

Chapter One

B Y THE END OF IT ALL, I'd got to know that picture very well. At the beginning, all I knew was its nationality.

'French,' Emmeline said, 'so you're probably the best person to handle it.'

We were sitting in her cluttered little office at our headquarters in Clement's Inn, just off the Strand. It was less than a year since our organisation had moved its headquarters from Manchester to London and since then things had been moving too fast to get unpacked properly.

'Not unless it talks,' I said. 'I speak the language, but I don't know anything about paintings.'

Emmeline disregarded that, as she tended to do with anything that got in the way of what she wanted. One of the secrets of her success.

'It's by Boucher.'

She looked at me and I looked back at her. I know now that I should have sat up, looked excited and said, 'You don't mean *the* Boucher?' But the name only rang the faintest of bells. To be honest, paintings have never been an enthusiasm. A friend says that's because I never stand still long enough to look at them, which may be true. But it wasn't time to think about that, because she was giving me my instructions.

'Probate's been granted on Mrs Venn's will so there's nothing to prevent us sending somebody down to collect it. I think you should call in to Christie's first and arrange to take it straight to them for a valuation. The solicitor thinks it might be worth as much as a thousand pounds, and we certainly need the money.'

The young man at Christie's was at least as beautiful as the things they sold. His hair was as fair as thistledown in the sun, hands moving when he talked as if on currents of some warm invisible sea. When I said the word 'Boucher' they wafted upwards above the tooled leather top of his desk, almost breaking the surface of his languid calm.

'You're quite certain it's by Boucher? What do you know about its provenance?'

I wasn't certain of anything.

'It was left to the Women's Social and Political Union by the late Mrs Philomena Venn. You've heard of her?'

He hadn't, of course. Not many people outside the movement had.

'She was a pioneer,' I told him. 'One of the women who signed the suffrage petition back in 1866.'

I could see that meant little if anything to the elegant young man, but we'd liked and respected Philomena Venn. She was Irish by birth and had joined the formidable band of women who'd fought for the Vote a good part of the previous century, before some of us were born. They hadn't got what they wanted but, a generation ago, they'd achieved a great step forward in the shape of the Married Women's Property Act, which meant women had a right to keep their own money instead of handing it over to their husbands. The year before, in her late sixties and already ill, Philomena had come from her home in the Cotswolds to visit us at our new headquarters and give us her blessing, from one generation to the next. She was a little grey-haired woman in an old-fashioned bonnet and black lace gloves, frail with the heart disease that would kill her within a few months, but with

4

lively eyes, a beautiful speaking voice and a surprisingly deep and wicked laugh. Because what happened in the next few weeks was the indirect result of decisions by the late Philomena Venn, I'd like to make it clear here and now that none of it was her fault. She made her provisions with generosity, good faith and – to some extent – in blissful ignorance and couldn't possibly have foreseen the mess we were going to make of her intentions.

'Yes, your movement.' Christie's young man made it sound as if it were happening in some faraway country. 'The Women's Social and Political Union, I think you said.'

'Or the Suffragettes, as the *Daily Mail* prefers to call us.'

The hands had sunk down again and were resting lightly on his desk like things in a rock pool.

'And Mrs Venn told you she was leaving you a Boucher?' He was frankly sceptical now.

'She didn't mention the artist's name. She thought our office needed cheering up and said she'd leave us a picture in her will. She died back in the spring and her solicitor got in touch soon afterwards.'

'Where is the picture now?'

'At her house in the Cotswolds. Her husband's still alive. I'm going down to collect it from him in the next day or two.'

'Her husband being . . . ?'

'Mr Oliver Venn.'

His expression changed, which surprised me. All I knew about Mrs Venn's husband was that he was a committee member of the Fabian Society and the young man at Christie's hardly seemed the type to know about socialist groups, even tame ones like the Fabians.

'I think I may have heard about Mr Venn. Is he an art collector?'

From sceptical, he'd turned interested again. I told him I

had no idea. I was already tired of the picture question and wanted to get it over.

'So shall I bring it in to you for a valuation?'

'By all means, but I should warn you, as we always warn our clients, not to set your hopes too high. It's always sad to have to disappoint people.'

I didn't tell him, as I suppose I should have, that our movement was used to being disappointed – and over a much more important thing than pictures. I let him show me out and went to consult a railway timetable.

Chapter Two

THE VENNS' HOME WAS ON THE Oxfordshire edge of the Cotswolds, near the Gloucestershire border. Two days later, sitting in the train from Paddington as it left the flatlands around Oxford and started its easy climb up the low hills, I was enjoying what amounted to a day off. It was late August, harvest time, with gangs of men out in fields that were half stubble, half standing wheat. One gang was using a steam reaper and the white vapour mingled with straw dust, turning the air to a golden haze. Although the leaves hadn't started their change to autumn colours there was a hardened, almost metallic green about the hedges and copses that goes with the end of summer.

It was the first time I'd been out in the country since spring. It had been a more than usually busy year for us, with the move to London and a new Liberal government that must be made to see sense, and I'd had my living to earn as well. I'm a freelance translator and the present job on hand was translating catalogues and other sales material into German for a Birmingham bicycle manufacturer. It paid quite well – or would do when they got round to handing over the fee – but working out the German for gear ratios and brake block specification tolerances was uphill work. So a simple day trip to the Cotswolds to pick up a picture was as good as a rest cure.

Two days before I'd sent a reply-paid telegram to Mr Oliver

Venn, asking when it would be convenient to collect the picture, and had received a lunch invitation by return. Another exchange of telegrams fixed the train I'd travel by and the assurance that the Venns' gig would be at the small railway halt that served the village to meet me. With luck, and if lunch didn't drag on too long, I might get the picture back to London in time to take it to Christie's before they closed for the evening. By taxi, not bus, we'd decided. Philomena Venn's legacy deserved that at least, even though I'd passed on the young man's warning about being prepared for disappointment. I had to kick my heels waiting for a connection at Chipping Norton Junction then travelled a few stops along the local line. The halt was no more than a wooden platform with a corrugated iron shelter, some empty milk churns, a rack for bicycles. The gig was waiting for me in the yard as promised, a smart little Lawton with the wheel spokes picked out in yellow, a strawberry roan between the shafts and a bowler-hatted groom in the driving seat. He got down to help me in – not that I needed it, but it was an occasion for ladylike manners – and we bowled along uphill between more harvest fields, trailing a light brown plume of dust behind us from the dry earth road.

'That's it, miss.'

The groom pointed with his whip to a gem of a manor house, set above a stubble field and just below a wood. It was built of the local limestone that glowed gold as if generating its own light, possibly Elizabethan, with a lot of narrow windows glinting in the sun and a cheerfully disorderly roofline of gables and tall chimneypots. Although it wasn't large as manor houses go it still looked a grand place for a veteran suffrage campaigner and her Fabian husband. I reminded myself not to be prejudiced. There were people who managed to combine wealth and socialism. Logically perhaps there should be more credit given to them than to poor socialists, since they had more to lose. I couldn't bring myself to be quite as logical as that but wouldn't think less of Philomena Venn because she'd lived in a beautiful place.

Looking away from the house and down at the road, I saw two hikers ahead of us. They were going in the same direction as ourselves, heads bent down and invisible behind huge knapsacks. The road was sloping quite steeply uphill at that point and if I hadn't been on my best visiting manners I might have suggested that we stop, and offer to carry their packs to the top of the hill. There would have been just about room for them on our laps, although the gig could carry only two people. But I said nothing, then felt guilty when we passed them and I turned back to see their sweating faces through a cloud of our dust. They were oddly dressed for hikers, in dark and crumpled suits like city clerks, with pale indoor faces. It seemed to me that they looked resentful and I couldn't blame them. I said something to the groom about it being hot weather for hikers.

'Oh, they're not hikers, miss. They're Scipians. Mr Daniel's got a whole lot of them coming here.'

'Scipians?'

'Yes, miss.'

He didn't seem to think it needed explaining, and soon after that we turned through a gateway and up a drive between two lines of elms with sheep grazing underneath them. When we drew up on a sweep of gravel outside the front door, a plump man in a pale linen suit came down the steps to meet me, full of anxious enquiries about my journey.

'Was your train on time? Isn't Paddington intolerably crowded these days? Aren't you simply gasping for a glass of lemonade?'

A kind man, a fussy man with a neat tonsure of grey hair that looked as soft as a baby's round an otherwise bald pate, eyes brown and protruding like a spaniel's. No obvious sign of mourning, unless you counted the mauve silk cravat that he wore instead of a tie at the neck of his crisp white shirt. The bereaved husband, Mr Oliver Venn. A maid appeared to take my hat and travelling coat.

'It's nice and cool in the studio.' He put a tentative hand on my elbow and guided me towards a door on the right. 'Unless you'd rather go upstairs first.'

His anxiety to make me comfortable came close to being irritating. I let myself be guided into the studio and stopped too suddenly a few steps inside it so that he cannoned into me.

'What a beautiful room.'

Because he and Philomena came from an older generation, I'd expected something mid-Victorian and heavy, but the big room was full of sunlight, light furniture in elm and oak, curtains and upholstery swirling with leaves and birds. Mr Venn had been spluttering apologies for stepping on my heel, but this seemed to calm him. He came alongside me, spaniel eyes shining.

'It's Carol's taste mostly. They use it as a display room for the workshop.'

I was too busy admiring it to ask who Carol was and what workshop. It was full of blues and greens in the curtains and upholstery, woven cream and blue rugs on the polished wood floor. Blue and white hand-painted tiles surrounded the fireplace. Long windows extended almost down to floor level on the side facing the garden, with late white roses and vine leaves framing them from the outside, echoing the leaf and flower patterns on the fabrics. I found out later that it had once been a Victorian conservatory. The size and lightness of it meant that it could take a lot of furniture without looking crowded. There were oak tables, robust enough for farm kitchens but finely proportioned, simple ladder-backed chairs with woven rush seats, carved and painted chests, an oak three-seater with immense cushions in a honeysuckle pattern. The pattern made me feel as if I'd come home – not that I'd ever lived in a place half so grand. In my earliest memories of my mother she was wearing a dress in it.

'William Morris.'

'You admire his work?' Oliver Venn sounded reassured.

'I certainly do. He and my father used to be friends.'

It was politics, not art, they'd discussed for hours on end, my father and that gentle bear of a man. My father was as ignorant of art as I am but he liked Morris for his ideas.

'Carol's a great admirer, of course. The workshop is run very much on his principles. That's his work too.'

More confident now he was talking about art, he turned me round to a tapestry that took up the whole wall behind us, a pale long-necked woman in a flowing blue dress holding a pomegranate, with doves and rabbits in the grass at her bare feet. 'That was one of my birthday presents to Philomena.'

A maid entered the room, with two glasses of lemonade on a tray. Mr Venn was too absorbed in the tapestry or his memories to notice her and I didn't like to help myself unasked so all three of us stood there in a row staring at the long-necked woman until the maid gave a little cough to alert him.

'I'm sorry, Annie. Do forgive me, Miss Bray. Would you care to sit over there?'

I liked the fact that he'd apologised to the maid as well as to me. He and I sat at opposite ends of a couch, looking out at the garden through the long windows.

'We thought perhaps, Miss Bray, that you might like to have lunch first and I can show you Philomena's picture afterwards.'

I thanked him, glad he'd brought up the subject. In spite

of the civilised surroundings, my main interest was getting back to London with it as soon as politely possible.

'Carol's not here but Felicia's out in the garden. If you'll excuse me, I'll go and call her.'

I nodded. He opened a door to a terrace and carolled 'Felic-i-a' out to the garden, every syllable as precise as a bird's call. While he waited, I puzzled over who Felicia and Carol might be. As far as I knew, the Venns had been childless. Felicia appeared between the swags of roses and when she stepped into the room, it looked as if she'd been designed by nature to match it. There was a simplicity and neatness about her that carried an invisible label of quality, much like the furniture or hand-painted tiles. She was wearing a cornflower-blue skirt and a white blouse with leg-of-mutton sleeves with a high neckline and a matching cornflower ribbon tied in a bow. Her hair was a light glossy brown, put up in a simple pleat at the back, her complexion creamy.

'Miss Bray, may I introduce my nephew's fiancée, Felicia Foster. Felicia, Miss Bray.'

We smiled at each other, made the usual murmurs. The ring on her engagement finger had diamonds and sapphires in an old-fashioned setting, quite small and modest. Her hands looked younger than the rest of her; rounded and childish, they had nails nibbled down to the quick. She and Mr Venn must have exchanged one of those little signals that well-run households have, because she left the room as soon as we'd been introduced and soon after that a gong sounded from the hallway. It was a tactful, unaggressive bong, in keeping with the atmosphere of this very civilised household.

Felicia was already waiting for us in the dining room, standing next to a good-looking man in his early thirties. Quite tall, dark brown hair, light tweed suit with a black mourning band round the right arm. Mr Venn introduced us.

12

'My nephew, Adam Venn.'

He smiled and asked some conventional question about my journey. Quite how you tell, from the first contact, that a person is intelligent I've never known, but it's unmistakable, like a little jolt of electricity. Adam Venn was intelligent. More than that, he was glinting me a look that said: Yes, I know this thing has its ridiculous side but let's see it through, shall we?

I said yes, it had been a very good journey thank you. Then we sat down and Annie served lamb cutlets and green beans. The picture wasn't mentioned over lunch. I suppose that would have counted as business. Most of the talk was of Philomena and her work in the suffrage movement, which her husband had supported with great enthusiasm. His admiration and love for her were clear in every look and word and more than once his bulging eyes filled with tears and his voice broke. When that happened, Adam and I would carry on talking about nothing in particular until he recovered. Felicia didn't say much, but organised unobtrusively the clearing of plates and the arrival of plum compôte and cream, then coffee. Over the coffee cups, Mr Venn apologised for his show of emotion.

'Philomena would have hated that, positively hated that. She even made me promise not to wear mourning for her.'

I glanced without meaning to at the broad band on his nephew's arm. Adam Venn said, catching the glance, 'It takes too much energy to defy all the small conventions. Don't you think so, Miss Bray?'

'But how do you decide which are the small ones?' I said.

I'd have enjoyed a discussion with him, but Mr Venn was still talking about Philomena.

'She said life would go on quite well without her. She was really quite angry when we decided to delay the wedding because she was taken ill. Young people shouldn't be made to wait for an old woman, she said.'

13

Felicia was blushing, an attractive peach shade. Was she so much in the grip of the small conventions that it embarrassed her to have her matrimonial arrangements discussed in front of a stranger? To give her time to recover I turned the conversation to Adam.

'Thoughtful of your aunt, not to want to delay your wedding.'

For a moment he looked alarmed. When he recovered, his eyebrows went up and the smile on his face told me I'd said something stupid. 'Not my wedding, Miss Bray. Felicia is engaged to marry my younger brother, Daniel.'

I dare say I blushed, and not as attractively as Felicia. I was annoyed too, feeling that Mr Venn had let me fall into a social trap.

'Adam's wife Carol is away for a few days in London,' he said. 'As for Daniel, he's hunting in Berkshire at the moment.'

'Hunting!'

It wasn't the season for it and anyway they didn't seem like that sort of family.

'In fact,' Adam said, a little edge to his voice, 'if all has gone according to plan – which it won't have necessarily with Daniel – by now he'll be in Faringdon workhouse.'

'Workhouse?'

Mr Venn came anxiously to the rescue again.

'Daniel has a great interest in collecting English folk-songs. He tells me that there are old men in some of the workhouses who know an astonishing number of songs that will be entirely lost to the world unless collectors can write them down in time. He's been spending most of the summer doing field work in Wiltshire and Berkshire.'

That at least got us back on safe conversational ground. I had several friends who were interested in the folk-song and dance movement, going along as it did with many of the left-of-centre political causes. Neither morris dancing nor

14

'here we come a-wassailing' were great interests of mine, though I'd been coerced into the occasional session. So we talked about that until Mr Venn, at long last, suggested that I might care to come up to his study and see Philomena's picture.

As I followed him up the beautiful curved staircase, something odd struck me. As fiancée of the missing Daniel, you might have expected Felicia to put in a word or two about him and his folk-song enthusiasms. She hadn't. Not one.

The picture was facing us when he opened the door. Standing on the floor, it was propped against a chair. I admit my first reaction when I saw it was: Well, we couldn't have hung that on the wall of the office. The woman in the picture was as naked as a baby, sprawled stomach down on a cushioned sofa, with one knee bent and the sole of her foot upturned. It rested on its own velvet cushion, offering a curve of little pink toes like sweets on a plate. Her rounded face, turned over her shoulder towards the artist, was part welcoming, part petulant as if she reserved the right to sulk but might be kissed out of it. Her flesh was as pink and puffy as cumulus cloud at sunset. You had the impression that if lawn tennis had existed in eighteenth-century Versailles it wouldn't have been her game. I felt Oliver Venn's eyes on me, sensed his anxiety.

'The model was a young lady who, um, gained quite a reputation at the French court. There's a more famous version, of course, *La Blonde* Odalisque at the Alte Pinakothek in Munich. Unmistakably the same model and much the same pose, but the angle of the head is different.'

He wanted me to like it. I did, in a way, only I'd expected something more in the line of swains and shepherdesses and didn't know what to say.

'She looks very, er, at ease with herself.'

15

He nodded several times, as if the comment had been sensible.

'Philomena and I spent our honeymoon in Paris. I bought it as a surprise for her.'

Surprise for me too. It was hard to connect the veteran campaigner I'd met or the decent elderly man standing beside me with a young couple of nearly half a century ago who'd carried this back as their souvenir.

I said, 'You'll miss it.'

That aspect of Philomena's bequest hadn't struck me until then. A glaze of tears came over his eyes. Quickly I turned back to the picture.

'She'll be doing good work for us, I promise you. We really are most grateful to Mrs Venn, and to you.'

There was a clean linen tablecloth lying folded on a chair. He picked it up and began to wrap the picture, as if he didn't trust himself to look at it any more. When I knelt to help him, I could feel his whole body shaking.

'Cord, on that table there, if you'd be so kind.'

Soft cord, so as not to damage the frame, everything carefully prepared. I felt guilty depriving him of his treasure, and tried to console myself by thinking of all the campaigning she'd pay for. How much for a picture like this? A thousand? Five thousand? Once we'd got her decently covered and corded up we wrapped her in another layer of brown paper and the job was done. He suggested sending for Joseph – the groom, presumably – to carry her downstairs but I thought we could manage. He walked down backwards, none too steadily, while I tried to take most of the weight. It was a relief when we got it down to the hall and propped it against the umbrella stand.

'I've asked them to have the gig ready. There's a good train in just over an hour you should be in time to catch – unless you'd like another lemonade first?'

16

As I was thanking him and declining more lemonade, Adam came in at the front door, looking annoyed.

'Uncle, have you got the key to the schoolhouse? Some of Daniel's confounded Scipians have arrived already and they want to get it aired.'

Mr Venn rummaged in his pockets.

I asked Adam, 'Who are these Scipians?'

'So the news hasn't spread yet? They're a breakaway group from the Fabians that my dear brother seems to have got himself involved with. He's invited them to hold a summer camp on Uncle's land.'

I knew that Oliver and Philomena Venn, as good middle-class socialists, had been among the founders of the Fabian movement and guessed that Adam was of the same persuasion.

'Philomena would have wanted it,' Oliver Venn said sadly, still failing to find the key. 'She'd have liked to think of young people from the factories having a few days of sunshine and country air.'

Adam gave me another of his looks that implied he and I knew things weren't as simple as that, but his tone with his uncle was patient.

'Don't worry, I'll see to them. We must hope Daniel remembers they're coming and gets home in time. Now, has somebody called the gig for Miss Bray?'

He said good afternoon to me and disappeared into the back of the house. Mr Venn came out to see me off and make sure the picture was safely stowed in the gig. As we turned into the road I looked back and there he was still standing there, like a fond parent watching his first-born going away to school.

I caught the train with ten minutes to spare and paid extra to go first class, so that the Odalisque could travel upright

17

on two seats. For the first part of the journey my mind was on her and Philomena, but as we got nearer London I started worrying about the unexpected result of my trip. The news about the Fabians and the Scipians was not good because it meant more campaigning work when we all had more than enough. All right, I know reformist groups are always splitting like seed pods on a hot day. It's one of life's little unfairnesses that while alliances of the cynical and greedy seem to rub along quite happily for decades, put three idealists in the same room and you immediately get at least two different parties. To those outside it usually doesn't matter one way or the other. But if – like the Suffragettes – you're a group fighting for one particular issue, you have to pick up allies wherever you can, from moderate Liberal to anything this side of revolutionary anarchist. It had taken us a lot of time and work to get the ever-cautious Fabians to put votes for women high on their agenda. Since, for my sins, part of my job for the WSPU was to know what was happening in other political groups, I'd been aware that two factions within the Fabians were fighting each other – one more radical, the other less so. A split had been on the cards for some time, but now it had happened and I hadn't known about it, which was careless. I'd have to spend some time finding out who'd ended up on which side of the split and whether the Scipians were worth cultivating from our point of view. This was where my mind was as we drew into Paddington and I realised I'd have to move fast if I intended to get the Odalisque into the safe hands of Christie's before it closed.

I let a porter carry her to the cab queue for the sake of speed and managed to get to Christie's as the doorman was just shutting up for the day. He wasn't impressed with me or my package, but as luck would have it the beautiful young man was coming downstairs on his way out, soft felt hat in his hand.

'Miss Bray, is that it?' Far more enthusiasm in his voice than when we'd last met. 'Since we spoke I've made some enquiries among my older colleagues. It seems Mr Venn may have bought some quite interesting pictures.'

I'd propped the brown paper parcel by the porter's chair. His eyes went to it as eagerly as they might have done to the lady herself.

'It's a version of the *Blonde* Odalisque,' I said. 'Is she worth much?'

From the little shiver that went through him, I could tell the question was indelicate. 'There's never an easy answer to that,' he said. 'I shall have to see the picture, check its condition and provenance.'

From the hungry look in his eyes I expected him to start tearing at her wrappings there and then, but I'd misjudged him. He wanted to be alone with her when he did it. The long-suffering doorman, annoyed at being kept late, was sent to find a porter. The porter carried the parcel upstairs with the young man watching every step. When they were out of sight at last he remembered I was there.

'I'll be in touch with you tomorrow, Miss Bray. Where may I find you?'

I'd given him the address already but I gave it to him again – 4 Clement's Inn – and left. As the door closed behind me I could hear his feet practically running back upstairs.

When Emmeline asked about it next morning I was able to tell her that Christie's seemed quite excited about our picture. The Fabian split was not such good news and I had the feeling – not for the first time in our acquaintanceship – that Emmeline blamed me for it. 'You'd better go down to this camp, Nell. Find out who the leaders are and bring them in line.'

'Must I?'

The fact was, I'd already survived one Fabian summer school that year. It took place on the Welsh coast, involved debates and lectures on things like housing and poor law from morning to night, an hour of Swedish drill before breakfast and sea bathing along with George Bernard Shaw in any spare moment. I'd enjoyed it, up to a point, but wasn't eager to repeat the experience so soon.

'Somebody has to and it might as well be you.'

I didn't argue, as it's always a waste of time with Emmeline, but decided privately that I'd find things that would keep me in London. I spent the morning doing various odd jobs, mostly concerned with organising meetings, waiting all the time for the message from Christie's. It came around two o'clock in the afternoon, by special messenger. The elegant young man would be very grateful if Miss Bray would come and see him as soon as convenient. I put my hat on and walked at a good hiking pace along the Strand, across Trafalgar Square, past the gentlemen's clubs and gentlemanly little shops of Pall Mall, weaving in and out of the crowds strolling in the late summer sun. All the time I was looking forward to bearing the good news back to them all at Clement's Inn. The face and voice of the young man the evening before had suggested that Philomena's windfall might be a lot bigger than any of us had guessed.

When one of the porters showed me into his office, the first thing I saw was our Odalisque propped on an easel. I felt proud of her and the lazy pink curves that would translate into so much useful activity for us. A hundred and fifty years ago she'd laid herself down on soft cushions, never dreaming that her flesh would be translated into leaflets, marches, speeches at factory gates. I smiled at the thought of it and looked up, expecting to see an answering smile on the young man's face. No smile. Instead the expression – half pity for

20

you, half pride at his own knowledge – of a specialist about to give bad news.

'Have . . . have I hurt her?' I was filled with sudden guilt about the gig, the train ride. She'd deserved to be treated more respectfully.

'No, Miss Bray. The picture's in very good condition.'

'What's wrong. Isn't it by Boucher after all?'

He gave a long sigh and walked out from behind his desk like a man coming to lay a wreath.

'May I ask, when the picture was left to your organisation, was there any mention made in the will of its being a copy?'

'Copy?' I stared at the Odalisque. She stared back, unconcerned.

'I'm afraid there's no doubt about it. I was certain as soon as I unwrapped it, but I asked several colleagues to look at it this morning. I'm afraid there is no doubt at all.'

'Poor Philomena. I'm glad she never knew.'

It was the first thing that struck me. I was disappointed for all our sakes, of course, but money comes and goes. The young man was looking at me as if I'd said something stupid.

'You think she didn't?'

'I'm sure not. Her husband bought it for her on honeymoon in Paris. They must have lived with it all those years, thinking it was genuine.'

'All those years?'

'Forty at least, I'd say. They'd been married for a long time.'

'Your understanding is that Oliver Venn bought this picture in Paris around forty years ago?'

'Of course. He said so.'

He walked three slow steps to his desk, picked something up and paced back to the picture on the easel.

'May I show you something?'

21

The thing he'd picked up was a magnifying glass. He held it over the bottom right hand corner of the picture and beckoned me to look.

'What do you see?'

'Initials, very small ones. It looks like JVD in a monogram.'

'John Valentine Dent.'

'Is he a well-known faker?'

'He's not a faker at all. John Dent is a very expert copyist of pictures. He's quite a young man – no older than his late twenties, I'd say.'

'But . . .'

'And he's only been doing work of this quality for the past two or three years.'

'But that means they . . . he . . .'

I stared at him, hoping that he'd say something that made sense of this – or at least some different sense from what was in my mind.

'Had it copied within the past two or three years? Yes. It's not uncommon, especially if people are worried about art theft. They commission a good copy and store the original somewhere safe.'

'He must have known.'

'Mistakes can occur, especially if a household is in some confusion.'

Oliver Venn's household had been one of the most orderly I'd seen in a long time.

'Of course, it's not my place to advise you on this, but if the will made no mention of a copy I'd suggest that you get in touch with the executors and let them know that a mistake has occurred. Naturally if you receive the original, we should be more than pleased to handle the sale on your organisation's behalf.'

'What would it be worth?'

This time I got an answer out of him, though it was given reluctantly and with many qualifications, but . . .

'It could be as much as two thousand guineas. Possibly considerably more than that at auction if the Americans took an interest, as they tend to do these days.'

'How can I get in touch with Mr Dent?'

'I can assure you, it's his work.'

'I'm not doubting it. I just want to speak to him.'

His eyebrows went up, but he sat down at his desk, consulted an address book, wrote something on a slip of paper.

'His studio's in Highgate.'

I took the slip of paper, thanked him and turned to go.

'Are you taking the picture with you?'

I looked at her. It struck me for the first time that there was a hint of mockery in those wide eyes.

'No. We'll send for it.'

John Valentine Dent lived in a road leading to the Highgate bathing ponds, on the east side of Hampstead Heath. I went there by horse tram, not bothering to go back to Clement's Inn first. Bad news would keep. There were two women on the lawn in front of the house playing with a plump baby on a rug, one of them in nursemaid's uniform, the other presumably the lady of the house, though she looked no more than about twenty. I said I'd come to see Mr Dent, trying not to scare them by looking as angry as I felt.

'He's up there.' She pointed to an open window on the first floor and raised her voice. 'John, somebody to see you.' Then, to me, 'Do walk up. First on the right at the top of the stairs.'

From the look of the house, Mr Dent was making a decent living from his copying. When I knocked on the first door on the right, a cheerful voice told me to come in. Mr Dent had a face like a friendly Afghan hound, bright brown eyes, sharp nose, blond wispy beard. He was standing by a still life of fruit with beetles and butterflies.

'One hundred and thirty-four, not counting the spider.'

'What?'

'Insects. I think some of the Old Masters enjoyed making life difficult for copyists.'

He didn't seem to need any introduction, but I told him who I was and mentioned I'd been given his name by the man at Christie's.

'Decent chap. Sends me clients occasionally. Are you one?'

'No. I've come to ask about one of your other clients. A Mr Oliver Venn.'

'Nice old boy. Is he well?' he asked. But he was more intent on the picture, stepping back from it then making little darts at it all the time we were talking.

'Look at that, now. Can you imagine the technique you need to paint a lacewing? You might say it looks simple enough, but one brushstroke wrong and . . .'

'You did a copy for him. A Boucher.'

'He showed you? One of the best things I ever did, although I say it myself.'

'I've seen it, yes. When did you do it for him?'

He had to stop and think about it.

'June or July, it must have been. June, probably. I seem to remember the dog roses were out and the barley was still green.'

'June this year?'

'Yes.'

Philomena had died in March.

'You went to his home to copy it?'

'Yes, some clients prefer that. I stayed there for ten days or so. Very hospitable they were too. Some places treat you like the man who's come to see to the plumbing.'

'Did he say why he wanted it copied?'

'Not sure. I think I gathered he had to sell it or something and wanted a copy to keep. I get a lot of work that way – families feeling the pinch and having to keep up appearances. You have to be a bit discreet about these things, of course.'

He was about as discreet as a five-year-old. I thanked him and left him still staring at the beetles and was sure that by the time I'd got to the tram stop he'd have forgotten he'd spoken to me. Now all I had to do was break the news to Emmeline.

Chapter Three

'PUT IT TO HIM, POLITELY BUT firmly, that there's been a mistake and we want the original picture.'

Emmeline had resisted the temptation to blame me this time, but made it clear that I was expected to sort out the mess.

'I don't think it was a mistake at all,' I said. 'That copy was made less than three months ago. He can't have mixed them up already.'

'No, Nell, of course he hasn't. But we want this settled without gossip or bad feeling. We owe that to Philomena if nothing else.'

'So you think if we give him an easy escape route, he'll take it?'

'Of course he will. I know Oliver Venn and he's not entirely unreasonable. You might put it to him that if he wants to keep the original so much he can get Christie's down to value it and we'll take the money instead.'

I suggested that since she knew him, he might listen to her rather than me. A waste of breath, like my alternative proposal that we should ask our solicitor to get in touch with the executor.

'These things are better done the direct way. It might be best if you go down there tomorrow and take that with you.'

A jerk of the chin towards the false Odalisque, back from

Christie's decently covered again in linen and brown paper and propped against the wall. I drew the line at that. The next day was Saturday. If I had to cancel my other plans for the weekend and travel back to the Cotswolds on a crowded train, I didn't intend to do it with her sitting on my lap.

I was right about the crowds. Usually the trains in that direction shed most of their passengers at Oxford, with only farmers and weekend hikers going on to the Cotswolds, but this one went on its way more than half full and the talk that came to me in snatches, over the noise of the train toiling up the gradient, wasn't about sheep or footpaths.

'The problem with you syndicalists is you assume that revolution is going to come automatically . . .'

'The eight-hour day isn't the be-all and end-all, it's only the start of it.'

'The future of the International Labour Party . . .'

There was some singing too, drifting from the third-class carriages on the warm air in a blue haze of cheap cigarette smoke. The passengers were mostly working-class young men in cheap best suits, jackets unbuttoned over dark waistcoats, shirts open at the neck or flaunting bright red ties. There were a few young women too, quieter than the men and with the determined look of people who've been taking on the world at unreasonable odds from the time they first stood upright. The luggage nets bulged with faded haversacks, rolled tarpaulins and battered suitcases made of brown-painted cardboard. In spite of the political talk, there was a holiday atmosphere with people shouting out joking insults or pointing out of the windows at the view as if they'd never been in the countryside before, which some of them probably hadn't. I'd obviously found the Scipians and they seemed to me cheerful company – more cheerful at any rate than the few hours ahead of me once we got to the halt for the Venns' house.

We changed trains together at the junction and when we spilled out at the local halt the porter took one look at the Scipians and vanished, judging rightly that there were no shillings to spare among this lot. With a lot of laughter and loud enquiries to each other about the route, they got haversacks on to their backs, and with cases in hand and tarpaulins over their shoulders they moved in an irregular crocodile up the road between the harvest fields. There was a particularly jolly group of girls with London accents who were singing more tunefully than the rest. When one of them accidentally dropped her haversack a muffled chime came from it, delicate as a breeze in a chandelier.

'Three bobs' worth of bells in there and she's just chucking them around,' one of the others said.

They formed into an impromptu morris line and danced away up the road, packs bobbing on their backs, feet kicking up the dust. I picked up my bag, more glad than ever that I hadn't brought the Odalisque back with me, and followed. Ahead of me, a man was bending to adjust his boot. I said good morning as I passed and he straightened up.

'Miss Bray, I didn't know you'd joined the Scipians.'

Tall thin frame, black hair and neat beard, profile like a benevolent hawk.

'Max Blume. What are you doing here?'

'Observing, as usual. Are you here for their summer school?'

Max was a friend from several years back, a freelance journalist and ferocious chess player. He scraped a living of sorts writing articles for left-wing newspapers and magazines which all too often went out of existence before they got round to paying him.

'No, I haven't joined. What do you know about them?'

'Interesting lot, mostly the younger and more left-wing generation. A fair bit of support from socialist students at Oxford and Cambridge, but mainly workers from the North and Midlands. Some London garment trade too, as you see.'

'Why Scipians?'

'Haven't you worked that out? You know the Fabians are named after Fabius Cunctator?'

The Roman general famous for delaying battles rather than fighting them. The timid Fabians all over.

'H.G. Wells told them they'd got the wrong general. They should have chosen Scipio, who fought battles and won them. The younger lot, and a few of the disgruntled seniors, took him at his word – so there you are.' A sweep of his long, flannel-shirted arm took in the column winding up the hill in front of us.

'Then,' he said, 'Harry Hawthorne's coming. He'll be the main attraction.'

Of all the quarrelsome political family, Harry Hawthorne was the liveliest and least predictable. He was the son of a Methodist preacher and had exhausted most of the available political organisations, from Liberal, through International Labour, communist, anarchist, socialist, syndicalist and even briefly Fabian (until he got thrown out by them for trying to settle debates with fists instead of statistics). In his forty years or so of life he'd been a fairground prize fighter, docker, steel worker, and deckhand. Above all, he was simply the best public speaker I'd ever heard. When Harry was on form, you expected the very stones to rise up and build themselves into the New Jerusalem.

'Quite a coup for the Scipians to get Harry,' I said.

'More like Harry getting the Scipians. He's up to something as usual and I'd like to know what.'

Which partly explained why Max, who was no enthusiast for rural life, had bothered to make the trip to the Cotswolds.

'Any suspicions?'

'Only that it's something financial to do with the Venns.'

I said nothing but must have made some surprised movement that alerted him.

'You know them?'

'A little.'

Max might be a friend of mine and our cause, but he was a journalist, after all. I asked him why the Scipians had chosen this place for their camp.

'It's on Oliver Venn's estate. You know he's a dyed-in-the-wool old Fabian?' I could think of a lot worse things to call him than that, so just nodded. 'Anyway, he's got a nephew called Daniel, a composer who seems to think he's a revolutionary. Daniel's fallen head over heels in love with the Scipians and invited them to camp in some old buildings on his uncle's estate. Not sure what Oliver Venn thinks about it, but I suppose he's having to put up with it.'

'What's Oliver's background?'

'Made his pile on the Stock Exchange back in the eighties, then discovered a social conscience, though that was probably his wife's influence as much as anything. You know about Philomena, of course. Would I be right in guessing that your presence here has something to do with her?'

No point in denying it. He could look up the will if he wanted to.

'Philomena left us quite a valuable picture,' I said. 'I'm here to make the arrangements.'

He didn't comment. Ahead of us the rest of the column had turned right through a gateway and was walking along a track beside a wood.

'It looks as if we part here. Should I wish you luck?'

'Can't do any harm. Enjoy the camp.'

He probably would, in spite of the countryside. Eight hours of political discussion would be Max's idea of a day well spent and he'd be capable of finding somebody to play chess with on an Arctic ice floe, let alone among all that earnest youth. I waved to him and went on up the hill to the house, wishing I'd had time to draw him out on Harry Hawthorne's interest in the Venns. This time, although the sun was on the house again and the stonework glowing as before, I liked it less. Smug and privileged, it seemed to me, curled up round its secret. I'd worked up a useful head of anger against Oliver Venn by the time I was ringing the doorbell.

It was wasted. I could feel it oozing away like seawater from a beached jellyfish once in the atmosphere of that wellordered household. The maid opened the door to me, entirely polite although I'd given them no warning I was coming. Would I care to wait while she went up and told Mr Venn I was here? She put me in the studio and while I was there Felicia Foster came running in, fresh and cool in a pale green dress with a broad ribbon belt, an annoyed look on her face.

'Daniel, you might have—' She stopped short when she saw me. 'Oh, I'm sorry. I heard Annie opening the front door and I thought it was him at last. He was supposed to be back yesterday but he loses all sense of time when he's out collecting.'

She sounded more like a bossy sister than a girl longing for her lover's return but she recovered and went into hostess mode. Had Annie offered me tea? Mr Venn would be down in a minute. She made no attempt to find out what I wanted with him or why I was back so soon, uninvited. I'd been wondering if the rest of the family knew about Oliver Venn's deception and thought probably not. Steps in the hall. She stood up, said she'd leave me with Mr Venn and whisked out in a swirl of cotton and lace.

'Good afternoon, Miss Bray. It's nice to see you again.'

But Oliver Venn's face said something else entirely. He knew the game was up.

I said politely but firmly, following Emmeline's instructions, 'I'm afraid there seems to have been a mistake.'

Stubbornness I know about. If you're in the campaigning business you come to recognise all varieties of it. Emmeline's stubbornness, simply refusing to accept that things won't arrange themselves the way she wants them. The padded stubbornness of a statesman (Tory or Liberal variety, they're each as bad as the other) whose family hasn't changed its mind in three generations and sees no reason to start now. The bone-headed stubbornness of somebody who believes what his daily paper tells him and won't hear otherwise. Oliver Venn's stubbornness was a new kind to me. He sat there on the fruit and leaf patterned sofa in his old smoking jacket with ink stains on his fingers, listened courteously to what I was saying and denied everything. Denied it as if the whole thing had happened in a different universe and it concerned him only because I would insist on talking about it. Round one, he flatly denied that the picture was a copy.

'Christie's say so.'

A wave of his plump little hand dismissed Christie's.

'I've actually spoken to the man who copied it, John Valentine Dent. He stayed in this house and did it just a few weeks ago.'

Widening eyes and a brief pursing of the lips suggested I was guilty of bad taste.

'I can see that it was hard for you to part with the picture, but we're sure we could come to some arrangement about that. If you could invite the man from Christie's down here . . .'

A small shake of the head.

'Well, what do you suggest, then?'

So it was round two and he went on the attack, if you could call anything an attack that came in such a gentle, regretful voice, with a tear trickling down his smooth old cheek. Philomena would have been so distressed by this. All she'd wanted was for us to have a nice picture to hang on our wall. He didn't see why we had to haul it off to an auctioneer, make this – he had to say it – this rather *mercenary* fuss about things. It almost worked, too. I started feeling grubby, penny-pinching. Why not leave this gentle old man in peace with his picture after all? I pulled myself together and reminded him that there'd been only a half-joking remark from his late wife about hanging the picture on the wall. She must have seen how inappropriate it would be so in the will she'd left it to the movement outright, no conditions on what we did with it. For all the impression that made, I might as well have been talking to a sad stuffed owl. In round three, I tried to appeal to his political instincts. The money the WSPU would get from selling the real picture would fund an expansion of our campaigning work that might even bring the Vote at last. Wouldn't that be a monument to his late wife more splendid than any picture ever painted? For a moment, I thought I'd won.

'Very well, you have my permission to sell it.'

'So we can send and collect it?'

I wasn't going to take it home on the train this time, not now I knew how valuable it was. He stared.

'But you have it already.'

I had to take a firm grip on the chair arm – carved vine leaves and tendrils – to stop myself yelling out in sheer frustration.

'I've told you, the one we've got is Dent's copy.'

'Never trust an art dealer, my dear lady. Never trust an art dealer.'

So we came to the next impossible scenario, delivered with

the occasional chuckle this time at the theoretical sharp dealing of Christie's and my naïvety in expecting anything else.

'You've told me you left the picture with them overnight. What was to prevent their substituting a copy and spiriting the original across the Channel to sell for a good profit? I shouldn't be surprised if poor Philomena's picture isn't on an easel at some Parisian art dealer's even as we speak.'

I could have gone on arguing, pointed out that even the most shifty art dealer couldn't have got a good copy painted and dried in less than twenty-four hours, but I knew there would be no point. Oliver Venn was becoming more confident as the discussion went on, convinced that he'd won and we could do nothing about it. I stood up, told him I'd let myself out. That at least seemed to disconcert him for a moment.

'You won't stay and have tea with us?'

His face fell again when I refused, like a child denied a small treat. I strode to the front door and opened it for myself, resisting, only just, the temptation to slam it behind me. Walking fast down the drive, hat in hand, I wondered where we went from here. The only prospect seemed to be bringing the lawyers in. We could prove the picture was a recent copy. Oliver Venn wouldn't have a snowball's chance in hell if it came to court so would obviously have to hand over the original. The trouble and expense involved would be bad enough, but even worse would be the near certainty of the story getting out. Suffragettes involved in a legal struggle with the family of one of their most venerable supporters, cause of war a nude painting, would be a gift to our opponents that it would take years to live down. Venn might be counting on that, sure we wouldn't risk it. Well, he was wrong. I felt I'd been made a fool of and had a personal stake in it. If I had anything to do with it we'd fight all the way for what was ours, ridicule or not.

*   *   *

There was just one other problem. Before we could discuss the next stage, I had to go back to London and report my failure to Emmeline. Not something to be done in a hurry. Even thinking about it slowed my pace from striding to walking, from walking to ambling. Out on the road between the cornfields, with stooks standing left and right, bullrushes in the ditch and irritating swarms of black harvest flies in the air, I stopped walking altogether. It was too feeble, unthinkable, to trail back tamely to London without another try. On the other hand, a second interview with Oliver Venn would be a waste of breath. So the only hope for diplomacy was to try to influence him through the two nephews. Both were left-leaning in their politics – Daniel very much so by the sound of it – and should be well disposed towards us. Adam had struck me as an intelligent man and Daniel probably wasn't stupid. The obvious thing was to talk privately to one or both of them, explain our dilemma and get them to persuade their uncle to see reason. I simply had to find somewhere to stay overnight and find an opportunity to talk to them.

At that point I noticed – or perhaps part of my mind had noticed already – that I'd come to a halt just above the turning the Scipians had taken on the way to their camp. Back in London I'd been unenthusiastic about joining them but now it seemed providential. I could do my duty by sounding out the Scipian position on women's suffrage, talk to the nephews and go back to London on Sunday night or Monday with a report of work well in hand on both tasks, rather than failure on one. On the downside, it meant at least one night in a communal dormitory, hours of political discussion and catering just one stage up from a soup kitchen, but we all have to make sacrifices. I opened the farm gate and followed the scuffed cart track across a field and round the edge of a copse to another field, this one dotted with faded tents, camp-fires and puzzled cows.

*　　*　　*

The men's dormitory was the old schoolhouse at the far end of the field by a road, the women's dormitory an old dairy about two hundred yards away along the road, both buildings Venn property. A young Lancashire woman, small and fierce, was in charge of accommodation and took an immediate dislike to my costume – second-best navy blue because of calling on Oliver Venn – and my accent. When I explained that I was a visiting delegate from the Women's Social and Political Union the welcome didn't get any warmer.

'You can't separate the question of women's suffrage from universal suffrage.'

'We don't. May I stay for the night?'

'It's just middle-class divisionism to work for the women's vote until all working men have got the vote without property qualification.'

'We want all men to have the vote too. What's divisive about that? So may I stay?'

'Did you book?'

'No.'

'Are you a member?'

'No.'

'Did you bring your own blanket?'

'No, I'm sorry.'

'That'll be five shillings non-members' rate for meals and accommodation, plus sixpence for hire of blanket. They've just started the debate on wage differentials over in the big tent. The one next to it is Midlands miners. Working party on trade union legislation by the elm tree.'

I paid up. There was still a smell of cheese lurking about the dairy and the beds were a ramshackle assortment of garden benches, old doors propped up on bricks, even a couple of abandoned chapel pews with folded blankets. I reserved a bedspace in the far corner by leaving my hat on it then went

36

dutifully out to spread the word, pausing on the way to beg a mug of tea from a cheerful group of anarchists who'd managed to bring a fire and a kettle into partnership.

By mid-afternoon I hadn't made many converts but there hadn't been much hostility either. Nobody was actually opposed to us, but all the different groups that made up the Scipians had their own agendas and urgencies. Variously, votes for women would have to wait until they'd achieved a national minimum wage, or a majority of working men's representatives in Parliament or total overthrow of the capitalist system and a workers' republic. I'd done enough to report back conscientiously that the Scipians were a likeable, even admirable, crowd but not much use to us at present. I saw Max Blume coming out of the Midlands miners' tent and went over to him.

'I thought you weren't going to join us,' he said.

'Changed my mind. It's a long way back to London.'

He gave me one of his looks. I asked him if he'd point out Daniel Venn when he arrived.

'He's here already.'

'Where?'

'Over with the bells and bouncers.'

He nodded towards a big elm tree. A group of people had gathered under it and I recognised some as the London girls. Even from a distance they seemed a less earnest group than the rest of the Scipians. Laughter and a few notes squeezed out of a concertina drifted over to us.

'Which one's Daniel Venn?'

'Smallish, dark-haired, pleased with himself. Anyway, you'll tell him by the voice.'

Max was right. You could hear it from yards away, the voice of a university man, sounding as if it should go with long afternoons on cricket pitches rather than gambols in socialist camps. None of the group seemed to resent it, though. They were trying out a dance in a tentative, walking-through way, with Daniel in charge. He was thin and active-looking, early twenties, a little below average height with dark curling hair ending just above the collar of his cream flannel shirt. His eyes were bright and there was a crackling feel of energy about him. He wore a red and white spotted neckcloth instead of a tie, a moleskin waistcoat, and dark trousers that looked as if he might have slept under hedges in them. I waited for a break in the conversation and intro-duced myself to him.

'I'm sorry to interrupt, but I wonder if I might have a word about your uncle, Oliver Venn.'

He looked alarmed. 'Is something wrong with Uncle Olly?'

'No. I saw him this morning and he seemed quite well. It's a business matter.'

He heaved a deep sigh and pushed his hands into his pock-ets. 'I'm no good on the business side. It's Adam who handles that.'

Judging from the question about his uncle, he hadn't been up to the house yet. It seemed odd to me, with his fiancée waiting for him, but that wasn't my affair.

'It's not complicated. Perhaps if you'd let me put the prob-lem to you, you could discuss it with your brother.'

'Problems.' Another deep sigh, as if he were unfairly loaded with them. And yet there was an air of openness and generos-ity about him. He wasn't good at turning people away.

'Tell you what, Miss Bray, I was thinking of taking a walk to the workshop to talk over something with my sister-in-law. If you'd care to hang on for a minute, we can stroll together.'

I thanked him. He went to a place in the shade of the hedge where a long bundle was lying, wrapped in a grey blanket, and knelt down beside it. At first I took it for a pack until I saw a long trail of red hair coming out of the top of the blanket. He got up, said something to one of the girls, who nodded, then came back to me.

'She'll sleep all right until we get back,' he said. 'It's been a long journey for her.'

Which was all the explanation I got.

Chapter Four

H E LED THE WAY PAST THE old school towards the church and cluster of houses that made up the village, walking fast and easily. I fell into step behind him and explained the problem of the picture. His first reaction was open and hearty laughter.

'Well, the old scoundrel. I do believe it's the best thing I've ever heard about Uncle Olly.'

'You can hardly expect us to see the joke.'

'I suppose not, but you must admit it's ripe. Then putting the blame on Christie's. You have to hand it to the old chap.'

'You can hand him anything you like as long as he hands over the picture to us. If he doesn't, this could end up in the law courts.'

That stopped him laughing at least. 'If you do that the lawyers will only get it all, and the scandal rags will have a field day.'

'Precisely. So what can we do to avoid it? I thought you and your brother might have a serious talk with him and suggest that if he really can't bear to part with the picture, we'd accept a cash equivalent.'

He whistled. 'Not sure about that. I think cash may be a bit tight with Uncle Olly at the moment.'

'It's a bit tight with us all the time. It's not as if we want it for our own selfish purposes. You must know how expensive political campaigning is.'

'Money, money, money.' His voice was bitter, no laughter in it now. 'What a hideous system this is, when you're not supposed to paint pictures or make music or be kind to people or fall in love or do anything human without thinking about money.'

'I'd like a better system as much as you would, but it doesn't come by just wishing.'

I thought I'd got his measure: spoilt young man mistaking his own itch of discontent for revolutionary fervour. But perhaps I'd misjudged him, for now he apologised.

'Yes, I suppose we'll have to try to get Uncle Olly to see reason. Trouble is, Adam and I aren't on the best of terms at the moment. I might ask Carol's advice. She's usually the one who sorts things out. I'm relying on that in any case.'

He went quiet, as if there were other things on his mind. We passed a couple of farms and came to the main part of the village. It seemed mostly to consist of one wide main street with a public house called the Crown at one end and a horse trough and pump in the middle, opposite a general store and post office in a cottage so lopsided that the thatch almost touched the ground on one side. A church was set back on a little hillock with a graveyard round it, and a school and schoolyard stood on more level ground on the other side. We walked past them and almost out of the far side of the village. At a forge on the right a big shire horse was standing patiently while the smith heated a shoe. Opposite was a rectangular stone building that looked like a barn recently altered for other purposes with a big window let into one side on the ground floor, a smaller window above. A yard on the far side was piled with stacks of timber. On our side was a door with a porch and a neatly lettered sign: 'Visitors Welcome'. A gentle humming noise came from inside.

Daniel opened the door and we stepped into a room of normal height at the front but the full height of the original barn at the back, stretching up to shadowy beams where sparrows twittered. The humming came from a pole lathe with a man standing at it, operating a treadle and holding a chisel to a revolving cylinder of wood. Behind him, fading into the shadows, were more pieces of furniture like those up at the Venns' house but in various stages of being made – bedheads propped against walls, chests without lids, chairs without seats. There were three people in the room.

The man who'd been working at the lathe stopped and straightened up as we came in. He was in his thirties, big and square-shouldered. His eyes were blue, face strong in the jaw and broad in the forehead, hands brown and workmanlike with some lines of old scars. A good-looking man who seemed mercifully unaware of the fact, shy even. 'Hello, Mr Sutton,' Daniel said. The man took his hand and said it was good to see him again, in a deep voice with a West Country accent. A woman was kneeling by the big window with another woman standing beside her holding a baby. When we came in they'd both been staring at a big wooden cabinet and the kneeling woman had her back to us. She turned when she heard Daniel's voice and got up in one easy movement, smiling.

'Daniel, we expected you yesterday.'

She was in her early thirties, stylish in an unconventional way: dark crinkly hair pinned up with a tortoiseshell comb, a few tendrils hanging down to frame an intelligent oval face with dark eyes that had a slight upward slant to them like a cat's, a straight nose and lips as finely shaped as on a classical statue, but with a satirical twist. Her dress was damson-coloured, softly draped from a high bodice with a few spirals of wood shavings clinging to it. She reminded me of the woman in the William Morris tapestry, only less yearning and more active. Her voice was deep-toned and attractive. When Daniel introduced us the hand she held out to me was slim

42

but had a firm grip. I was surprised that she seemed to take my presence for granted until Daniel said, 'I'm afraid she's not a customer, Carol. There's a little problem. Tell you in a minute.' A moment's disappointment showed in Carol's dark eyes, but she recovered well.

'When wasn't there a little problem? Have you been up to see Felicia yet?'

Daniel shook his head and turned to say hello to the baby, giving it his finger to grip. The woman holding it – mother, presumably – smiled but seemed a little nervous of our invasion, although she'd looked quite at ease with Carol Venn. She had a round face, a mass of red-brown hair, and wary grey eyes.

'You should have, Daniel. She's waiting for you.'

'She won't mind.'

Daniel pulled his finger gently away from the baby, took Carol by the arm and guided her towards the shadowy back of the room. 'You'll excuse us for a minute, Miss Bray. Get Mr Sutton to show you the pole lathe. He's an artist.'

The big man went back to the treadle. Behind him the long pole that powered the lathe rose and dipped to the rhythm of his foot and the machine hummed. He was making a chair leg, pale shavings curling away from his chisel blade like apple peelings. The woman with the baby watched him, smiling. The air was full with the sweet smell of wood. Above the noise of the lathe I could hear the murmur of Daniel and Carol's conversation, but not what they said. Once she gave a sharp little laugh. Mr Sutton finished his chair leg, took it out of the lathe and fitted in another cylinder of wood. Daniel and Carol came back.

'Carol's going to ask Adam about it,' Daniel said. 'You're staying at the camp until tomorrow, aren't you? I'll let you know what he says.'

I think that was probably my signal to go. He'd mentioned

that he had something else to discuss with Carol and I supposed it was family business. But she had other ideas, perhaps reluctant to give up the idea of me as a customer. If she'd seen my home or my bank balance she'd have known better.

'Do look round while you're here, Miss Bray. We encourage people to come in and see things being made.'

She led me round the big room, talking lovingly about different kinds of wood, glowing red cherry wood, dark burr yew with its grain patterned like clouds in a stormy sky, coromandel, rosewood, ebony. I asked her if she designed the furniture herself.

'I'm not trained as a designer. I have ideas and do sketches and Mr Sutton makes them work. He's a kind of genius. Would you believe that before we rescued him he was working in a factory at Swindon fitting out railway carriages? Isn't that terrible? Like making a thoroughbred pull a milk cart!' She put a hand lightly on my arm to stop me by a chest of drawers painted in a wild rose pattern. 'That's mine. I do the painting, though wood's so beautiful it sometimes seems a crime to paint it at all.'

'Do you and Mr Sutton do all this on your own?'

'There's another craftsman and two apprentices from the village, but we give them Saturday afternoons off. In time, we hope to be employing a lot more people from round here – maybe encourage them to set up their own workshops all over the village. The point is to show what can be done by craftsmen working with love, not having to think of profits all the time.'

I noticed a small oval mirror in a carved stand on top of the chest of drawers, of an unusual design. The mirror was cradled by two beautifully worked female hands in some glowing golden wood.

'Your hands?' I said.

I'd noticed that hers were particularly fine and slim. She laughed and blushed a little.

'You're observant, aren't you? Yes, we can't run to professional models.'

But in spite of the casual tone I could see it pleased her. She stared into the mirror and the reflection of her face was clasped between her golden carved hands. The sound of the lathe faltered and when I turned Mr Sutton was watching her, a little smile on his face like a man trying to contain his pride. Not surprising because the mirror stand was a masterpiece. While we'd been walking round, Daniel had followed us, looking fidgety and trying to get Carol on her own again. We almost completed our circuit and came up to the big cabinet she'd been examining when we came in. It seemed out of place. The rest of the furniture in the workshop had a light and airy feel about it. This thing was massive, made in dark bog oak and corrugated with carvings.

'This isn't one of ours. It's Jacobean. It belongs to a friend of mine who wants it restored. It's not the kind of work we normally do but it's an interesting piece.'

The front of the cabinet was divided into eight panels, four on each door, with what looked like scenes from a play or story carved on them. The top left hand one showed a man riding away on a horse and a lady waving him goodbye from a tower. Below that was a window in a house with what looked like some demon or hobgoblin creeping through it. The carving was rough but spirited, showing the creature with unnaturally long fingers and a grisly grin. The next panel had the hobgoblin standing full length with a girl who might be a serving wench, each on one side of a cradle. The hobgoblin figure was carrying a short sword and the wench a bowl. The bottom panel on that side and the top one on the other had been damaged so it was hard to make out what was happening but the next one showed the wench and the hobgoblin with a lady. He had his long fingers in her hair and her body was tilted backwards, mouth open in a little dark 'O'. The last two panels showed the wench burning in a fire and the hobgoblin creature hanging from a gallows, eyes popping and tongue lolling all the way down to its splayed knees. I asked what the story was.

'Janie and I were just trying to work it out when you came in. Janie doesn't like it one bit, do you?'

The young mother had moved aside, clasping the baby to her more tightly than before. Her hands were square and blunt-fingered. She shook her head but didn't say anything. Carol turned to Daniel.

'You know about legends and ballads. See what you make of it.'

He came over, but more to please her than because he was interested. While he was looking at it, the workshop door crashed open and a man came in like a sudden gust of wind.

'All right then, where's this workers' co-operative?'

I'd seen Harry Hawthorne at various meetings so recognised both him and his method of making an entrance: in a hurry and loudly. He was tall and broad in any case, but had a rough confidence and vitality that made him seem even larger. He carried more superfluous weight than in his days as a docker and prize fighter and his unkempt beard had acquired some grey hairs since I'd last seen him, but he was still straight-backed and quick on his feet. His hair, untidy and not recently washed, came down almost to his shoulders.

At the sight of him Janie clutched her baby even more closely. Daniel sounded pleased to see him.

'Hello, Harry.'

'Good afternoon, you bourgeois renegade. Where have you been?'

'In Wiltshire on the Marlborough Downs, song collecting and so on.'

46

'So where's this workers' co-operative you told me about?'
Carol gave Daniel a reproachful look. 'We don't call
ourselves a workers' co-operative,' she said. 'We're a craftsmen's federation.'

He paused, sizing her up. On the one hand she was a
good-looking woman and Harry was notoriously susceptible
to that. On the other she looked and sounded like what she
was – a member of the hated middle classes.

'And you're one of the toiling masses, are you?'

'My name's Carol Venn. I help design things.'

'Oh, another Venn, is it? His sister?' He looked at Daniel.

'My sister-in-law,' Daniel said. 'Carol is married to Adam.'

At the mention of that name, Hawthorne's attitude vis-
ibly shifted towards hostility. 'Making a good profit, I
suppose,' he said.

'Harry.' Warningly, from Daniel.

Carol said calmly, 'At present, we don't make any kind of
profit.'

'I'm not surprised.' He looked at Mr Sutton, who was still
carving away at his chair leg. 'You won't till you get some
proper machinery in.'

Harry would know that this was heresy to Carol and people
like her in the Arts and Crafts movement. He probably didn't
mean it and was only trying to annoy. She was cool enough
not to rise to it. In fact, she seemed quite amused. Hawthorne
moved towards a small round ashwood table.

'So how much do you sell this for?'

'Yours for six pounds.'

She smiled at him. Hawthorne threw back his head and
roared with laughter. 'Six pounds! A man's wage for a month
and you charge that for a table. How's that supposed to help
working people?'

'By giving them a chance to make something beautiful.'

'The middle classes all over,' Hawthorne said. 'They want

to rob you and feel virtuous about it.' He moved over to Mr Sutton and the lathe.

'That doesn't look too difficult.'

Mr Sutton smiled, rather nervous.

'Let him try, then,' Carol said.

Reluctantly Mr Sutton took out the chair leg he was working on and put in a new cylinder of wood. He explained the working of the lathe, while Hawthorne nodded impatiently as if he knew it already, then surrendered his place to him. But he wouldn't let Hawthorne use his chisel and fetched another from a row of tools on a table. The treadle started again, its rhythm less regular. Daniel turned his attention back to the chest. Uninterested at first, now he was absorbed in the thing, particularly the panel with the hobgoblin squeezing itself into the house.

'It's Long Lankin.' He started singing. '"The doors were all bolted and the windows all pinned, Except one little window where Long Lankin crept in".'

'But what is he?' Carol asked.

'An outlaw, Old Nick, anybody's guess. It was probably a Scottish ballad originally but you get versions all over the place. I heard one in Berkshire and another one just now near Ogbourne. The story's much the same in all of them. Long Lankin gets into the house while the lord's away. He and the wicked nursemaid prick the baby with a pin to make it yell and when the mother comes down to see what's wrong, they kill her.'

Janie Sutton's expression had changed from nervous to horrified and the baby started grizzling. Not noticing, Daniel sang again:

'Here's blood in the kitchen. Here's blood in the hall.
Here's blood in the parlour where my lady did fall.'

48

Unexpectedly, a second voice joined in, Hawthorne singing as he tried to operate the lathe, in a loud baritone, word-perfect. The lord comes riding back and hears what has happened to his wife:

'Long Lankin was hung on a gibbet so high
And the false nurse was burnt in a fire close by.'

Janie was shaking, tears pouring down her cheeks. Her husband moved across and put his arm round her. She burrowed against his chest so that the baby was protected between them. The treadle stopped with a snap of wood. Hawthorne said, 'Oh dammit.' Absorbed in singing, he'd gone on gouging with the chisel in the same place so that the chair leg was snapped right through. Carol went over to disentangle things.

'You see, Mr Hawthorne. It's not so easy.' Then to Daniel, 'I think you've solved it at any rate.' She caught Mr Sutton's worried look over his wife's bent head. 'Don't cry, Janie. We'll have this carted up to the studio on Monday and Daniel can help me work out some sketches for the damaged panels.' She found an old sheet and draped it over the front of the cabinet. 'There, you don't have to look at it.'

I said goodbye and thank you and left them there, Hawthorne looking crestfallen, Carol making arrangements with Mr Sutton to have the carter come on Monday, Daniel still looking like a man with a problem. Not my problem, at any rate, though whether I'd got any nearer to our picture was anybody's guess.

I strolled around the village for a while, taking my time about getting back to camp. I'd had enough political discussion for one day. By the time I got back a queue for supper had formed outside the kitchen of the old schoolhouse. Max Blume joined me while I was standing in it and was amused to hear about Harry Hawthorne's encounter with arts and crafts. We collected our portions of corned beef hash and pickled cabbage on tin plates and strolled across the field, avoiding cowpats, to find a clean patch of grass to sit and eat on.

At this late stage of summer the sun was already well down below the hedge at the western side of the field and the air had a crisp edge to it. People were gathering in groups round fires, most of them still debating as if a day of talk hadn't been enough. Somebody was squeezing a plaintive tune from a concertina. There was a general drift over to a group in the far corner of the field, first in twos and threes, then a steady stream. The attraction might be the bonfire, bigger and brighter than the rest, or the sound of a violin and a stamping of feet that vibrated through the hard ground.

'Sounds like a party,' I said. 'Shall we go over and have a look?'

We took our plates back to the kitchen and followed the general movement. By the time we got to the big bonfire most of the camp was standing round it with a space cleared between the audience and the flames. In the space two lines of silhouetted figures were dancing to the music of the violin, sticks in their hands, feet thudding in unison.

'Yes, I was afraid they might be committing morris,' Max said.

The lines moved towards each other, clashed sticks three times as precisely and solemnly as duellists, danced away. The crowd watched mostly in silence until the music stopped in a gliding arpeggio from the violin and the two lines of dancers came to a halt. They were all women, the Londoners I'd noticed on the train. Some applause, some friendly insults flung between the dancers and friends in the crowd. One of them called, at a man who must have said something critical, 'Well, you come and try it if you think it's so easy.'

Laughter and mock struggles as the man was pushed forward by his friends, more horseplay as two apprentice morris sides were pulled into the space in front of the fire. The violin struck up again, with the concertina artist playing alongside, but less expertly.

The violinist was a real musician, with some of the fire of a gypsy fiddler. I glanced over and saw it was a woman, or rather a girl with long red hair. The girl in the blanket, now out of her chrysalis and seeming to fly in the firelight like some exotic moth. She was as thin and mobile as the flames, her whole body swaying with the music, booted foot beating the ground, sweeping the bow at full stretch of her long, bare arm.

The new dancers got in a terrible muddle even though the experts tried to push and pull them into line: they hit each other's shoulders with their sticks and yelled out, stumbled and had to be grabbed by their arms to stop them falling backwards into the fire. After all the earnestness, it was good to watch the Scipians having fun. Max touched my arm and pointed to Harry Hawthorne, galumping like a cart-horse among ponies, half-empty beer mug in one hand, stick in the other. He wasn't trying to keep time or attending to the experts. As we watched he dropped the stick, grabbed a plump girl by the waist and twirled her round and round, faster and faster, still keeping a firm grip on the beer mug with his other hand. The dancers drew back from the whirling menace the two of them made, then gave up dancing altogether and formed a circle round them, laughing and clapping. And all the time the thin fiddler girl went on playing her wild music, with a face as blank as a hired mourner at a funeral. The plump girl tripped, Harry Hawthorne fell over on top of her and the beer went flying. The music stopped and a chant started, 'Speech, speech, speech!'

He was breathless. He was at least half drunk. He had

51

grass in his unkempt hair and beard, beer soaking into this thick flannel shirt. He roared at them from the ground, 'You want a speech?'

Yes, after a day of talking, they wanted a speech from Harry. Several people helped him up. He started in a rambling way, glad they were all there, glad they were allowed a few grudging days off by their money-grubbing bosses who sweated the life out of them in factories or crushed it out of them in mines and foundries. A few shouts of support, but this was nursery stuff for the Scipians. They wanted more from Harry Hawthorne and they got it. You could hear him climbing out of the beer fumes and the twopenny-halfpenny oratory into what he really wanted to say.

'You deserve more, you know that, I know that. But do you know *why* you deserve more?' He waited.

'Because we're the producers of wealth,' somebody shouted.

Harry shook his head. 'True, but that's not it.'

'Because we need more.' From the fierce Lancashire woman.

'True too, but that's not it either. Anybody know?'

He let the silence stretch out for some time, then answered his own question in a voice now so soft that it was almost a whisper. They had to move inwards to hear him; light from the bonfire flickered over their intense faces.

'Because you can *enjoy* more.' He waited for it to sink in, then let his voice roar out, so that the people who'd crowded in got the full blast of it.

'Enjoy! That's the word to remember, my friends and comrades. If you can't enjoy – if you haven't got strength and appetite and laughter in you – then you can have as many meetings and minutes and votes and amendments and statistics and percentages as you like – and they're all as useless as a picture of a mug of beer to a man dying of thirst. And

52

that's the big difference between the likes of us down here and those up there.'

He was pointing up the hill to Oliver Venn's neat little mansion. It was perhaps unfair to Oliver Venn, given that he was after all a socialist of a kind and the host of the gathering. Still, somebody had to stand in for the capitalist system and as far as I was concerned Harry could be as unfair to him as he liked.

'They keep the best things for themselves but the pity of it is they're so full of fear that somebody will come and take them away that they can't enjoy them. They have food and they can't enjoy it because they've lost their honest appetite. They have music and they can't hear it because they're too busy listening to their cash registers . . .'

I noticed Daniel Venn standing opposite us, nodding vigorously when Harry talked about music.

'They have their womenfolk dressed up in clothes worth six months' wages, but there's no honest love or beauty there because they'll sell themselves to the highest bidder in the marriage market . . .'

Felicia? Surely not. Harry was firing at random, knowing nothing about the Venns. Anyway, why should I assume there was no honest love there?

'So remember, demand your fair wages, demand your better working conditions, demand your eight-hour day.' A thump of his great boxer's fist into the palm of his hand on each 'demand'. He dropped his voice again. 'But remember, you deserve more than that. You deserve the fine food and wines, the pictures and the music and all the beautiful things they hug to their mean and frightened little hearts, because you're the ones who can enjoy them best. And if they won't give them – and believe me, they won't willingly give them – then it's your work and duty in life to go and take them. And enjoy them.'

53

Back to a roar for the last three words, and a storm of clapping and cheering. I thought: If he led a charge up the hill to the Venns' house, I do believe they'd follow him, and more than half liked the idea. But he didn't. He grabbed a mug of beer from somebody, put his arm back round the plump girl's waist and drank like a man with a steelworks thirst. The music started up again, the concertina at first then the fiddle joining in. The expert dancers formed up in the space lit by the bonfire, this time without sticks. They seemed less sure of themselves, probably a new dance they were learning. They appealed to Daniel and he took over somebody's place in the dance, calling out the moves when they wavered. In motion he was a jumping jack of a man with such buoyancy that you could tell he was having to rein himself in so as not to bound higher than the others. At one point the dancers got themselves in such a tangle that even Daniel was at a loss and the music died away. He ran a hand through his curls and called to the girl fiddler, 'Daisy, how does it go? Is it leaders change places, then straight to two bars clap hands?'

'No. Four bars change places, six bars side step, then clap hands.'

The fiddling girl's voice was working class with an accent that might be Wiltshire or Berkshire.

'That's not the way I learned it from Mr Sharp,' he said.

'Well, he learned you it wrong then. It's like I tell you.'

'Six bars side step it is, then. Thank you, Daisy.'

The fiddle and concertina started up again and the dancers circled. I wondered if Daniel Venn had managed to get home yet to see his fiancée. I was curious about the relationship between the two of them. Why was he capering down here in a field instead of spending time with her? There was a pause in the music and I thought of going over to ask him if there'd been any progress about the picture, but then the violin and concertina started again and his head went up like a horse hearing the feed buckets clanking. This time it was a different kind of dance, with just four men taking it in turns to outdo each other in high leaps and fancy footwork and the crowd cheering them on as if at a sporting match. The girl fiddled faster and faster, the concertina player gave up in despair on a last dying wheeze and Daniel spun, leapt and capered like a man possessed until the other three simply gave best and stood back, admiring. One more run of notes from the fiddle and he spun until he was no more than a blur and collapsed panting on the grass.

Max had got into conversation with a Welshman about some detail of trade union politics that sounded as complicated as the Trojan war and would probably go on as long. I left them to it and went for a walk round the margin of the field, in no hurry to claim my uncomfortable bed in the cheesy dairy. On the whole my day had been difficult but not, I hoped, entirely wasted. Daniel might be a wild lad, but I'd got him to take the problem seriously. I cut across the field back towards the bonfire, which was no more than a red glow now, hoping for another word with him. Only a dozen or so people were left around the dancing place, with most people gone to their beds or elsewhere. The girl was wrapping up her fiddle in a cloth, a group of men and women were discussing something quietly together and Daniel was still there, sitting by the fire with a bottle of beer in his hand, talking to Harry Hawthorne. It looked like an intense conversation. I noticed Harry glancing up at the girl with the fiddle as if she were part of what they were talking about.

It was coincidence that I happened to be there just when Daniel made his announcement. It's likely that he was a little drunk, not so much from the ale as from the excitement of the dancing or Harry's speech, or perhaps from nerving himself for what he was going to do. Anyway, Daniel leapt up from a sitting position straight to his feet and spun round as if starting another dance, with only the last of the flames this time for accompaniment.

'Everybody – friends, comrades, don't go. I've got something to announce.'

They all stared at him except the girl who went on calmly wrapping up her fiddle. They probably thought, like I did, that he was going to make a political speech, but what he said was, 'I'd like to introduce you all to my fiancée.'

I looked round for Felicia, enchanted by this latest turn in their puzzling romance. So the demure young lady had got tired of waiting for her wandering lover up in the manor house and come down to meet him in the field, like the raggle-taggle gypsies-O. Appropriate in view of all the folk music, although surprising. But there was no sign of Felicia: not in the group of men and women, nor by the fire, nor in the direction that Daniel was looking. His eyes were on the fiddler girl and her mouth was wide open, swathed violin dangling in her outstretched hand. Daniel walked over to her, took the fiddle and tucked it under his arm, then took her right hand in his free hand.

'Comrades, my fiancée, Daisy Smith.'

Chapter Five

AFTER THAT BOMBSHELL, DANIEL AND HARRY Hawthorne walked away with Daisy in between them. From the only glimpse I had of her face, she looked more dazed than delighted. There'd been a few puzzled murmurs of congratulation from around the fire but most people were too dumbfounded to react.

By the time I joined the other women in the old dairy to get ready for bed the news had spread. A good gossip was going on, which was a relief. High-mindedness and political dedication were all very well, but these women would have been less than human if they hadn't been interested. On the whole, they were in favour of Daniel Venn. Several of the girls from London were dance and folk-song enthusiasts and had met him at classes and displays. He wrote good tunes for singing, they said, and although he came from a rich family there was no side about him. He'd just proved it – with his money and looks he could have married nearly any girl in England and here he was, in front of everybody, getting engaged to that . . . And this was where they hit difficulties. They didn't know what to make of Daisy Smith. None of them, folk enthusiasts included, had known of her existence until she turned up at the camp. Simply, a brilliant traditional fiddler who had all the dances in her head better than any of them had dropped like a gift from the skies. Both gift and gifted, musically speaking, the ones who cared about folk had no doubt about that. What they couldn't understand was why nobody had heard of her before. But it was perfectly understandable that a musical man like Daniel should be interested in her. Politically, it was right too. From her voice and her attitude she was clearly one of the working class and Daniel was putting his theories into practice instead of, as one of them said, 'scuttling back home to the bourgeoisie as soon as there's a whiff of wedding cake in the air'. But another woman wasn't so impressed: 'Touch of the King Cophetuas, if you ask me.'

'King whats?'

'Didn't they teach you your Tennyson? "Cophetua sware a royal oath: This beggar maid shall be my queen!"'

'She's not a beggar, is she?'

'Janet didn't mean it literally. I see what she means, though. It was a bit, well. . . a bit stagey, as if he'd got carried away by the dancing and so on.'

'You mean he might be regretting it in the morning?'

'Too bad if he does. He said it in front of witnesses.'

I took no part in the debate because the thing I knew and they didn't would have been gunpowder on a bonfire. As far as Tennyson told it, when King Cophetua stepped down from his throne and took the hand of the beautiful beggar girl, he didn't have another fiancée stored away in his castle up the hill. So far, there weren't many people who knew that Daniel Venn had equipped himself with two prospective wives. If the decision had been as impulsive as it looked, it was possible that Daniel and I were the only ones. Normally I'd have been angry with him and concerned for the two women, but I have to admit that my reaction was a more selfish one – with the row that seemed certain to break out in the next few hours in the Venn household, how in the world could I get anybody to listen to sense about our picture?

*   *   *

We slept after a fashion but it wasn't a restful night, what with the hardness of the benches, the scratchiness of the blankets and patterings and scufflings around the floor that might have been rats, cockroaches or both. It was a tribute to the other women's strength of mind that after a morning wash in cold water from an old milk churn and a breakfast of dry bread and strong tea they were ready for another day of debating and resolution making. But we all knew that the first big question of the day was the one posed the night before – would Daniel have second thoughts in the morning? Then somebody spotted two figures walking along the cart track towards us, a little space between them. The man had dark curly hair and a red and white neckcloth. The woman was thin and young, with red hair scraped back from her face and a cloth-wrapped object in her hand. Daniel Venn and Daisy Smith.

When they reached the gateway at the back of the dairy yard he held it open for her. She glanced up at him and walked through, eyes on the ground. We murmured good morning to her, uneasy. By firelight with her swaying body and her flaring red hair she'd looked as exotic as a tropical moth. Now she looked as sad as that same moth pinned out in a collector's cabinet. Her face was the blue-white of skimmed milk, lips pale, her hair, partially tamed into a thick and untidy pigtail, the glowing red of a wire held in a bunsen flame. Sticking out from the cuffs of a cream flannel blouse her wrists were as thin as a child's. The ankles were probably just as thin, but they were hidden in clumsy laced boots that looked like hand-me-downs, much too large for her. In spite of that, there was a kind of dignity about the way she stood, eyes down but body upright, arms clasped to her chest over her violin.

Daniel said, 'I want you all to look after Daisy.'

He'd come to stand beside her. One of our party said, 'Of course we will.'

That broke the spell at least. A bench was brought out for them to sit on, two mugs of tea produced, all with the unnecessary bustle of people wanting something to do to hide their embarrassment. Daisy sat on the bench with the violin beside her and drank, clasping both pale hands round the mug the way old men do. Daniel accepted the tea but remained standing.

'Daisy slept under the hedge last night. I rigged up a tarpaulin for her. I slept outside it to keep watch on her.'

It was absurd and perhaps touching in its way – but absurd mostly. Here he was in an open field, carefully preserving the middle-class conventions and Daisy's reputation. Or perhaps in his own eyes, a knight from the Middle Ages with drawn sword laid in the bed between him and his beloved. Still, it seemed to go down well. Our party relaxed a little. Yes, of course they'd look after Daisy. She might enjoy the class on the history of the trade union movement for new members, then in the evening more music and dancing. At the mention of music Daisy looked up at last and gave a fleeting smile. Her teeth were gappy and uncared for. While all this was going on, I'd kept carefully to the back of the group, avoiding Daniel's eye. Considering what I knew, my presence must be an embarrassment to him. Now he looked my way.

'Miss Bray, do you think we might have a word?'

With several pairs of eyes on us, we went out of the gate and on to the farm track.

'Miss Bray, I hope . . . I mean I'd take it as a favour if you wouldn't . . .' He was as nervous as a nice boy caught apple scrumping.

'Tell Miss Smith about Miss Foster, you mean?'

He nodded.

'They're both going to have to know sooner or later, aren't they? Or are you contemplating bigamy?'

He winced, but I'd meant it to hurt. 'I've got to go up to the house and explain to Felicia. Uncle Olly and Adam too, come to that.'

'I'd advise starting with Felicia.'

'Yes. I know it must look from the outside as if I'm behaving pretty badly to her.'

'That will be the general impression, yes.'

He ran a hand through his curly hair and looked miserable. If he expected comfort from me he'd come to the wrong shop.

'The thing is,' he said, 'if I can get Felicia on her own and explain to her, I think she'd understand. She's a nice reasonable girl in a lot of ways.'

'Explain to her what exactly? That you got carried away by dancing and bottled beer and announced your engagement to a girl who looks hardly old enough to be away from home? She'll have to be more than nice and reasonable. She'll have to be downright saintly.'

'What I want her to understand is that Daisy needs me a lot more than she does. Felicia can marry practically anybody she likes, any time she wants to. She's got friends and she'll inherit quite a lot of money of her own. Daisy's got nothing. I'm her only hope.'

'For getting married? I don't suppose any woman's that desperate, particularly one as young as Daisy. She can't be much more than sixteen.'

'Seventeen. And I don't mean I'm her only hope of getting married. I mean only hope of . . . well, of surviving.'

I stared at him. 'Surviving what?'

He turned red and looked at me pleadingly, as if I were deliberately making things more difficult for him.

'You can't believe the . . . the beastliness out there. Oh look, do you mind if we walk? I honestly find it hard to think about it, let alone talk.'

His problems were the last thing I wanted, but there was no escaping. We turned and walked along the track and the thing came out disjointedly, sometimes in a torrent, sometimes with long gaps between the words.

'I'd been wandering around the Berkshire Downs and bits of Wiltshire, collecting folk-songs. There's a treasury of them. It's the one hope for British music, tapping into this tradition that's been neglected for centuries and there's so little time left. Most of it's just hanging on in the heads of old men and women who won't be here in a year or two . . .'

'Yes, I've heard about it. Can we come back to Daisy Smith?'

'It's about Daisy Smith. I'm trying to explain how this started. I'd picked up a rumour that there was a singing pub just over the Wiltshire border on the Marlborough Downs. So I decided to drop everything and get over there before some other collector got wind of it. They can be a competitive lot, folk-song collectors. Would you believe Percy Grainger actually hid under an old woman's bed to get a tune she was singing to her granddaughter? She wouldn't . . .'

'Can we keep to your story?'

'Look, it *is* the story. I'm just trying to make you understand. Anyway, I found the pub, rough place in a village of about ten houses, and it was a goldmine. Two completely uncollected songs and three variants of known songs just in the first evening. So there I was, buying beer and tobacco as fast as I could get the money out of my pocket to keep them singing. There was one man in particular, rough farming type in his thirties, leading the singing. That was something in itself. Usually it'll be some old gaffer in his seventies or eighties. Luke Fardel, the man's name was. Trouble was, he sank so much of my beer he got fighting drunk and the landlord slung him out. I was sure there were more songs

62

in him if only I could get at them, so I stayed the night in the pub. Next evening, there he was again but by now he's done some thinking and realises his songs may be worth money. He says he's got his old dad bedridden back home with a head full of songs – forgotten everything else but remembered the songs. So he suggested I should come home with him, which I did.'

Daniel took a deep breath that turned into a long sigh.

'And that's how I met Daisy. Tell me, have you ever seen poverty?'

'Yes, of course I have.'

'I don't mean just threadbare clothes and not much food on the table. I mean real, foul-smelling, pig-like poverty.'

'Yes.'

'Well, I hadn't. Oh, I thought I knew about it. I'd read the books and the newspaper articles, heard the speeches, even made the speeches sometimes. But this was the first time it had really hit me. This . . . this hovel of a place with the thatch falling off, a midden up against the wall, flies everywhere and the smell . . . and so many children, all ages, dressed in rags with their backsides hanging out and a scrawny woman with her dress open and a baby sucking at . . . oh God, I shouldn't be saying this to you.'

'Don't worry, I know.'

'It was like a foreign country. And in the middle of it all, this toothless yellow-skinned old man on a bed, the father I was supposed to be getting the folk-songs from, only he couldn't remember them and Fardel, his son, got impatient with the old man and . . . and, actually hit him in the face, hit his own father to try and make him remember. Now, I'm as keen on collecting as the next man but I couldn't have this so I told the brute to stop. Well, he sulked for a bit then he said his niece knew a lot of the old tunes from her grandad and he'd get her to play them for me on her fiddle. So he yelled outside, and in came Daisy looking as scared as if he was going to hit her too. Anyway, he told her to go and get her fiddle and play the tunes and as soon as I heard her I knew this was the biggest thing I'd ever hit on in the collecting line. It wasn't just the tunes. She knew the dances that went with them – all from the old grandad. She played and played, and any time she looked like stopping Fardel told her to go on, play for the gentleman and she looked like . . . like something in a trap. So I felt ashamed of myself and said she was tired and I'd come back tomorrow. So I did, and the next day. And gradually I got her to trust me and start talking to me when we were on our own and . . . I'm not even sure I can tell you the next bit.'

'Go on.'

'He was brutal to her, I'd guessed that. She showed me the bruises on her arms where he'd grabbed her and shaken her when she wouldn't do what he wanted. But the worst of it is – what he wanted. Her own uncle, and he wanted her to . . . you know.'

'Yes.'

'You can't believe the simple way she said it, as if it was only to be expected, what all uncles did with all nieces. She . . . she even thought she was being wrong and disobedient in not wanting to. I swear to you, when I think about it I get so angry I could go back there and . . .'

'So what did you do?'

'Went to him and told him it had to stop.'

Which showed nerve, at least. Daniel was a lightweight and didn't look as if he'd trained as a fighter.

'Did he knock you down?'

'No, he did something worse.'

'What?'

'Offered to sell her to me. He thought I was . . . interested in her in *that* way. So he said I could have her for twenty pounds.'

64

'You didn't accept, did you?'

'If I'd had twenty pounds in my pocket I'd have done it just to get her away from him and be blowed to the consequences. But after all that beer and tobacco I'd had to buy I didn't even have twenty shillings. So Fardel laughed and said he'd keep the goods until I came back with the money. That's what he called her – the goods. So what could I do? What would any decent man have done?'

'You ran away with her?'

'Yes.'

'And what did you intend to do with her?'

'At first all I could think of was getting her here and asking Carol and Felicia to look after her. Then I started wondering – what happens after that? She can't go back where she came from and anyhow I've compromised her. Even though I haven't . . . you know . . . everybody will think I have, so her reputation's gone and nobody else will marry her and she'll end up on . . . oh God, I can't even bear to think about what would happen to her. So it came to me last night, the only solution is to marry her myself.'

I didn't know whether to laugh or cry. So much desperate gallantry and even more desperate stupidity – but then perhaps they always go together.

'Even though you're engaged to be married to Felicia Foster?'

'Yes. I suppose there'll be a terrible row.'

'Quite likely.'

'I've got to go up to the house and tell them all now. Will you do something for me?'

'All right, I promise not to tell Daisy about Felicia – although I think you'll have to tell her yourself sooner or later.'

'I mean, something else. Would you explain to Felicia for me?'

65

'What!'

'It might come better from another woman and there are things I'd be embarrassed to say to her, like the uncle and so on. If you can get her to . . .'

'Mr Venn.' He was rushing on but the tone of my voice pulled him up short. 'Mr Venn, there are things a man has to do for himself and breaking off an engagement is one of them.'

'I mean afterwards. I suppose when I tell her it's off she'll cry or get angry or faint or something and that's when she'll need another woman there.'

'What about your sister-in-law?'

He looked even more ill at ease. 'Carol will be furious with me too, but I've got a feeling that she and Felicia don't always see eye to eye. It might come better from somebody outside the family.'

'But I hardly know her.'

'It would be better than nothing. And I can't say all this to her – really can't. Please.'

He was a young man used to getting his own way. That look, from under a sweep of black eyelashes, must have melted a succession of nursemaids' hearts. He was too old for nurse-maids. What he needed now was a keeper.

'I've got other things to do.'

'I know, the picture. Look, let's make a bargain. If I promise to do anything I can think of to see you get your picture, will you do this for me?'

He couldn't have guessed it, but even without that bargain I'd already decided to do what he wanted. The whole thing was a mess, but it was only partly his fault and I felt sorry for both women. After an explosion like this threatened to be, somebody had to pick up the casualties.

'All right. I'll do what I can.'

'Thank you. I think we should go straight up to the house now before . . .'

'Oh no. You're going up there on your own and you're telling Felicia and your uncle on your own. I'll come up later.'

'How much later?'

'An hour or so. Let some of the wreckage settle first.'

He looked terrified. I think the implications of what he'd done were only now rushing in on him. In the end I had to take him firmly by the shoulders, spin him round and give him a little push up the field towards the house. No spring-heeled Jack now. He went like a man in lead boots.

I gave him three hours' start. Around midday I went the way he'd gone, up the field and through a little gate in a hedge into the Venns' garden. It was at the back of the house, and must have been a pretty place once, gravel paths bordered with herbs, arches of roses and honeysuckle, a south-facing wall in Cotswold stone with espaliered fruit trees and the thatch of what was probably a summerhouse in the angle where the wall met a yew hedge. But it looked as if it had been neglected all summer or probably longer. The paths were overgrown with weeds, half blocked by untrimmed lavender and rosemary, the arches sagging from a weight of sprawling foliage, the fruit trees pulling away from their nails, the yew hedge shaggy as an old dog. The half-wild effect was attractive in its way, but so unlike the neatness and order inside the house that I wondered if the Venns had quarrelled with their gardener. When I negotiated the arch nearest the house there was Daniel's anxious face looking out of one of the studio windows. He opened the door to let me in.

'What kept you?'

He looked as if he'd got several years older in the last few hours. A house with a row going on has a particular atmosphere to it – as if the air's too thinly stretched.

'How did Miss Foster take it?'

He collapsed on to a sofa. His neckcloth was untied and his curls were practically standing on end from his hands running through them.

'I don't know.'

'Do you mean you haven't told her?'

'Of course I have. Twice over. I told her and she said "Say all that again". So I said it all again and she burst out laughing, ran upstairs and locked herself in her room.'

'Hysterical laughter? Relieved laughter?'

'Not hysterical, I don't think, but not happy either. Can you laugh in a minor key? Anyway, Adam tried to talk to her but she won't say a word to him. He's furious with me.'

'What about your uncle?'

'Not pleased. I had hoped he'd see things from my point of view. After all, he and Aunt Philly spent most of their lives making speeches and drafting reports about giving poor people a fair chance, so you'd have thought he'd be pleased I was doing it for one of them at any rate.'

'Has he forbidden you to marry Miss Smith?'

'He can't. I'm over twenty-one. But he says I'm treating Felicia disgracefully and I'll ruin my life if I marry Daisy. Anyway, he's having a family conference with Adam and Carol in the dining room now. If we're lucky, I can get you upstairs without them knowing you're here.'

'You didn't tell your uncle I was coming?'

'He wasn't open for being told things. He was too busy telling me what a lunatic I've been.'

For once I agreed with Oliver Venn but I let Daniel lead me up the curving staircase like a conspirator. From the first floor landing, corridors carpeted in sage green led to left and right, with lines of white-painted doors, panelling picked out in the same green. Very calm and tasteful, but still the feeling of domestic thunder in the air.

'Hers is second on the right.'

Daniel pointed it out to me, then bolted. I called a protest but if he heard it he took no notice. I walked along the clean carpet in my dusty shoes, knocked on the second door on the right and announced my name. With luck, she'd tell me to go away. But the door opened within seconds and there was Felicia, at first glance reasonably self-possessed. At second glance, her cheeks were flushed and the brightness of her eyes came from unshed tears. But she did her brave best.

'Good afternoon, Miss Bray. Wasn't there anybody downstairs? I'm afraid Mr Venn's rather occupied with a . . . a family crisis.'

'I know. I've just been talking to the cause of it.'

'Daniel?'

'Daniel.'

She sighed. 'You'd better come in and sit down.'

Another lovely room, willow pattern curtains and upholstery, blue cushions and carpet. A blue and white desk by the open window had a few sheets of notepaper and an ink bottle on it, so I'd probably interrupted her writing a letter. A difficult letter, judging by the three sheets of screwed-up paper on the carpet. I sat down and she perched on the edge of the chaise-longue.

'I'm sorry,' I said. 'I'm intruding. Daniel seemed to think it might be a good idea for me to talk to you.'

'So are you his ambassador?'

'Ambassador would imply I approve of what he's doing.'

'You don't?'

'It isn't my business to approve or disapprove. But if I'm honest, no I don't. He was in a difficult situation but I think he's chosen the wrong way out of it.'

'By trampling over me? He doesn't care though, as long as he gets what he wants.'

'I'm not even sure it's a case of what he wants.'

'Why's he doing it, then? Why's he doing it if he doesn't want her more than he wants me?'

'He thinks she needs him more.'

'That's what he was trying to tell me, I think. I laughed at him. Of all the ways to jilt somebody. You meet a girl who's more interesting and more beautiful and you like her better, so you make it sound as if you're giving yourself away to charity, like an old coat. Only he's giving me away as well, giving my whole future away.'

Her face and body, her nice manners, the whole neat package of her was at odds with the distress and anger in her voice.

'She's not more beautiful than you,' I said, 'and I don't think he likes her better. But he does feel sorry for her. Will you let me tell you why?'

Up to then she'd been looking me in the face, now her eyes dropped to her clasped hands with their bitten nails, twisting against each other in her lap. They went on twisting while I told her, as gently as possible, Daniel's story of rescuing Daisy. At the end of it she looked up at me again.

'Is that supposed to make me feel better? Am I meant to feel all forgiving about him and her?'

'No in both cases, I should say.'

'Do you know what he said to me, Miss Bray – that it was all right for me because I could marry anybody I liked?'

'Yes.'

'I'll have my own money in a few months when I'm twenty-one. He seemed to think that helped. Perhaps I should put an advertisement in the papers: "Damaged goods. Open to any reasonable offer."'

'Of course you're not damaged goods.'

'Aren't I? My mother will say so. Most people will say so. If I'm not, what am I?'

'A human being. And one who's being very badly treated, whatever the motive.'

'Are you saying you're sorry for me? No, please don't apologise. There are going to be a lot of people feeling sorry for me so I might as well get used to it. Poor Felicia, jilted you know, and for a fiddling girl. Poor Felicia.'

'What will you do?'

'What does a woman do? Put willow leaves in my hair and throw myself in the brook?'

'I shouldn't. You'd only get pulled out by Scipians who'd give you tea with sour milk in and read you lectures on trade union history to cheer you up.'

She looked at me, then started laughing – a little loud and shrill, but real laughter.

'Well then, answer my question. What do I do?'

'You might go back to your family and friends for a while.'

'To my mother? No, thank you.'

'What are the possibilities?'

'Goodness knows. Ship myself off to India and pick up some major who's under orders to find himself a wife before he gets promoted.'

'Does it have to be marriage?'

'You mean I'm such a failure so far, it's no use . . .'

'No, but there are other things.'

'What things?' She leaned forward, eyes desperately sad. 'Please don't start lecturing me about teacher training college or learning type-writing. I wanted to be married because I lived in a dark little house in a boring little town and my mother's a clergyman's widow who organises sewing circles and breeds spaniels and plays hymns on Sundays and Gilbert and Sullivan on weekdays on a piano that's always out of tune and . . . oh, you can't imagine being so bored that every nerve aches from it. Then I met Daniel because his Uncle Olly had been a friend of my

71

father and we . . . we liked each other and there was an escape at last.'

'From the boredom?'

'Yes. Uncle Olly's wife was still alive then and when Daniel and I got engaged she suggested I should move in with them, be a companion to her. Daniel and I would have been married last March, only she was so ill that we put it off, then she died so we had to put it off again.'

'I'm sorry.'

'Yes, it could so easily have been different. So I moved in and . . . fell in love.'

'With Daniel? But . . .'

In spite of her distress, I still wasn't convinced that she'd loved him. She hesitated, as if wondering whether to say the conventional thing and deciding against it.

'With all of them – the family. You've seen it, how light and beautiful it all is here. Daniel with his music, and Philomena was such a darling and Uncle Olly such fun . . .'

Not a view of him I shared, though I didn't say so. She was running on, tears pouring down her cheeks.

'He thinks it's just a matter of finding somebody else, only it isn't like that. Couldn't he understand, I needed rescuing too? It's not only people who live in pigsties who need it. He rescued me once – the whole family did – now he's just throwing me back again and I don't know what I'll do.'

'I wish I could do something for you.'

'Tell me to pull myself together? Plenty more fish in the sea?'

'Not that, no.'

I stood up, aware that I'd been worse than useless to her.

'Are you going to report back to Daniel?'

'Do you want me to?'

I'd have to see him, I supposed. The wretched picture had gone out of my mind while she was talking, but now it was back. She shrugged.

'Do what you like. He'll marry his fiddler girl and that will be an end of it. Daniel's made up his mind.'

I closed the door behind me and stepped out into the corridor. From downstairs a voice called softly, 'Miss Bray?'

Daniel was standing by the door to the studio, looking up.

'You can come down. The coast is clear.'

I went down, not bothering to be quiet, tired already of being conspiratorial.

'Well, how did she take it?'

'If you mean does Miss Foster understand and forgive you, the answer's no.'

'Oh.'

'Did you really expect otherwise?'

'Well, no. But I suppose I'd hoped . . . Oh *hell*. I'm sorry.'

'For the swear word or the mess? So what's happening about Miss Smith?'

'I've just been talking to Adam. Our parents left us both some money, with Uncle Olly as a trustee. I get my share when I'm twenty-five or when I get married, whichever's earlier. And there's no nonsense in it about the trustees having to approve of who I marry. I think Adam was surprised I'd remembered that because I haven't got a head for business like he has. Anyway, I told him I was going to ask Uncle Olly for the money whether he liked it or not.'

'Would it be enough for you and Miss Smith to live on?'

'Not for ever. It's just a few thou. But if I find a room somewhere and get work as a music teacher . . .' His voice trailed away. He was looking round the big, beautiful room, probably contrasting it with the life of a jobbing music teacher in rented digs. Then, fiercely, 'I'm not abandoning that girl, whatever happens.'

'Won't it take time to get married and get the money out of the trust?'

'That's what Adam says, but I don't see why it should. Anyway, for the sake of peace and quiet I've had to promise them that I won't run off and marry her straight away. In return, Adam and Uncle Olly have agreed to do what they can for Daisy while we get something sorted out. She's to move in here and Carol can chaperone her.'

I thought of that elegant and confident woman and wondered what on earth she and Daisy would find in common.

'Only we'll have to wait for Felicia to move out first,' Daniel said. 'Carol seemed to think it wouldn't do for them both to be in the house at the same time.'

I gave him a glare. 'That hadn't occurred to you?'

'Oh I say, don't make me out to be a monster. I'm trying to do my best in the circumstances, I really am, only there are so many conventions.'

'Like having only one wife at once? Maybe you should take yourself off to Utah.'

'I'll have to take myself off to Outer Mongolia if the atmosphere here doesn't get any better. Do you mind going out through the garden?'

He opened the door on to the terrace. I stayed where I was.

'Did you get a chance to talk to your brother about the picture?'

'The picture. Oh yes. Yes I did.'

He hesitated as if trying to remember, then came back into the room and shut the door behind him.

'I had a word with Adam. He doesn't think we've got a prayer of a chance persuading Uncle Olly.'

'So I've been wasting my time, then.'

'Well, not exactly. The thing is . . . I mean, I've discussed it with Carol too and she's come up with an idea and I really think it's not a bad one.'

'So?'

'She thinks – I suppose we both think – that the best thing for you to do is to steal it.'

Chapter Six

IT TOOK ME A SECOND OR two to recover. Quite a few more seconds to make it clear to Daniel what I thought of him, his uncle and the Venn family's way of doing business. When I'd finished he shook himself like somebody coming in from a storm.

'So you don't like the idea?'

'No.'

'I didn't mean to offend you. I just didn't expect you to be so conventional.'

'I'm not conventional. I'm not an art thief either.'

'Maybe I shouldn't have used the word "steal". After all, your case is that the picture in Uncle's study is the rightful property of the WSPU.'

'It's not just my case. It's a fact.'

'So if you were to take that and substitute the other one, it wouldn't be stealing. It would just be claiming what was yours.'

There was some sense in that. He'd stung me too by calling me conventional. Above all, the idea of wasting a whole weekend and still having to go back to London and admit failure wasn't a pleasant one. Perhaps Daniel saw a change in my expression – he wasn't entirely stupid after all – because he leaned forward and started talking quickly about practicalities. The house was never locked at night. His uncle had suffered from insomnia after Philomena's death and the doctor prescribed a sleeping draught that put him out by eleven o'clock promptly. The picture was hanging over the desk in his study at the far end of the upstairs corridor, with Daniel's room on one side of it and Adam and Carol's suite on the other. Simplest thing in the world to come in by the studio door, creep upstairs, unhook picture, substitute other picture, and get the early train back to town. And the beauty of it was that even if his uncle noticed the substitution—

'He will,' I said.

'Yes, but he won't be able to do anything about it, because he'd have to admit he'd hung on to the real picture in the first place. Can't fail.'

'In that case, why don't you just bring the picture to me and we'll swap?'

A tactical mistake that, admitting I was now seriously thinking about it. Daniel didn't miss it.

'Because if he notices and there is some sort of row, I'll be able to swear I never touched it. I'm in so much trouble at the moment I can't afford more.'

'Have you consulted Adam?'

'Well, not as such. But I think he'd be glad enough if the problem just took itself away. Besides, Carol could bring him round if there happened to be any trouble.'

'I need time to think about it.'

'Why not do it tonight and get it over?'

'The fake picture's still in London.'

'Tomorrow, then, or Tuesday. If I hear a noise in the night I'll just turn over and go back to sleep and Carol will distract Adam some way or other.'

'Servants?'

'Annie and Cook sleep up on the top floor, and Uncle Olly isn't the sort of slave-driver who keeps them working late at night.'

'What about Miss Foster? I take it she's not in on the plot.'

His face fell again. 'I suppose she'll be wanting to move out as soon as she can. It seems a shame . . .'

Back to the dark house, the boring little town and the out of tune piano. There was a shade of regret in Daniel's voice but that wasn't my business.

'I'll think about it. Where can I meet you to let you know?'

'I'll be down at the Scipian summer school now and then to see Daisy. I think it's your best chance, I honestly do.'

He saw me out and I went across the garden, through the gate into a field then down a footpath to the Scipian camp. Some of the tents were being packed up and a little column of people was winding along the track to the road. A fair number of the Scipians had to be back at work on Monday morning. Only enthusiasts who were spending their week's summer holiday at the camp would stay drafting resolutions, proposing amendments and arguing. The Lancastrian, less angry now she was getting used to me, collared me when I went back to the dairy.

'Are you staying on?'

'Yes, please. Tonight at any rate.'

'That's another shilling.'

I handed it over and asked where Daisy was.

'Over there blackberrying.'

Screams of laughter from the hedge, where a group of London girls were discovering that blackberries had prickles attached. Daisy wasn't laughing though. She was standing there holding a big saucepan while the others threw the berries into it, but her head was bent and she took no interest in what was happening round her. I begged an envelope from the Lancastrian, found pencil and paper in my bag and knelt by one of the old pews in the dairy to write a note to

Emmeline. 'Please send the picture by somebody discreet and reliable as soon as possible. I shall meet trains from London at Chipping Norton Junction from Monday late afternoon onwards, through Tuesday.' The less said the better. Emmeline would not approve my methods, but if all went well she need never know about them.

By the time I'd got the envelope sealed and grubbed in my purse for a stamp, the London girls had arrived in the dairy, mouths and fingers stained purple. Most were returning on the evening train and there was a lot of giggling about how they were going to carry their squashy harvest with them. One tipped a lot of them into her felt hat saying she hated it anyway and didn't mind going home bare-headed. All the time Daisy watched from a shadowy corner where she'd stowed herself as if these cheerful people were things from another planet. The girl with the blackberry hat was quite happy to post the letter for me when they got to Paddington. That meant, with luck, that it would get to Clement's Inn tomorrow morning and even if Emmeline acted promptly, as she probably would, the messenger with the picture couldn't arrive before the evening, which gave me most of twenty-four hours to kill.

Luckily Max Blume had decided to stay on too. I met him in the supper queue. With only two dozen or so of us left, we were all eating at the schoolhouse now. When we'd collected our plates of stew and found a place on our own at the end of a trestle table I asked him if he wasn't needed back in London.

'Yes, but there are interesting things happening here.'

'Daisy Smith and Daniel Venn?'

Not Max's usual line. He shook his head and my conscience, guilty in advance, made me think he'd guessed I was seriously considering burglary. I was wrong.

'I've been finding out more about Harry Hawthorne, talking to him and to other people about him. He interests me.'

'He was in typical form last night.'

'The dancing and the beer and so on? Oh yes, Happy Harry, your genuine working-class rebel, not too sound on political economy but heart in the right place. Wants to use capitalists for maypoles and strangle them with red ribbons but always kind to children and puppy dogs. Just the kind of revolutionary the English think they can cope with.'

'You think that underrates him?'

'Yes. Under all the rhetoric and capering there's a much more intelligent man than people think – and a much colder one too. He's ambitious and he knows exactly the effect he has on people. If he makes what looks like an impulsive move you can be pretty certain he's worked it out carefully in advance.'

I remembered Harry Hawthorne and Daniel sitting heads together by the bonfire, just before the bombshell, and saw where Max was driving.

'Like the engagement?'

'Exactly.'

'But he didn't have time. Daniel and Daisy had only arrived a few hours before.'

'You don't need much time if your mind moves quickly,' Max said. 'And his does. You must have noticed that he was encouraging Daniel, practically pitched him into it.'

'Daniel didn't need much encouragement. He was already deep into playing the rescuer.'

'All right, he couldn't have known that Daniel would arrive with Daisy in tow, but once it had happened he knew exactly how to use it for his own ends.'

'What advantage could it possibly be to him – apart from simple mischief making?'

'In this case, complicated mischief making. It was all part of the great plan to embarrass Oliver and Adam Venn.'

'Like that visit to Carol Venn's workshop?'

'Yes. He never misses a chance.'

'But they're being quite generous to him and the Scipians, letting them camp on their land.'

'Through gritted teeth.'

'Quite elegantly gritted.'

'Oh, I dare say they managed polite smiles once the thing was a *fait accompli*. But it wasn't Oliver or Adam who invited them, it was young Daniel. And once the invitation was given they had to go along with it or face the embarrassment of being socialists throwing other socialists off their land. That's their weak point, fearing embarrassment. Hawthorne saw that.'

'Still, he's got what he wanted. He's here with the summer school. Why not leave it at that?'

'Because the camp was only stage two in the campaign. Stage one, he meets Daniel at some folk-dancing event, mentions in the middle of the hey wassailing, or whatever it is these people do, that the Scipians need a place for their camp and Daniel puts the ancestral acres at his disposal. Stage two, the camp. Stage three, the unexpected opportunity to get Daniel engaged to a girl from the agricultural working class.'

'But why this great campaign against the Venns? It's a nice house they've got here, but it's not exactly Versailles.'

'Because Hawthorne thinks Oliver and Adam owe him money.'

'What!'

'Not him personally, but the whole socialist movement. It all goes back to Philomena Venn's will.'

'Philomena's?' I jumped, sending an undercooked carrot rocketing off my fork. Luckily Max was too busy explaining to notice.

'Yes. She was wealthy in her own right. She left five thousand pounds to the Fabians, with the proviso that it was to be used for the education in socialist principles of working people below the age of twenty-one. Hawthorne maintains that's the job the Scipians are doing, so the money should come to them. Only Oliver's an ex-treasurer of the Fabians and Adam's a lawyer and they don't see it that way. It's the sort of dispute that could go on for years.'

We finished as much as we could of the stew. As I helped with the communal washing-up I thought over what Max had told me and the irony that Philomena's good socialist bequests seemed to be causing trouble all round. The common factor was that the Venns seemed very reluctant to part with money or valuables. They deserved a little breaking and entering in a good cause. Or perhaps I was only trying to find reasons for a decision I'd already made. When it was getting dusk Daniel reappeared, looking chastened. He had a few words with Daisy on her own, which seemed to leave neither of them happier, then came over to me.

'Have you thought yet?'

'I've sent for the picture. It might be tomorrow, if we're lucky.'

'Make it tomorrow if you can.'

I explained it wasn't up to me but he was too keyed up and nervy to listen. Later, as we sat around on benches in what had been the school yard, somebody found a few bottles of beer, Daisy unwrapped her violin and there was music. No dancing this time though and no wildness, mainly sad ballads in Daniel's good tenor voice. There was one I'd heard before, 'A varmer he lived in the West Countree (With a hey down, bow down) And he had daughters one, two and three (And I'll be true to my love if my love'll be true to me.)' Now and again he'd forget the words and Daisy would prompt him in that authoritative way that she had only when music and dancing were concerned. 'They hanged the miller beside his own gate, for drowning the varmer's daughter Kate. The sister she—' What was it, Daisy? 'The sister she fled beyond the seas And died an old maid among black savagees (And I'll be true to my love, if my love'll be true to me.)' Around ten o'clock, Daniel said good night to Daisy and came over to me.

'Does somebody always end up getting hanged?' I asked him.

'What?'

'In folk-songs. That's two so far.'

I think he'd intended to have another chat about burglary but this distracted him, as I'd intended.

'I'd never thought about it. I suppose it does happen quite a lot, come to think of it. But then they were wild times.'

He said good night and started back over the dark field to the house, whistling dolefully. With most of the women gone home there were only half a dozen or so of us sleeping in the old dairy so I swapped my plank bed for a more comfortable straw pallet against the wall. As it happened, Daisy was sleeping on another pallet not far away. We'd left a little oil lamp burning on a table in case anybody needed to go outdoors to the yard during the night. By the light of it, I saw that she'd put her cloth-wrapped fiddle carefully between herself and the wall then had curled up under the blanket like a small child, face to the fiddle, legs drawn up to her chest.

There were the usual sighs and snores through the night of people sleeping uneasily. At some point the oil ran out and the lamp died. I dozed for a while, then was jerked wide awake by a scream from somewhere near me. 'No. No, don't let him take me. Don't let him take me!'

Daisy. We were all awake in the grey of pre-dawn, getting out from makeshift beds with a clattering of planks and cries of what was up, what was happening? I was nearest to Daisy so got to her first and she struggled, trying to push me away. 'No, no, no!' I pinioned her as gently as I could in the blanket, talking to her all the time, telling her that it was all right, she was safe, we'd protect her. She stopped struggling but was trembling so violently that I could feel it vibrating through my own body. Somebody managed to find a candle and light it and that seemed to help. At least we could look round the room and tell her truthfully that there was nobody there. The woman whose bed was nearest the door was sure nobody had come in and nothing could have come near Daisy without disturbing the rest of us who slept round her.

'Nightmare.'

'She's had a nightmare, poor thing.'

'Leave the candle on the table. She doesn't like the dark.'

So we hugged Daisy, reassured and settled her and I moved my pallet closer to hers so that, for what was left of the night, she could reach out and grab me if the fear came back. As we were falling asleep again she murmured so softly that I could only just hear, 'I thought he'd come for me. I thought he'd come to take me back.' I whispered that he wasn't there, that we'd all protect her. Like the rest, I knew it had been a nightmare. Unlike them, I knew from Daniel what her nightmare was.

Chapter Seven

NEXT MORNING DAISY WAS PALE AND quiet but that was normal with her and nobody said anything about the scare in the night. We all trooped over to the old school-house for breakfast of bread and tea. Harry Hawthorne shambled out of the men's sleeping quarters like a dishevelled bear from its cave, drank three mugs of tea and teased Daisy gently about where her young man had got to.

Around ten o'clock Daniel arrived with the look of a man who hadn't slept much and a pocketful of tin whistles. It turned out that Hawthorne had ordered him to give the Scipians an illustrated talk on Everyman's Music. As we all moved over to the big tent where lectures were held he trailed behind the others, obviously waiting for me.

'Well, is it tonight?'

'I shan't know till later. The earliest anybody could get here with the other picture would be late afternoon.'

'How will I know?'

I said I supposed he'd be down at the camp again in the evening and I'd try to get word to him then. Through a not very restful night I'd been giving some thought to my new career. Mostly to its drawbacks. 'I suppose you realise,' I said, 'that I'll be carrying a valuable painting through fields at the dead of night.'

'Can't you cut it out of its frame and roll it up?'

I knew that was what proper picture thieves were supposed

to do, but the thought of putting a knife even to the edge of it terrified me. I could practically hear the squeals of the beautiful young man at Christie's.

'No, I'll take it in its frame. But it will have to be properly wrapped up and I can't risk doing that in your uncle's study.'

'So what will you do?'

'It's a question of what *you* do. There's a summerhouse at the back of your garden. It doesn't look as if it's used much.'

'It isn't.'

'Could you leave me a sheet or a thin blanket there, and some string? A paraffin lamp and matches too, if you can.'

'Yes.'

'Another thing – if the fake picture arrives this evening, I'm going to have to find somewhere to put it until after eleven when your uncle's asleep. I thought the summerhouse for that too.'

'How will you get it there?'

'Up the fields and in at the back gate.'

It would be a useful rehearsal for the more intimidating task of taking the real picture back down by the same route.

By now everybody else, including Daisy, had disappeared inside the tent. Hawthorne called, 'Come on, Daniel. We're waiting.'

I left him at the entrance, walked away with the chorus of *John Barleycorn* fading in the distance and spent the next hour or so making myself familiar with fields and footpaths around the village, plotting as inconspicuous a route as possible from the railway halt to the Venns' back gate. It consisted of a few hundred yards of road, a cart track, four fields, three gates and a stile. The thought of all that twice over, once with the false Odalisque and again with the true one, was so discouraging that I'd have called off the whole thing if I hadn't already sent the letter summoning her. Cravenly, I even hoped the blackberry hat girl had forgotten to post it. The next part of the preparations involved a trip to the village shop. It had occurred to me that oil lamps and valuable paintings might not be a good combination and a battery-powered flashlight would be a great help in an art robber's life. The woman behind the counter was friendly enough but mildly shocked at the idea that her crowded shelves would have anything so newfangled.

'Chipping Norton would be your nearest, or if you could wait till tomorrow you could have a word with Mr Bestley.'

'He sells flashlights?'

'No, he runs the carrier's cart. Tuesdays and Fridays, he'll fetch nearly anything as long as you pay him in advance.'

So, with plenty of time to spare, I took the train a few stops along the line to Chipping Norton and managed to buy a battery-powered bicycle lamp, rather bulky but giving a fair beam of light. Then I had lunch and, still with time to spare, caught a train back along the line to the junction with the express route from London.

I'd proposed the junction rather than the local halt in my letter to the office on the grounds that the messenger with the picture would attract less attention at a busier place. She could deliver it and take the next train back to town without being involved in any illegality or embarrassment if the thing went wrong.

Trains came and went without any sign of a discreet person with an indiscreet picture and I began to think it wouldn't arrive till the next day, which was a relief in a way but meant another earnest evening and uncomfortable night with the Scipians. Towards the end of the afternoon a London express drew in – also without result – until the moment after it began to pull out. It picked up speed from walking to running pace then stopped with a hiss of steam and banging and clattering of couplings with the last carriage just alongside the platform. Before it came to a halt a door opened, nearly knocking me off my feet, and a huge paper parcel came flying out, with an angry female voice shouting from somewhere behind it.

'Well, it's not my fault. I told you to tell me when we got there.'

Above the hiss and clatter, an equally angry male voice from the train was saying something about fines and emergencies. A pair of fashionably shod feet hit the platform below the parcel and a face emerged round the side of it, bright-eyed and wild-haired, with a smudged nose.

'Good afternoon. It's Miss Bray, isn't it? Would you hold this?'

The new arrival propped the parcel up against me before I could say anything and went on arguing with the man in railway uniform hanging out of the guard's van.

'It was an emergency. This is a valuable picture and it's needed urgently.'

I thought if this was their idea of discretion at Clement's Inn, I was lucky they hadn't sent banners and a brass band as well.

'It's not me delaying the confounded train anyway, it's you. Oh go on, for heaven's sake.'

She flapped her hand at the train driver, who was craning out of his cab to see what was going on behind him. Amazingly, he made a gesture that might have been an ironic salute and did drive on, with the guard shaking his fist at us from the open door of his van as he was carried away. She stood on the platform, cheeks flushed, grinning in triumph.

'At least I got it here.'

I'd never seen her before. She couldn't have been much older than twenty; not tall, she was as slim as a cigarette.

Her face was like a pretty street urchin's, surrounded by the kind of dark wiry curls that are designed by nature to ping hairpins out of place like water drops from a dog shaking itself, and sure enough her hair was coming down. If she'd started the day with a hat it must have got left on the train. In spite of my annoyance, it was hard not to look at her and laugh, partly because of the contrast between her appearance and her voice. It was unmistakably upper class and had the tone of a family who'd been telling other people what to do since the Conqueror landed. I put out my right hand, keeping the parcel upright with my left. Her ungloved grip was muscular. She probably played a lot of lawn tennis.

'You're . . . ?'

'Roberta Fieldfare, but for goodness sake call me Bobbie.'

'Have you been with us long?'

'Three days. My mother took me along on Saturday to help with addressing envelopes. Then this morning they asked her to bring this down to you in no end of a hurry, only she couldn't because she'd got an appointment in town, so I said I would. I was sick of envelopes by then, anyway. Actions not words, that's what I say.'

It was beginning to fall into place. Lady Fieldfare was one of our solidly useful workers, younger sister of a notorious firebrand called Maud, in her late sixties but always causing rows in committees because things weren't moving fast enough for her liking. Bobbie apparently took after her aunt.

'So what are we going to do with Bessie Broadbeam now I've got her here?'

'Um?'

She gave the parcel a little slap. 'I had a look at her on the journey. Reminded me of one of my aunt's brood mares.'

'You unwrapped it in a railway carriage?'

'I wanted to see what all the fuss was about. I suppose we

89

take it up to the old man and go back with the real one. Is there a cab?'

Worse and worse. If this did go wrong, she'd now provided us with a carriageful of witnesses, plus train driver and guard.

'Don't worry about a cab,' I said. 'Thank you for bringing the picture. If you go over to the other platform you've got plenty of time to catch the next train back.'

She didn't move. 'She's quite heavy. I'll help you with her wherever you're going.'

I told her I could manage, but seeing the picture again I was disconcerted by the size of it. Already we were attracting the hopeful attention of porters. I compromised.

'If the local train gets in before the London express, you can help me get it into the carriage, that's all.'

The local train arrived about half an hour later. Fortunately there were only two people waiting for it besides ourselves and they looked like farmers' wives too deep in gossip to take much notice. I got in and Bobbie helped manoeuvre the picture after me. We settled it against the seat. I thanked her, wished her a good journey back and slammed the door. More doors slammed. As the train slowly drew away from the platform I thought I was in for it now: no taking the thing tamely back to London and admitting failure. That must have distracted me because I wasn't aware of a person moving through the compartment until somebody was standing beside me. Guilty conscience made me jump then:

'You!' I said.

Bobbie Fieldfare was swaying as the train got up speed, looking a bit abashed.

'I've been thinking . . .'

'You're not supposed to be thinking, you're supposed to be going back to London. What are you doing here?'

'I got on at the other end. I thought I could see you to where you're going at any rate.'

90

She sat down on the seat opposite. I felt like pitching her out of the train but that might have attracted attention so I ignored her until we stopped at the local halt. When the train went on its way there were just three of us on the wooden planks of the platform, Bobbie, Bessie Broadbeam and me. By then I'd managed to get over some of my annoyance and admit that Bobbie might have her uses in a limited way. It was around half-past six, less than two hours of daylight left. With her help I could use the time to get the picture stowed in the Venns' summerhouse and still, with luck, send her back to London on a late train.

Bobbie stared round at the fields and copses and remarked that it looked like quite good hunting country. I pointed out the Venn house, half hidden by trees.

'That's where we're going, over the fields.'

The cheerful way she accepted this put her up a point in my estimation. We each grasped one side of the picture, getting a good grip on the knobbly frame through the wrappings, and carried it along the road, up the cart track and into a stubble field. The farmworkers had gone to their tea, so there was nobody to see us except a couple of pheasants getting plump on harvest gleanings. A copper glow was on the birds and the stubble and the horizontal light threw our grotesque shadow across the field, like a rectangular beast with two sets of unmatched legs. We went slowly across two more fields, stopping now and then to change our grip on the frame or massage aching wrists and fingers. Although I wouldn't admit it to Bobbie and discouraged her attempts to chat and ask questions, I wasn't altogether sorry to have help and worried even more about how I'd manage getting the real Bessie back over the same ground in the dark on my own. She'd be every bit as awkward and heavy and so much more valuable that an accident with a toe or tree branch would be a disaster.

91

At one point on our uphill journey we stopped for a rest only a field's width away from the road and heard hooves and wheels coming down it from the direction of the Venns'. I took Bobbie by the shoulder and pressed us and the picture into the hedge. On the road, the Venns' gig came past at a brisk walk, the oil lamps on the front already lit and glowing like pale lemon sweets in the evening light. A man sat in the driving seat on his own, staring straight ahead. Although I couldn't be sure from across the field in the dim light I was pretty sure it was Adam Venn; the figure looked too respectable for Daniel and too active for Oliver.

'Is that one of them?' Bobbie said when he'd gone past.

'Yes.'

My heart was beating faster than I liked. Daniel's view of the operation seemed over-optimistic to me now that action was getting closer. At any rate, I didn't want to be the one to lead this infant any further astray.

'Thank you,' I said. 'I can manage now. If you cut across to the road then down to the railway you should be able to get the late train back to the junction.'

'I'm not going back.'

'Oh yes you are. You've delivered Bessie, and I'm very grateful. That's your job done. Back to the envelopes.'

'I'm sure I'd be a lot better at burglary.'

'Who said anything about burglary?'

I certainly hadn't in my letter. As far as anyone at Clement's Inn knew, this was simple exchange, all above board.

'We're going in the back way and you're as twitchy as a filly her first time out. So we're leaving this picture and snitching the real one. Good idea.'

'I am not twitchy.' I was so annoyed I practically shouted it. Here was this fledgling, probably around ten years younger than I was, questioning my nerve. 'Now will you go, please.'

'You'll need somebody to keep a lookout. And how are

you going to break in? There's a trick with treacle and brown paper for taking out window panes quietly. My brother taught me.'

'So does everybody's brother. Firstly we haven't got any treacle and secondly it doesn't work anyway.'

I'd no intention of telling her that two of the Venns were part of the plot.

'At least let me help you get it up to the house.'

Her tone was so submissive that I was idiot enough to give in.

'All right, but no further.'

As we walked on I wondered where Adam was heading and guessed it would have something to do with the Daniel and Daisy problem. We came to a farm gate with a rickety barn on the far side of it, old dry hay sticking out from gaps in the timbers. At that point only one small field separated us from the back of the Venns' house. We went slowly over tussocky pasture, keeping in the shadow of a tall hedge to our left then round the corner towards the small garden gate, the wall protecting us against being seen from the house. When we reached the gate I propped the picture up and told Bobbie to wait. With Adam away, and Felicia probably too miserable to care, the only person I had to worry about was Oliver Venn, and some caution was needed from now on in case he happened to be out for an evening stroll in the garden. I had my hand on the latch of the gate when it happened.

A single gunshot. It came from the garden at the back of the Venns' house and was loud enough to set the drowsy blackbirds into a flurry of alarm calls and make orange and brown butterflies rise up from the bramble flowers. A sharp, stinging sound. Then, after it, a sound of human distress, like a strangled sob. It took a second for my brain to register. I looked at Bobbie and after that comment about my supposed twitchiness was pleased to see that she was as shocked as I was.

'It sounded like—'

'Stay there.'

I left her with the picture and went through the gate into the garden. My first panicked thought was Oliver shooting at us, but the sound had come from away to the right, towards the summerhouse. I pushed my way towards it through archways sagging with vegetation, purple cardoon flowers flopping across the path, nettles shoulder-high, white convolvulus looped between bushes with stems as tough as parcel string. The summerhouse was in the angle between the wall and the unkempt yew hedge, artistically built with knobbly timbers and trelliswork, but neglected now. A woman in a white blouse and a skirt with a pattern of peacock feathers was standing just inside the trellis, staring out at me. Felicia Foster. Her brown hair was tangled and scattered with bits of leaves. Her face was creamy pale, damp with sweat and tears, eyes scared. The hand by her skirt, pale against the purple and turquoise swirls of the pattern, was weighed down by something heavier than feathers. A gun. A revolver. I raised my eyes from it, back to her face.

'What's happened? Are you all right?'

There was a change in Felicia's eyes, recognising not me in particular but the fact that somebody was there.

'I . . . I found this. Under there.'

Her right hand lifted slowly as if coming up from deep water, bringing the gun with it, pointing at a blanket on the bench in the corner of the summerhouse. A ball of twine lay beside the blanket, matches and a paraffin lamp.

I stepped forward and held my hand out for the gun. She hesitated for a moment then let me take it. The barrel was still warm and it reeked of powder and hot oil.

'I heard a shot,' I said, 'a few minutes ago.'

94

'It went off. It was under the blanket. I picked it up and it went off. I didn't mean . . .'

Her empty hand was shaking against the skirt.

'I'll take you back to the house,' I said.

'Flissie. Flissie, are you there?' Carol Venn's distant voice calling from the house, high and anxious.

'It's all right, Carol. I'm here.'

It was a brave try. From where I was standing I could hear the tremor in Felicia's voice, but Carol probably couldn't.

'Is it the boys shooting rabbits again?'

'I don't know. Wait there, I'll come in.'

She stepped out of the summerhouse and looked at me.

'Go to her,' I said.

Slowly she walked in the direction of the house. Carol was family – she'd manage better than I could. After a while I heard Carol's voice again, asking 'Are you all right, Flissie?' If there was a reply I didn't hear it.

I looked at the gun, pointing it at the ground in case of accidents. I'd never taken much interest in the things but a cousin who went into the army had been knowledgeable about them and I remembered him saying that revolvers didn't usually go off accidentally. At any rate, with a shot just fired the chamber would be empty so it was safe for carrying. I slipped it into the pocket of my jacket and went back to Bobbie. She was waiting more or less where I'd left her. I now had three things on my hands I wanted to get rid of: the revolver, the picture and her.

'What was happening?'

'Nobody's hurt. But I think we'd better leave the picture in the barn down there for now. I'll come back for it later.'

We went back down the field with the picture, the hedge shadow now dissolved into dusk. The barn door was open. We edged the picture inside and propped it against a pile of hay. Then, as bad luck would have it, the revolver fell out of my pocket. They never make them strong enough in women's clothes. Bobbie's eyes widened.

'Is that yours?'

'No.' I picked it up and shoved it in the other pocket, glaring at her to show that further questions weren't welcome. 'That's it, then. Off you go to the train.'

She didn't move. 'Are you staying here?'

'No, I've got things to do. The picture will be safe here for an hour or two.'

Daniel would be paying his evening visit to Daisy at the Scipian camp. I had to see him and tell him that the substitution was on for tonight. That and something else.

'You can't leave Bessie Broadbeam on her own. She'll be a lot safer if I stay here and keep an eye on her.'

I gave in. Arguing would take too long. Also, against my will, I was beginning to have some respect for Bobbie. She'd been uncomplaining in carrying the picture around and hadn't panicked at all about the gun.

'It will be a long time, probably midnight,' I warned her.

'That's all right. I suppose you wouldn't care to leave that gun with me? I could amuse myself shooting rats.'

No, I told her, I would not. As I walked fast downhill towards the camp the wretched thing hung heavy in my pocket, banging against my thigh.

I didn't join the Scipians, not wanting to face questions from Max. Instead I walked up and down the field at the back of the old schoolhouse, watching for Daniel. He came loping along the path at around ten o'clock, a darker figure against the darkness, whistling a sad little tune I hadn't heard before. I came up behind him.

'Mr Venn.'

He spun round. 'Have you got it?'

'Yes.'

'Tonight's the night, then. Can you give me a couple of hours? I want to talk to Daisy, then I'll go back and see to things. I'll make sure the studio door's unlocked. Uncle Olly will be snoring by the time I get back so I'll unhook the picture from the wall for you. You remember where his study is? Left at the top of the stairs and along to the end of the corridor.'

'I saw your brother going out in the gig. Won't it be embarrassing for him if he comes back late and bumps into me?'

'He'll be back by now. He was only going to see a friend in the village.' He seemed to sense some reservation on my part. 'You're not going off the idea, are you?'

'No. But there's something you should know. Did you hear a gunshot in your garden this evening, just as it was getting dark?'

'No, I was playing the piano. But Carol and Uncle Olly were going on at dinner about boys shooting rabbits.'

'Was Miss Foster at dinner?'

'No. Felicia had a headache and they sent something up to her on a tray. To be honest, I think she's avoiding me.'

He said it with that hurt little boy air, as if she were being unreasonable.

'It wasn't a boy shooting rabbits. It was Miss Foster with this.'

I took the revolver out of my pocket. With only starlight to see by he had to bend his head close to it.

'Oh God, it looks like . . .' I let him take it from me and got out my bicycle lamp to give him a better look at it. 'I think it's Aunt Philly's.'

'Your aunt had a revolver?'

I thought of Philomena in her old-fashioned bonnet and black lace gloves.

'A Smith and Wesson .38 calibre. A friend brought it back

97

for her from California. She'd play with Adam and me, shooting lemonade bottles off the wall. She was a pretty good shot, as a matter of fact.' He broke open the gun and signed to me to bring the lamp closer. 'It's a five shot. Looks as if two of them have been fired.'

'I only heard one. Did your aunt give it to Miss Foster?'

'Of course she didn't. What would Felicia want with a thing like this?'

'She was in the summerhouse at the back of the garden, holding it. I heard the shot and went running to see what the matter was. She said she'd found it under the blanket you left for me, picked it up and it went off. She'd been crying.'

A long silence.

'Did you put it under the blanket?' I asked him.

'Of course not. Why should I do that?'

I hoped I wouldn't have to say anything else and in the end he got there.

'You don't believe her, do you?'

'I think there's another possible explanation.'

'She gets Aunt Philly's gun, goes to the summerhouse and . . . oh God.'

'Tries to kill herself? Yes, I think so.'

Chapter Eight

I LEFT THE GUN WITH HIM, but the idea of it was still weighing me down as I went back up the field in the dark. Poor Felicia. Poor Daisy. Even poor Daniel. Stupid, yes, but well meaning. Come to think of it, there's probably more damage done in the world by well-meaning stupidity than calculating malice. He'd behaved like a boy, thrilled with his power to alter lives. Then suddenly and belatedly he'd looked at the gun and had to grow up. Goodness knows where it would end, but that wasn't my problem. By the time it got light, I should be on the milk train back to London with the picture and that would be my last contact with the Venns. Sooner or later, perhaps, I'd hear which one he'd married. No point in even thinking about it. Stick to what you've come for. But, trudging in the dark, I started to hate what I was doing. What did a picture or money matter when lives were being torn apart? I had to conjure up Emmeline to give me a talking to about battles to fight, not everybody's duties being pleasant, not letting down the cause. Yes, Emmeline, I know, I know. But if you'd seen . . . All right, I'm *doing* it, aren't I?

I went quietly, keeping to the hedges, avoiding the pale smudges in the dark that were sleeping sheep. But Bobbie Fieldfare must have had good hearing. She was outside the barn waiting for me.

'Are we ready? I'll get Bessie.'

'Give it another hour.' I wanted to give Daniel a chance to get back to the house and make his small contribution by checking the door and unhooking the picture. 'Have you been all right here?'

'Pretty well,' Bobbie said. 'I had to scare off a drunk tramp, but he was no trouble.'

'When?'

'Just after it got dark. I was sitting here wishing I had a cigar to pass the time, then there were these footsteps outside and somebody shambling round whistling. Then he came to the doorway and mumbled something. I told him to clear out and he went.'

'He went because you told him to?'

'I said I'd got a gun, which was pretty nearly true. I knew you should have left it with me.'

'What was it he mumbled?'

'Couldn't make it out because of the accent and him being drunk, but it didn't sound friendly.'

'A local accent?'

'Country. They all sound alike to me. I can do the tune he was whistling if you like.'

She whistled, off-note but recognisably, the first few bars of *Long Lankin*.

'What did he look like?'

'Too dark to see. Why worry about him? He'll have found some other barn to sleep it off in by now. Have you worked out a way to get us in?'

I said yes and left it at that. By now I'd accepted that I couldn't get rid of her, but the less she knew, the better. We sat in silence outside the barn until I judged that about an hour had passed. It was almost totally dark and the countryside quiet apart from a hedgehog snuffling somewhere in the hedge. Bobbie was on her feet as soon as I moved, following me into the barn for the picture.

'Hup, Bessie old girl. Time to go home.'

Bobbie was having the time of her life. As we carried the picture up the field alongside the hedge she moved with the bounciness of a dog let out for an unexpected walk. The back garden gate creaked on its hinges, something I hadn't noticed by day but at this time of night it sounded as loud as a trumpet call. I said quietly in Bobbie's ear that I'd go ahead to check that nobody was about and she should wait with Bessie. Trailing briars and roses came out of the dark and slapped me in the face and other vegetable stuff twined round my ankles and squished underfoot. As I got nearer the house I saw a faint light coming from the studio windows and cursed, thinking Adam or Oliver must be up late. As quietly as I could I moved across the terrace and looked in at a window.

The light was coming from the hall, through a door left partly open, possibly Daniel's idea of being helpful. But there was something wrong about the room, something that hadn't been there before, a big dark shape looming in the middle of it. Then my eyes got used to the light and the thing was only the massive dark oak cabinet I'd seen in the workshop. No sign of anybody in the room. The brass handle of the door into the studio was cold against my palm. It turned and the door opened with hardly a sound. I took a deep breath, waited for a minute then went back through the garden to Bobbie. We carried the picture sideways on along the narrow path, up the terrace steps and into the studio. As we were going past the oak cabinet Bobbie stumbled and let out a muffled curse.

'Rug or something.'

We propped the picture against the wall and I signed to Bobbie to wait again while I looked into the hall and up the staircase. The light I'd seen was coming from an oil lamp hanging just inside the front door. This was the bit I didn't like at all. The staircase as I remembered it was wide and imposing, sweeping up to a broad landing. Once embarked on it we'd be as obvious as two dogs on a cricket pitch, even in the dark. I was tempted to find a less obvious way, perhaps through the kitchen and up the back service stairs that must exist in a house like this. But I didn't know the house, and blundering around backstairs in the dark might be a worse risk. We'd stick to Daniel's plan, such as it was. I went back, collected Bobby and the picture again and we shuffled out into the hall. If Oliver or Adam happened to be looking down from the floor above we were done. I went up backwards with Bobbie walking forwards and the picture in between us, the stair carpet muffling our steps.

At the top of the stairs we paused. Below us the hall in the dim light was silent and empty. Up here, almost total darkness and deep masculine snores from somewhere to the right. They sounded like an old man's and I hoped they were Oliver's. We turned left, the corridor wide enough for us to walk side by side with Bessie in between. By now I felt as if we'd been welded to her for life, like a trio of badly matched Siamese triplets. We went on to the far end of the corridor. The last door on the left was the one I'd seen Daniel disappearing into a few days before, so presumably his room. No sound came from inside it. The corridor ended at the door to Oliver Venn's study. It opened noiselessly and we bundled ourselves inside. Bobbie let out a sigh of relief. A big window faced us with the curtains drawn back and starlight coming through it, dim enough but seeming bright after the dark of the corridor. I took the battery cycle lamp out of my pocket and switched it on. Light of any kind was a risk but we couldn't do without it. The small yellow glow made a kind of cave, with parts of the room still in darkness. A big desk to our right, crowded with papers. Above it, a picture in a gilt frame. The light just reached to the pink cloud of her haunches.

102

'Well,' Bobbie whispered, 'Bessie Broadbeam's twin sister.'

I was annoyed to find the picture still up there on the wall instead of unhitched and waiting for us as Daniel had promised. I signed to Bobbie that she should hold the lamp while I got on the desk to unhook it but she scrambled up herself, brisk as a monkey on a barrel organ.

'Can you hold the light closer? The wire's all twisted up round the picture hook.'

In the end I had to climb up beside Bobbie, support the bottom of the picture with one hand and hold the lamp with the other while she struggled with the wire. Although we tried to be quiet we must have made some noise. I imagined Daniel, still awake probably and listening on one side of us, Adam and Carol on the other. If Adam woke and heard, how was she supposed to distract him? That idea seemed like another piece of Daniel's breezy optimism that might collide with reality. Although things had gone more or less smoothly so far my heart was thumping with fear that the study door would open and a voice shout out. Once the wire was untwisted we had a bad moment when several thousand guineas' worth of picture nearly fell on us but we managed to get her to the floor safely. Then we unwrapped the false Bessie and used her coverings to wrap up the real one for her journey as far as the summerhouse. By then the lamp battery was nearly gone and we still had to get the false Bessie in place.

'Can't we just leave her?' Bobbie whispered.

But I needed to buy time for ourselves and Daniel. With the false Bessie high on the wall it was just possible that Oliver Venn wouldn't notice the substitution for some time – until, say, we'd got the proper one safely sold and the money in the WSPU bank account. Unlikely, but just possible.

I hitched my skirt up, clambered on the desk and waited for Bobbie to hand her up. While I was waiting, we heard a noise. It sounded like a door opening and closing some distance away.

'Miss Bray, somebody's about.'

Bobbie's voice came from the level of my knee. Oh, the wonders of formality. We were burglars together but naturally she, as the younger woman, couldn't use my first name until asked. I signed to her to be quiet and turned off the lamp. It sounded to me as if the noise had come from downstairs but it was difficult to be sure through the closed study door.

'What do we do now?' Bobbie whispered.

'Wait.'

I scrambled down off the desk. Even if somebody were still up and about, it didn't necessarily mean we were in trouble. A servant perhaps, checking that doors were locked. Only Daniel had said doors weren't locked and his uncle didn't keep the servants working late. We waited five minutes, maybe longer, but there was no other sound. I thought we could be crouching there all night, losing our nerves, so switched on the lamp again – not that it helped much – and we finished the job of hitching the false Bessie up on the wall. Then we were out in the dark corridor, doing our familiar Siamese-triplet shuffle towards the stairs.

We'd almost got to the top of them when I froze. Bobbie, halting a step later, drove the frame sharply against my ribs but that was the least of our problems. Somebody was still moving about downstairs. It's difficult to say how we were so sure of it. The footsteps, if there were footsteps, would have been muffled by the hall carpet and the person was moving cautiously anyway. Perhaps it was breathing we heard, or even just the animal-like sense of somebody down there. In any case, I could feel the hair on my scalp rising, my heart skittering. Just standing there and hoping not to be seen wasn't possible. The instinct to run and hide was too powerful – but how do you run and hide when there are three of you, inextricably clasped together? To our right were the stairs, to our left a closed door with snores still coming from it loud and untroubled, behind us Adam and Caroline's rooms. I took an instant decision to go forward, past the top of the stairs to unknown territory at the end of the corridor. The snores followed us, blotting out any softer sounds there might be from downstairs. When we got to the end of the corridor there was another door facing us. I opened it and somehow we bundled ourselves through it, into the total darkness on the other side.

We were on level ground at least, a landing probably. When I pushed the door shut the back of it felt soft under my palm. Baize. Green baize, I guessed, to shut off the noise of the servants' quarters from the rest of the household. Miraculously we'd found the back stairs. Now it was only a matter of getting quietly down them and— A gasp from Bobbie, cut off so abruptly she'd probably bitten her lip. A footstep at the bottom of the stairs. A cautious footstep but not muffled, because there'd be no thick carpeting on these stairs. By bad luck or bad judgement I'd chosen the wrong staircase after all and somebody was coming up it. My guess was that one of the maids had been out late, meeting an admirer possibly, but that didn't matter because however guilty her conscience she couldn't fail to set up an outcry if she bumped into two people and a picture in the dark.

I leaned against the wall, judging our chances of abandoning the picture, running back along the corridor and down the main stairs. Then realised that it wasn't a wall I was leaning against but another door, at right angles to the baize-covered one. I found the knob, twisted it and fell sideways into deeper and disinfectant-smelling darkness, taking Bessie and Bobbie with me. I don't think we'd even got the

105

door properly closed by the time the footsteps came up and past us but whoever it was can't have noticed because they went straight through the door to the corridor, and then there was total silence, apart from the thumping of two hearts. It stayed that way for several minutes, broken by a sudden crack of china.

'Oh dammit,' Bobbie said, too loudly.

I reached for her shoulder, to give it a warning squeeze but she was somewhere around my knees, the weight of the picture was on me and what felt like a damp mop was pressing against the back of my neck. I told her under my breath to leave it for goodness sake, but she only started giggling. Nerves, probably. So much for twitchy fillies.

'It feels like a bedpan. At least it was empty.'

I kicked her, not hard but to bring her back to her duties. She asked what we did now.

'Down the stairs, and for goodness sake be quiet.'

If it had been a maid, she'd be in her bed by now, relieved to have got away with truancy. We went down the dark stairs with the picture, coir matting underfoot, elbows brushing against the walls. The last few stairs were lit by a dim red glow and when we negotiated them we found we were in the kitchen, with the light coming from the firebox of the cooking range, left low for the night. It was tempting to find our way out by the kitchen door, but that might lead to collisions with empty bottles or pig bins, so instead I steered us across the room, making for what I hoped would be the family side of the house. Another baize-covered door to negotiate and there we were back in the hall with the dim lamplight gleaming just as we'd left it, then through the door to the studio. After what had happened, it almost felt like home. Not enough, though, to make us want to linger.

In my mind we were already several fields away, making for the railway by dawn and back to town in the early train that carried churns of good Cotswold milk to Oxford and London – milk and us and Bessie. It had been harder than I'd expected but we'd done it. I even felt quite kindly towards Bobbie. Until, that is, she tripped over a footstool, landed on a rug, went skating across the polished floor windmilling her arms and crashed against a carved oak sideboard with a noise that would have woken a hibernating tortoise. The only good thing was that she'd let go of the picture by then so that wasn't included in the wreckage, but I was past caring. The fates had been against this from the start or they wouldn't have sent her. Now the only thing to do was save ourselves. I put down the picture, grabbed her by the arm and pulled her up.

'Out. Run.'

She went for the picture.

'No. Leave that.'

But she was still argumentative. In spite of my anger, I had to give her marks for determination.

'If we hide it somewhere we can come back for it.'

She went to the dark oak chest and pulled the door open. Voices from upstairs were asking each other what was wrong, what was happening? A man's voice and a woman's, Adam and Carol I thought.

'It's big enough, and—'

Footsteps coming fast down the stairs now. Bobbie's voice died away. I had her arm again, trying to pull her away from the cabinet, but she seemed frozen. Then I looked over her shoulder and in the dim lamplight saw what she was seeing.

'Leave that,' I said. 'Get away from it.'

There must have been something convincing in my voice because she did. The footsteps reached the studio door and Adam's voice, sharp and angry, asked what was happening.

Chapter Nine

A T FIRST, IN THE SHADOW INSIDE the cabinet, it looked as if it might have been a figure carved from black oak like the rest, wedged at an angle with one foot sticking out. Then my hand touched something rough but yielding. Wool, some kind of wool fabric. There was a musty smell. Dried sweat, dead leaves. Something else, sharper and metallic.

'Who's in there? What's going on?'

The door from the hall was opening wide, a dark silhouette standing there speaking in the same angry voice. By then I had the bicycle lamp out of my pocket and was fumbling with it.

'Daniel, is it you?'

As Adam came towards the cabinet I got the lamp switched on and shone it on the thing inside. Her head was turned away from us into a corner, sideways on as if trying to escape from the light, but the neck was bent in a way no neck could ever be in life, her whole body propped on the diagonal across the width of the cabinet, one foot sticking out a little way and upturned so that light glinted on metal segs in the sole of the clumsy boot, newish segs put there to make the boots last longer. The shin coming out of the boot, even in its thick woollen stocking, looked as thin as a bird's. When I shone the lamp up again I saw dead leaves and grass in her red hair. Shrivelled brown oak leaves from last winter. Adam had recognised me by now.

'What's happened? What have you done?'

I stood back to let him look.

'Oh God,' he said. Then, fiercely to me, 'Who is it? What were you doing with her?'

'Nothing. We've just found her.'

'Adam. Adam, what is it?'

Carol's voice from out in the hall.

'Don't come in,' he shouted at her. Then, to me again. 'Is she . . . ?'

I nodded.

'We'd better get her out,' he said.

It was the wrong thing to do, I know that of course. Yet somehow, even though I knew very well she was dead, it seemed out of the question to leave her stuffed in the cupboard that terrible, casual way like something unwanted. Bobbie moved forward to help. I waved her back. So far Adam gave no sign that he'd noticed her. He shuddered, reached into the cabinet, and took hold of the hunched shoulders.

Together we got her out. It wasn't easy. Her body bent a little but the arms and legs felt as stiff and brittle as wood, the bent neck rigid. We laid her on one of the rugs. I'd left the cycle lamp standing on the floor and by its waning yellow light we could see the blood on her hair and neck. The iron smell of it was clogging the air. There must have been a lot of it to smell so much, but her thick dark clothes had soaked it up. Silently Adam stretched out his palms to me, dark red from where he'd taken hold of her shoulders. There was a gasp from the doorway. Carol was standing there carrying a lamp. She wore a blue velvet dressing gown, crinkly hair down to her shoulders, feet bare. The lamplight wavered over the carved panels, the hanging demon figure with its lolling tongue, the murdered lady and her surprised wooden O of a mouth.

109

'What's happened? Is somebody hurt?'

Then she must have seen the body on the floor, because she screamed and would have dropped the lamp if Bobbie hadn't jumped forward and taken it. She went on screaming, not loudly but with a terrifying concentration, like an injured stoat. Adam ran and took her by the shoulders.

'Stop it. Please.' Then, to us, 'Cover her up, for goodness sake.'

There was a beautiful embroidered cloth on one of the tables. Bobbie and I gathered it up in armfuls and put it over the body. It settled as lightly as leaves. Adam was sitting on a sofa, Carol curled against him, not moving. He asked me, 'Who is it?'

So he'd never met her, I thought. Discussed her, dealt with her as a family crisis, settled her immediate future and never as much as set eyes on her. For some reason – shock, probably – that made me desperately sorry for Daisy and furious with the Venns.

'It's Daisy Smith,' I told him. 'The girl your brother was going to marry.'

Carol said something to him that I couldn't hear. He shook his head. Meanwhile things were happening outside, footsteps coming from the direction of the kitchen, a wavering voice from the stairs.

'Carol? Adam?'

Adam groaned. 'Uncle Olly. Get him to go back to bed. Tell him I'll come to him in a minute.' Then, as I was halfway to the door, 'No, ask him to go up and get Daniel. Don't tell him what's happened.'

When I went out to the hall, two people converged on me. The first was Oliver Venn at the bottom of the stairs in an old-fashioned nightgown and cap, looking dazed with sleep, eyes gummy. The other was the maid Annie, in nightdress and dressing gown with her hair in a plait.

110

'There's been an accident,' I told them. 'Would you go upstairs and ask Daniel to come down.'

Anything to get them away. Annie grasped the situation before Oliver, seeing from my expression that the accident was serious, and led him back upstairs. When I went back to the studio Carol was sitting upright on the couch beside her husband, pale and shaking but more composed. Bobbie had settled herself on a chair some way from them and Daisy's body, head in her hands.

'Now, Miss Bray,' Adam said, still shaky but judgemental, 'can you explain to us what's happened?'

The hardness of his voice told us, if we hadn't known before, how bad things looked for Bobbie and me. So I told him, as calmly as I could, from the start. Daniel had suggested the substitution, I said. (I left Carol out of it. She had enough to deal with already and I wasn't certain anyway how much she'd known about the details of the plan.) He listened, arm still round Carol.

'But where did Daisy Smith come into it?'

'She didn't, not at all, until I found her in the cabinet when we tried to hide the picture in there.'

Carol spoke for the first time. 'In the cabinet? She was actually in the cabinet?'

'I'm afraid so.'

'But how . . . ?'

'It looks like a head injury,' Adam said.

I thought she was going to collapse again but she bit her lip and kept herself upright.

'And Daniel suggested you should break in?'

'More than suggested, he planned it. If you don't believe me, you'll have to ask him. But I can promise you that all we came for is the picture, and we've no more idea than you have what happened to Miss Smith.'

Carol said, 'Where is Daniel? And where's Felicia?'

Until then, I think we'd all forgotten about Felicia. There was a silence, then Carol pulled herself away from Adam and got to her feet.

'Somebody's got to tell them. I'll go and see Felicia.'

I thought Adam might protest, but perhaps he thought: Anything to get her out of the room. We were all so carefully not looking at the thin shape under the embroidery that had been Daisy.

'I'll go with you,' I said.

She was trying hard, but didn't look fit to get up the stairs on her own. In the hall Annie was waiting for us, terrified.

'I've got Mr Venn to go back to bed, but we can't find Mr Daniel anywhere,' she said.

Carol asked, 'Isn't he in his room?' Then, when Annie shook her head, 'Well, you'd better go and make tea for everybody. Serve it in the morning room and make up a fire there, please.'

She still sounded near tears but her mind had obviously started working again. When in doubt, ask for tea. Keep everyone occupied. She was right about the fire too. Even an August morning strikes cold at two or three o'clock or whatever it was by now. We climbed the stairs together in silence and went to the door of Felicia's room. It surprised me that the noise that had been enough to wake Oliver from his drugged sleep hadn't brought her down. Carol tapped on the door gently.

'Felicia, are you awake?'

No answer. Another knock, louder this time.

'Felicia?'

No answer. We looked at each other. There was the slightest of noises from the other side of the door, maybe a bedspring creaking. We waited, but heard nothing else. Carol took hold of the handle and pushed the door open. The blue and willow-patterned room was different shades of grey in the light coming through from the corridor, the curtains half drawn back. There was no head on the big white pillow, only a hump under the quilt. The hump rocked and quivered and, as the door opened, let out a little moaning noise.

'Felicia, what's wrong?'

Carol and I barged into each other in our hurry to get through the door. It was in my mind, hers too I supposed, that Felicia was tied up or injured under the quilt. We grabbed it, pulled it back, and there was Felicia in her nightdress, hair down and twisted round her, curled up on her side with her mouth open.

'No, no, no, no.'

A sobbing protest, like a child's, at being revealed. She grabbed for the quilt, tried to pull it back over her.

'What's wrong? Are you hurt? What's happened?'

Carol was on her knees by the bed, catching hold of Felicia's flailing hand. I found a lamp on the bedside table and lit it. Felicia's 'no, no' had turned to a low moaning. Her eyes were huge and horrified. Her bare arms where the nightdress sleeves had fallen back were criss-crossed with scratches. Her clothes lay on the floor in a heap, including the peacock skirt she'd been wearing in the summerhouse. The bottom of it was thick with dust, bristling with fragments of grass and straw. By now Carol had got Felicia's hand flat on the eiderdown, and was stroking it. After a while she persuaded her to sit up and propped bolsters and pillows behind her. I pulled the quilt back, unhooked a warm wool dressing gown from the back of the door and draped it round her shoulders. She'd stopped moaning but was still as tense as a violin string. Carol and I knelt on the sheepskin rug by the bed. Her eyes caught mine and I could see a question in them: What do we say about this? Mine were probably asking the same question, so neither of us got an answer.

'Would you like anything, Flissie? Some hot milk?'

This at least got an answer in the form of a little nod, although I doubted if she'd even understood the question. Carol stood up.

'Do you mind staying with her, Miss Bray? I'll go down and get it from the kitchen.'

Time passed. There were movements from downstairs and I wondered where Bobbie was. I held on to Felicia's unresponsive hand, pulled the dressing gown up over her shoulders when it slid down, and said nothing. There were two reasons for saying nothing. One was that I doubted whether Felicia would understand, whatever I said. The other was that there were questions in my mind that it would be inhuman to ask a person in this condition, even if they did get answers.

Questions like: How did you know something terrible had happened?

Or: Why didn't you come out of your room when everybody else did?

Or: How did you get those scratches on your arms?

When, after a long time, she spoke at last I was so surprised that I almost missed what she was saying.

'There was a shot.'

Not quite her normal voice but not far off it.

'Yes,' I said. 'There was a shot.'

'I had a gun, didn't I?'

She was looking at me, aware now that she'd seen me before.

'In the summerhouse, is that what you mean?'

She didn't answer, just crinkled her forehead as if trying to remember. I didn't dare ask anything else and she hadn't said another word by the time Carol came back with a mug of milk on a tray and a medicine bottle. At least having to look after Felicia had helped her get back her self-possession.

'Adam suggested we should give her some of Uncle Olly's sleeping drops. How is she?'

114

'A bit better, I think.'

I didn't tell her what Felicia had said. I needed time to think.

'Felicia, would you like some of Uncle Olly's drops? You'll feel better when you've slept.'

She nodded silently. Carol slid six precise drops from a pipette into the milk and handed the mug to Felicia. We watched while she drank like a good child, kept on watching as her head sank back into the pillows, her eyes closed and her breathing became normal and regular. Then we tucked the quilt round her, drew the curtains all the way across and tiptoed out with the tray and the medicine bottle. Once we were out in the corridor with the door closed behind us, Carol heaved a deep sigh. Her face looked as drained and tired as mine probably did, but her voice was firm.

'I've told Adam. He thinks you'd better join us for a talk downstairs, if you don't mind.'

Told him about Felicia, I supposed. I didn't ask questions, just followed her down.

Chapter Ten

THE ROOM WHERE WE HAD OUR discussion was on the same side of the house as the studio, curtains drawn back giving a view of the dark garden with a vine crowding the glass from outside. Inside, soft light of oil lamps, ash logs fizzing sap in the newly lit fire, tea things on the table.

When we came in Adam was standing staring out at the garden wearing the same clothes he'd had on when he first came downstairs, trousers and a woollen pullover, sockless feet in leather slippers. His face when he turned and looked at us was strained and questioning. At first I didn't notice there was anybody else in the room until a weak voice said 'Carol, Carol, my dear . . .' and Oliver Venn made a clumsy effort to get to his feet. He'd been hunched in the corner of a sofa by the fire. Carol sat down beside him and took his hand.

'We thought you were in bed, Uncle Olly.'

'He came down again,' Adam said, not sounding pleased about it.

Carol looked a question and he nodded.

'I've told him.'

'The poor girl,' Oliver said. 'Such a dreadful, dreadful accident.'

Nobody corrected him. He'd changed out of his nightgown into flannels and a blue smoking jacket, but still looked more asleep than awake and his voice was quavering. 'That

awful cabinet. You should never have brought it here, Carol.
I don't like it. Philomena would have hated it.'

'He thinks it fell on her,' Adam explained, as if his uncle
weren't there. 'What about Flissie?'

'She's asleep,' Carol told him.

A nod, as if something had been agreed between them.
By this time I'd sat myself down on an armchair, uninvited,
legs shaky. Adam turned to me.

'You understand, Miss Bray, I shall have to go for the
police – in fact, I should have done it by now.'

'If there's any question, you can say you had to deal with
the hysterical womenfolk first,' Carol said.

Was she joking? She gave no sign of it. She was still holding Oliver's hand, her long bare feet sinking into thick carpet.
There was no sign of Bobbie.

'Your friend's in the kitchen with Annie and Cook,' Adam
said. 'I realise that you have a difficult decision to make about
what you tell the police to explain your presence here.'

'There's no decision to make. I shall tell them what
happened. Only I want my friend kept out of this if possible. Everything she did was under my direction and she
couldn't have heard or seen anything that I didn't.'

'Are you suggesting that we keep things from the police?'

Adam Venn was a lawyer, after all, and his tone made
me feel as if I were already in the witness box, so I hit
back.

'I suppose that's what this discussion is about. Otherwise
you'd have gone for them already.'

I was still angry on Daisy's behalf, angry with us all. The
Venns had tried to manage the inconvenience of her in life;
now we were sitting around in this comfortable room trying
to do the same thing with her death.

'Please,' said Carol, 'don't let's start quarrelling.'

'I'm not intending to quarrel, but a young woman's

been killed. That's not something that can be tidied away,' I said.

'There's no proof she was killed,' Adam said, but he didn't sound convincing.

'What are the alternatives? If it was an accident, somebody must have put her body in the cabinet. Or are we suggesting that she crept in there and shot herself?'

'Shot?' Adam said. 'Why do you say shot?'

'Or killed herself any other way, come to that.'

'Shot,' he insisted. 'You said shot.'

'*Please*—' Carol interrupted us, practically shouting the word. Then, when she'd got our attention, 'Adam, this wasn't what you wanted to talk to her about. Miss Bray, please listen to him.'

Adam took a deep breath and sat down at last so that his eyes were level with mine. There was anger in them, but he was trying to control it.

'Miss Bray, please accept that we're not trying to tidy anything away. But when something like this happens, it's not only bad in itself, it can lead to all sorts of unpleasant consequences that have no direct connection with the event itself. You agree with that?'

I nodded, biting my tongue.

'Thank you. The police will naturally make inquiries about Miss Smith's identity and how she came to be in this part of the world. Inevitably, they'll hear she came here with my brother Daniel. We can't avoid that.' He paused again.

'Where *is* Daniel? What's happened to him?' Oliver's voice was pathetic and querulous. Carol shushed him gently. Adam ignored him and went on.

'The question is, whether it's equally inevitable that they should know about his . . . his so-called engagement to Miss Smith.'

'Considering the announcement was witnessed by about

a dozen people, including myself, it probably is inevitable,' I said.

'And you intend to tell the police?'

'I honestly don't know what I'm going to tell them. I suppose it will depend on what they ask me. But I'm not going to tell lies to protect your brother's reputation.'

'It's not Daniel he's thinking of,' said Carol softly. 'It's Felicia Foster.'

The name hung in the air.

'What about her?' I said. I could guess, but I wanted Adam to say it. He took his time, with long gaps between the words.

'Miss Foster has suffered great distress in the last few days because of my brother's actions. I think it's our responsibility – yours as well as ours – to see that she doesn't suffer any more from intrusive police questioning.'

'How can what I say affect that?'

'I gather from Carol that Felicia was in a state of great distress just now.'

'Yes.'

'I think you'll agree that you would not have been in a position to witness that distress if you hadn't come into our house stealthily and uninvited.'

'I might have come into the house stealthily, but I went to Miss Foster's room quite openly.'

'This isn't a matter for legalities.' (I thought that rich coming from Adam, who'd been trying to take a high legal tone, but said nothing.) 'It's a matter of, well . . . decency. If Felicia said or did in her distress anything she might regret later, it would be inhuman to pass that on without very good reason.'

'I agree. But suppose there were good reasons?'

'Such as?'

I let my eyes go where most of our minds must have been, towards the studio.

119

'Somebody's done this terrible, grotesque thing to us,' Adam said.

'To you? I thought it was to Miss Smith.'

'To all of us. Are you going to let that ruin Felicia's life? She's distressed anyway. If she's subjected to police questioning, she could break down entirely.'

'Perhaps she already has,' I said.

I made my decision. I'd already told Daniel what I'd seen in the summerhouse. Now they'd have to know it as well. I told the story as flatly as possible, from the time I heard the shot at the gate to taking the gun from Felicia. Three pairs of eyes were on me, Adam's hostile, Oliver's bleary, Carol's scared. When I finished talking, she was the one who broke the silence.

'She said she'd found the gun there?'

'That's what she told me. It might not have been true.'

Adam ran a hand through his hair, ruffling it so that he suddenly looked much more like his younger brother. Up to that point, I guessed, he really had believed he could control the effects of what had happened. Now he doubted it.

'Is that why you said she was shot, Miss Bray?'

'I don't know she was shot, but the gun was in my mind, yes.'

It must have occurred to him, as to me, that we could find out one way or the other by going next door and lifting the cloth from Daisy's body. He didn't suggest it, so neither did I.

'What became of the gun after you say you took it from Miss Foster?'

I tried not to resent his use of 'you say'. He had another shock coming to him.

'It was in my possession for perhaps two or three hours, then I gave it to Daniel.'

Carol flinched and let go of Oliver's hand.

'In *your* possession?' Adam said. 'You're admitting you had a gun for most of the evening?'

'I'm telling you, not admitting. I had it in my pocket, I didn't fire it, I told Daniel what had happened and gave it to him.'

'When was this?'

'About ten o'clock, I think.'

Carol had her fingertips together, pressed against her forehead. She said, from behind them, 'If she was shot, wouldn't we have heard it?'

'Perhaps you did,' I said.

'What?'

'I gather you and Mr Venn were having a conversation at dinner about boys shooting rabbits.'

The fingertips came down, showing dark, horrified eyes. 'No!' But it was an appeal, not a denial.

Oliver said, presumably catching at something he could understand, 'Lads from the village with shotguns. I wish they wouldn't.'

'You must have heard something,' I said to Carol. 'You were out in the garden calling Felicia. You even asked her if it was the boys shooting rabbits.'

'Yes. Yes, I did. I remember I did hear a shot but . . . oh God.'

'A shot or shots?'

'Don't answer.' Adam got up and sat beside his wife on the arm of the sofa. 'Carol, you don't have to answer that.' He looked at me. 'What are you trying to do?'

'I think what the rest of us are trying to do. Decide if there's anything we don't tell the police.'

'Are you seriously intending to put into their heads the idea that Felicia took a revolver, shot Miss Smith with it and hid her body in the cabinet? Is that what you're going to say to them?'

121

'She won't. Of course she won't,' Carol said.

She was nearly crying. Oliver just stared.

'Of course I'm not,' I said. 'I've no idea how Daisy Smith died. But it is a fact that I took a revolver from Miss Foster and later handed it to your brother.'

Impasse. Adam drew in a deep breath of air and let it out slowly.

'I can't delay going for the police much longer. They'll want to question us all about who she is and how her body was found, then there will be a post-mortem. We might not face the sorts of questions we're anticipating until after that. Perhaps not at all if there turns out to be a simple explanation for her death.'

I wondered how he thought there could be, but didn't say so. I was impressed in spite of myself by the way he was trying to keep in control of himself and us.

'If there is a simple explanation, then we might very much regret anything we'd said to throw unjust suspicion on Felicia and increase her suffering. After all, attempted suicide is a crime. Of course, it could only be an assumption that she was attempting any such thing.'

'That's quite true.'

'So the police will want to know how you came to find the girl's body and about her staying at the Scipian camp . . .' (Neat, I thought, keep it away from the family.) '. . . but unless you bring up the subject, they'll have no reason to question you about anything involving my brother or Felicia.'

'So,' I said, 'you're suggesting that we conceal Daniel's two engagements, Miss Foster's probable attempt to shoot herself and the fact that I handed over a revolver to Daniel?'

Conceal something else, too, something that only I knew about. Six words from a woman almost dissolving from fear and grief. *I had a gun, didn't I?* It felt like a theft even to have heard them, and the last thing I wanted to do was to pass them on to the police.

'I'm not suggesting we should keep anything from the police, only that we should be careful to tell them only what is strictly necessary to—'

As Adam was speaking, a face appeared in the mirror behind him. A pale face, desperate looking, surrounded by wild dark curls. I noticed it first because I was facing the mirror. It took me a second to realise that I was seeing a reflection from the window behind us. I turned and there was Daniel, mouthing something, jiggling at the closed window catch. Adam had seen him too by then and stopped what he was saying. He looked scared. I think we all were, as if letting him in would bring some new horror. Carol recovered first. She got up, released the catch, opened the window.

'Daniel, where have you been?'

'What's happened? What are you all doing up?'

Daniel squeezed through the narrow window frame and into the room, looking for a moment horribly like the creeping Long Lankin in the carving. Then he noticed me and some of the alarm went out of his eyes.

'Oh so that's what it's about, is it? You went and got caught after all.' Then, to his family, 'For goodness sake, don't make such a performance about it. It's only a picture. Listen, I've got something a lot more important to tell you. Seeing as you're up anyway, you might as well hear it together.'

He was keyed-up, unstoppable. Adam stood up, took a step towards him.

'Daniel, hold on. If you say something now you might regret—'

'Regret? It's all regrets. I've made a god-awful mess of things and the only thing I can do now is make a clean breast of it and—'

'Daniel!'

Adam actually tried to grab his brother but Daniel side-stepped him with a dancer's quickness and took up position on the rug in front of the fireplace.

'Listen, everybody. I've behaved like an idiot. I wanted to help Daisy, but I was wrong to do it at the expense of Felicia. So I'm going to wake Felicia up and tell her that if she'll have me, the engagement's on again.'

We were staring at him, speechless. Adam was frozen, the hand he'd reached out to grab Daniel fallen back at his side.

'Well, don't look at me like that,' Daniel said. 'It was what you all wanted, wasn't it? And you've got Miss Bray to thank. She made me see what I was doing. She told me . . . told me about something Felicia might have been thinking of and—'

'Daniel, will you please listen.'

Adam had found his voice at last, but Daniel swept on.

'I still care about Daisy. She's not going back to that hovel and that awful family, whatever happens. We'll find her a place to live—'

'Daisy's dead.'

Adam flung it at him, not being able to stop him any other way. Even then, Daniel was so intent on what he was saying that he didn't take it in at first.

'. . . get her qualified as a music or dance teacher – What did you say?'

'She's dead. Daisy's dead.'

He just stared, mouth open, eyes blank. Then, 'How? What happened?'

Nobody said anything. He started swaying where he stood. 'No, no, no,' he said.

Adam went over to him, put an arm round his shoulder and walked him away to the far end of the room. Daniel went as unresistingly as a puppet. An upholstered bench stood against the far wall, in half shadow away from the lamplight. Adam let him slump down there and sat beside him. The brothers' heads were close together and Adam was talking in a low voice, out of our hearing.

Oliver looked at Carol, scared and fretful. 'What's he saying to him? What's happening?'

She didn't answer. We were all poleaxed with weariness. A clock struck, low and mellow from the mantelpiece. Three o'clock. The sky outside was still dark. From the other end of the room, the murmuring went on. When I glanced that way, Daniel's head was down and he was moving it from side to side, but there was no way of telling whether that meant disagreement or bewilderment. It was half an hour before they came back to us, Daniel walking on his own now but tentatively, as if he didn't trust the floor under his feet.

Adam said, 'I'm taking the gig and going to tell the police. We can't put it off any longer.'

'Down to the police house?' Carol asked.

'No, this isn't a matter for the village bobby. I'll go straight into Chipping Norton and tell them at the police station.' Adam looked at me. 'When the police come, it's up to each of us what we tell them.' But he'd made his opinion clear enough, and his eyes told me what he expected.

'I'd better go and find my friend,' I said. 'On your way to the police, perhaps you'd be kind enough to drop her off at the railway station.' Just a nod from him, an agreement sealed almost before I knew I'd made a decision.

Bobbie didn't like it. I found her in the kitchen, sitting at the big scrubbed wooden table, drinking tea with Annie and the cook. From the way they had their heads together when I came in I knew they'd been deep in conversation. I took Bobbie outside to the corridor.

'Mr Venn's taking you to the junction,' I said. 'With luck,

there'll be a train back to town in a couple of hours. Don't ask him any questions.'

'Am I taking the Bessie Broadbeam with me?'

'No. Forget about her.'

By now the picture was so far from my mind that I'd forgotten we'd left it propped up in the studio.

'I don't see the point, then. I might as well wait until the police get here.'

I tried to keep a hold on my temper. My doubts about what I was doing made it difficult to take the firm line needed in dealing with Bobbie.

'There's nothing for you to tell them. I saw and heard everything that you did.'

'I've been thinking, if Daisy and Daniel Venn had an arrangement that she'd come to meet him and—'

I could have throttled her. 'Why in the world should she have come to meet him?'

'Well, they were engaged, weren't they and—'

'How did you hear about that?'

'Annie and the cook were talking about it. Apparently there was this fearful row when he announced it because he was engaged to the other woman and . . .'

It was dawning on me how impossible it would be for Adam to keep this hidden. Still, I did my best.

'Things are bad enough without gossip. I'd strongly suggest that you don't repeat it and you say as little as possible about anything that's happened here to anyone.'

I was almost past caring about the Venn family. What mattered was getting Bobbie off the premises.

'But there'll have to be a court case, won't there?'

'Yes. And if you stay here you'll end up in dock on a charge of attempted burglary, or in the witness box in a murder case. Or possibly both. Is that what you want?'

'I shouldn't mind.'

'Well your mother would, and your aunt.' (Emmeline too, but I hardly dared think about what she'd say.) 'I suppose you'll have to tell them something. You can say that you delivered the picture to me as arranged, then somebody in the Venn household got killed and I said you must go home. That's true at least, as far as it goes. Apart from that, don't talk about it any more than you have to.'

Normally I'd have hesitated in coaching a young woman in concealing things, but Bobbie was a special case.

'But what will happen to you?'

'Don't worry about me. I'm older than you. I can deal with it.' I'd serious doubts about that, but luckily Bobbie didn't seem to hear them in my voice. She sighed.

'If you're sure . . .'

'I'm sure. You'd better get out on the steps and wait for the gig.'

Perhaps it took Adam a long time to wake up the groom, because the sky was getting light by the time the gig came round to the front of the house. It was going to be another fine day, the air warm, a cock crowing. Bobbie scrambled up beside Adam and I watched them going away down the drive, relieved that one problem was out of the way at least. I went back into the house and found Carol waiting at the foot of the stairs.

'Daniel wanted to see her. I couldn't stop him.'

I didn't know whether she meant sleeping Felicia or dead Daisy, but her face gave me the answer.

'He pulled the cover back, took her hand and kissed it. Now he's gone to his room.'

She was much less hostile to me than Adam. Looking after Felicia together seemed to have brought us close in a short time, almost as if we were family. I offered to go up and see if Felicia needed anything and she said she'd come with me.

127

I wondered if that was simple need for companionship or whether she wouldn't run the risk of Felicia waking up and saying something to me unguardedly. She wasn't to know that it was too late already. When we opened the door and looked in Felica had turned on her side but was sleeping peacefully. Carol closed the door and took a long breath, looked down at her dressing gown and bare feet.

'She's all right for the while, then. I suppose I'd better go and get dressed before the police get here. Do ask Annie for some coffee or anything else you'd like.'

Left alone in the big house, I went back to the room where we'd had our discussion. It felt rancid with all the talking and the smell of the lamps, the furniture smeared with our plotting and bargaining. Because that was what we'd been doing, no getting away from it. We could claim it was in a good cause – or at least in the cause of not making a bad situation even worse – but it didn't feel good to me. I went round turning out the lamps and opened the windows wide to let some air in. Full light now, roses waving in a dawn breeze. How long before the police got here? Would Bobbie be on a train soon? When I turned back into the room, Annie was already there with a tray of coffee.

'Should I take some up to Mr Venn?'

Asking me, a stranger. A picture robber. I said leave it for a while, sat down and poured myself a strong cupful. I was hardly halfway down it when Oliver Venn walked in.

'Good morning, Miss Bray. Is that coffee I smell?'

He'd managed a miracle and turned himself back into the rounded and confident little man he'd seemed when I first met him. Or almost. He'd changed into a freshly laundered shirt and a dark brown linen suit, a white silk cravat at his throat, eyes rinsed and bright, tonsure of grey hair carefully combed. But he couldn't stop his hand from trembling a little when I handed him a cup of coffee. The skin on the back of the hand was thin and tight-stretched, pied with brown liver spots. He gave me a wan smile of thanks and settled himself in an armchair.

I said, 'Did Daniel give you back Philomena's revolver yesterday evening?'

I hadn't intended to come out with it like that, but his resilience annoyed me. I couldn't forget that he'd used his charm and nice manners to deceive me once already. He stared at me, eyes hurt, slopping coffee.

'Why do you ask me that, Miss Bray?'

'Because the police are going to be asking us all about that revolver sooner or later, and we'd better have our stories ready.'

'I have no story, as you put it, Miss Bray. I simply have no notion what happened to poor Philomena's gun. Until this appalling business, I'd even forgotten she possessed one.'

'Where was it kept?'

He blinked. 'In the drawer of the bureau in my study, I believe. I have a vague memory that Philomena asked me to take it some years ago. She used to keep it in her glove drawer, but apparently the oil on it made her gloves smell unpleasant.'

He wrinkled his neat little nose at the thought of it.

'Have you checked if it's in your bureau now?'

He shook his head.

'Not checked, or not there?'

'The latter.'

He admitted it reluctantly, voice low.

'And Daniel didn't give it to you or say anything about it to you yesterday evening?'

'No. Why should he? Why should Daniel be talking to me about guns?' He was indignant and it was a fair point. Daniel had believed, because of what I'd told him, that Felicia had taken his aunt's gun to kill herself. If he'd given it back to his Uncle Olly he'd have had to explain why, which would have been another betrayal of Felicia. The sensible thing would have been to lock it up somewhere until things calmed down. But had Daniel been in any condition to be sensible? I needed to talk to Daniel before the police arrived, but could hardly barge into his room.

Oliver and I sat in silence, drinking our coffee. After a while, Carol came in. She'd changed into her damson-coloured dress with a black jacket over it. As it happened, the colour of the dress matched exactly the tired crescents under her eyes, but I don't suppose she'd chosen it with that in mind. Her crinkly hair was screwed into a tight knot at the back of her head. Oliver's eyes went to her and I could see the relief in them, probably because he knew she'd protect him from me.

'How is Daniel, my dear?'

'Pacing up and down his room. I could hear him, but I didn't go in. I think he's best left to himself until Adam gets back.'

We were on to our third pot of coffee and the garden had warmed up and was beginning to spread its scents into the room by the time we heard wheels on the gravel. Oliver gave a little shiver then stood up and went to meet his guests, Carol following him. There were heavy official boots in the hall outside, deep voices speaking staccato words with Oliver's lighter twitterings underneath them. Asking, I shouldn't have been surprised, if they'd had a good journey and would they like some lemonade. I stayed where I was, regretting a lot of things.

Chapter Eleven

A S I SAT THERE I HEARD the murmur of voices and heavy feet in the studio next door. They'd want to see Daisy's body first. Adam must have given them some account of what had happened before they left the police station. A long halfhour passed then Adam came into the room with a police officer behind him, an inspector. He was a big broad-shouldered man, nearly a head taller than Adam. He stared at me. It wasn't a hostile look exactly, but it wasn't reassuring either. His grey eyes were watchful and his otherwise clean-shaven face had a tuft of bristles on one cheek, as if he'd been summoned from his home in a hurry. I'd expected them to start questioning members of the family before getting round to me and felt off balance.

'Miss Bray, I'm Inspector William Bull. I gather that you discovered the body of the deceased. I'd be grateful if you could spare us a few minutes of your time.'

Sarcastic too. He must have known I'd been sitting there waiting. Not a countryman's voice. At a guess, he'd started his career in Birmingham, although only the trace of an accent was there. An ambitious man, I thought, pleased rather than disconcerted by a murder in his area. Later I found out that he came from headquarters in Oxford and had happened to be seconded to the Chipping Norton station working on another case. He was in his mid-thirties and probably set on being a superintendent by the time he was forty. Not being a country man he showed no particular deference to land-owning families like the Venns.

'Certainly,' I said.

I expected him to sit down at the other side of the coffee table, but he stayed where he was.

'Upstairs, if you wouldn't mind.'

Adam stood aside to let me through the door. I gave him a long look as I passed, trying to pick up any message from his expression, but saw nothing there but concern. The inspector said 'Excuse me', very politely, as an apology for preceding me up the main staircase. I followed him along the corridor, through a doorway and up another staircase to a room that must have been directly above Oliver Venn's study. It looked like an architect's afterthought, small and narrow with a long window giving a view of the the gravel sweep outside the front door. The furniture was solid school-room stuff, with none of the elegance of the rest of the house, a battered table with three upright chairs round it, a book-case stuffed with dusty books, most of them on property and company law. A constable, young and round-faced, got up from his chair as I came in. The inspector, still too polite for comfort, pulled out another chair for me, facing the window, and settled himself opposite me.

'Now, Miss Bray, would you be kind enough to give us your full name and address?'

The constable had a notebook and pencil and wrote down painstakingly Eleanor Rebecca and the rest.

'I understand from Mr Venn that you recognised the deceased as a Miss Daisy Smith. Was she an acquaintance of yours?'

'She was staying at a camp on Mr Venn's land and so was I. I spoke to her a few times but didn't know her well.'

A creature as insubstantial as the bonfire flames, playing wild violin. A scared girl watching other girls pick black-berries. A scream in the dark, *Don't let him take me.*

132

'Do you know anything about her family?'

'I think she came from somewhere around the Marlborough Downs. I don't know the family.'

Daniel could tell them about the farmhouse where he found her. Daniel could tell them a lot of things, but would he?

'We need to find a member of her family for a formal identification of her body. After all, if you'd only seen her a few times, you might have been mistaken.'

'I might have been mistaken, I suppose.'

But I knew I hadn't been. If not exactly telling lies, I was implying untruths. It was like trying to find a way down a scree slope, with stones sliding away underfoot faster than you wanted to go. Inspector Bull leaned forward, painfully polite.

'What I don't entirely understand . . .'

Which was when everything started avalanching. There were a lot of things I hoped not to have to tell him – for Felicia's sake, Daniel's sake, even Bobbie's sake – but at some point or other we had to touch fact and this particular lot of facts were a threat to nobody but me. So that was when I told him I was in the house because I'd been trying to remove a picture from Mr Oliver Venn's study. He took it calmly enough, but the constable made a gulping sound and got a glare.

'Are you in the habit of stealing pictures, Miss Bray?'

'I've never tried it before. I shouldn't have tried it now except that I didn't regard it as stealing.'

I explained, because at least this was one of the things I could explain, about Philomena's bequest to the WSPU, Oliver Venn's bad faith and my regrettable decision. All the time the constable's pencil went scratch scratch and I had to stop twice for him to catch up. I noticed that the inspector's dishwater-grey eyes narrowed when I mentioned the WSPU. He didn't like suffragettes any more than socialists.

'You realise that you have admitted to being in Mr Venn's

house without invitation with the intention of depriving him of an item of property. I shall have to inform him and it will be up to him to decide whether to bring charges.'

'I understand.'

I thought, He won't dare, but didn't say it.

'And was Miss Daisy Smith your accomplice by any chance?'

'She most certainly was not. I didn't even know she was in the house until I saw her in the cabinet.'

'Why did you open the cabinet?'

'I needed somewhere to hide the picture. I'd . . . made a noise in the studio and I knew somebody would be coming down.'

'Had you equipped yourself with a gun for this enterprise?'

'Of course I hadn't. Was it a gun that killed her?'

'How did you gain entry to the house?'

'The studio door was unlocked.'

'So you went through the studio twice, on your way in and on the way out?'

'Yes.'

'What time was it when you came in?'

'After midnight, I think. I didn't look at my watch.'

'How much time in between coming in and going out?'

I thought of the struggle to unhook the picture, hiding in the broom cupboard.

'Probably about half an hour, or more. I'm not sure.'

'On the first occasion, did you look in the cabinet?'

'Of course not. I didn't need to.'

'So you've no idea whether the deceased was in the cabinet on that first occasion?'

'I suppose she must have been.'

But even as I was saying it, something struck me that made me hesitate. Bobbie had stumbled in the dark going past the cabinet on the way in. I'd assumed she'd tripped over a rug, but if Daisy's stiff foot had been sticking out . . . Bull didn't miss the hesitation.

'And why should you suppose that, Miss Bray?'

'If somebody had brought her in while . . . while I was upstairs, wouldn't I have heard?'

Another hesitation, with two reasons for it. One was that I'd nearly said 'we' instead of 'I'. The other was that I *had* heard somebody downstairs and it might have been Felicia.

'So you opened the cabinet and found the body. What did you do then?'

'Adam Venn had heard the noise and come down. We lifted her out and . . . laid her on the floor.'

'Why did you lift her out instead of leaving her for us to see? Did you think she might be still alive?'

'No. I don't know why we did it.'

Useless to explain the impossibility of leaving her there looking so uncomfortable and undignified, even though she was dead. He'd got me off balance, so I said something I hadn't intended.

'I noticed her body was quite stiff already, the neck and the arms and legs.'

'You're an expert on rigor mortis, are you?'

'My father was a doctor.'

I was tempted to tell him a story from the Liverpool slums, about a very fat man and the undertakers having to remove a door and doorframe to get him out, but decided against it.

'Pretty cool of you, wasn't it, noticing something like that?'

It certainly wasn't admiration in his voice.

'You can't help noticing things,' I said.

'Was there anything else you noticed, anybody hanging about the house?'

'There was a tramp,' I said, suddenly remembering. Then regretted it because he was Bobbie's tramp, not mine.

'Where and when?'

135

'I . . . I was waiting with the picture in a barn just down the field. A tramp tried to get in and I told him to go away.'

'Did he say anything?'

'I couldn't make it out.'

'What did he look like?'

'It was dark. I couldn't see.'

'So how did you know he was a tramp?'

'I suppose I assumed it.'

He sighed and gave the constable a God-help-us look that was probably intended to annoy me and did. I'd been wondering whether to tell him about the tramp whistling the *Long Lankin* song but that wouldn't help. He paused while the constable turned a page and sharpened his pencil.

'When did you last see Daisy Smith alive?'

'At the Scipian camp on Monday morning. She was going into a tent for a lecture with all the others.'

'Did she have any particular friends?'

'I didn't know her well.'

He must have noticed it was an evasion but didn't say anything. A pointless evasion too. He'd have to talk to the people left at the camp and the story of her and Daniel must come out, but I didn't want to be the one to tell it. I don't know if he'd have pressed it further or what I'd have said if he had, because at that point the sound that had been there in the background for the last few minutes got so loud that we couldn't ignore it.

When I first heard the music I thought it might be in my own head, because I'd been thinking about the whistling tramp. But it wasn't *Long Lankin* or any other song that I could remember hearing. A strange and antique kind of tune for a wild dance. It was being played on a concertina and not very well either – some wrong notes that added to the strangeness of the thing, the rhythm broken.

'What in the world is that row?' the inspector said. He stood up, opened the window and leaned out. 'Stop that. Stop it at once.'

A moment's check then the music went on defiantly. A voice started singing, loud and hoarse.

> *'Bring away the beggar and the king,*
> *And every man in his degree'*

Inspector Bull snapped at the constable, 'Come on,' and the two of them hustled out of the door. I went to the open window, expecting to see Daniel down below on the gravel. It didn't sound like him but if grief had driven him off his head it might have got into his voice as well. Looking down I saw a bare and shaggy head, booted feet scuffing the gravel in a kind of stationary dance, strong arms pumping away at the concertina. Only it wasn't Daniel. I was so surprised that at first I didn't guess who it was. It wasn't until the inspector and constable came hurrying down the steps on to the gravel and the singer turned up his big bearded face to look at them that I recognised Harry Hawthorne. Inspector Bull strode up to him, commanded him to stop, but Harry went on playing and pawing the gravel.

> *'Bring away the old and youngest thing,*
> *Come all to death and follow me'*

'Harry!' A shout from the top of the steps. Daniel Venn came running down them, hair as disordered as Harry's, voice high and sharp. 'Harry. Stop it. Stop playing that.'

He pushed past the inspector and made a grab for Hawthorne's arm. Harry took a few clumsy dancing steps away, still playing and singing.

'Make ready, then, your winding sheet,
And see how ye can bestir your feet,
For Death is the man that all must meet,
For Death is the man that all must meet.'

Daniel was yelling at him all the time to stop. It turned into a wild howling, a descant over the death music. The combination seemed to stop even Inspector Bull in his tracks. He just stood there staring until Daniel managed to get a grip on Hawthorne's right arm with both his hands and drag it away from the concertina. The music stopped, Hawthorne stood there panting with Daniel still shaking his arm yelling 'No, no!' The two policemen moved in and parted them. I craned out of the window, desperate to hear what was said.

'What do you think you're doing?' Inspector Bull to Harry Hawthorne.

'Lamenting.' Just the one word flung back at him. Hawthorne didn't retreat an inch, unkempt beard jutting at the police officer's clean-shaven face.

'*The Shaking of the Sheets.* He was playing *The Shaking of the Sheets.*' From Daniel, who could have mimed the title from the way he was looking, white-faced and trembling with anger.

'And who are you, sir?'

In spite of Daniel's state, the inspector had registered that he merited a 'sir', even if it was a sarcastic one. Adam clearly hadn't got round to introducing his brother to the police yet. At least the sharpness of the question seemed to make Daniel more sensible.

'Daniel Venn. I live here. And this man's got no right to be here.'

A roar of harsh laughter from Hawthorne.

'Defending your family property, are you? Young squire seeing the riff-raff off the premises? Arrest him, constable and have him clapped in the stocks!'

138

'I might just do that if you don't keep quiet.' The inspector, annoyed at being referred to as a constable. And to Daniel, 'Who is this man?' But Daniel had turned away, head down.

'My name's Hawthorne,' Harry told the inspector. 'Mr Hawthorne to you. And it's no good threatening me because I've been arrested more times than you've pissed in a pot. I've come here to mourn a member of the working classes slaughtered by the middle class in defence of its stolen property and you've got no right to stop me.'

The inspector said, 'What are you talking about?'

Adam called, 'Daniel, come in. Come in at once.' I couldn't see him, but from his voice he must have been standing at the top of the steps. Daniel gave no sign of hearing him.

'Miss Daisy Smith is what I'm talking about,' Hawthorne said.

'So what do you know about Miss Smith?'

'I know she was alive and now she's dead and I know what killed her.'

'If you have any information about Daisy Smith's death . . .'

'I'm telling you, they killed her. Arrest the lot of them. Arrest the whole bloody family and all the other families who think holding on to what they've got is more important than the flesh and blood of the people who made it for them.'

Adam had joined the group now. Standing beside the inspector, he was apparently listening quite calmly to what Harry Hawthorne was saying. 'I think this has probably gone far enough, Inspector. Mr Hawthorne is clearly under the influence of alcohol—'

'I am not.'

(Debatable point, I thought. Like a lot of good speakers, Harry Hawthorne could get drunk on his own anger and eloquence.)

'Drunk or sober, you're committing a breach of the peace. If you're not off these premises in one minute you're under arrest.'

They stared at each other. Hawthorne hitched his concertina on to his shoulder and whether he intended it or not it made a derisive wheezing noise.

'I've said what I came to say. If anybody wants any more, you'll find me down at the schoolhouse.' He looked round the half-circle of them, the two brothers and the two police officers, turned and went down the drive in no hurry.

'What did he mean about the schoolhouse?' the inspector asked Adam.

'He's the leader of a group staying down there – with my uncle's permission.'

'Funny way he's got of returning a favour,' the inspector said.

They all went inside. Soon after that two sets of footsteps came back along the upstairs corridor and the door opened. I was still standing by the window, to let Inspector Bull know I'd heard what was going on. I didn't think he'd come off well and he seemed to think so too, because he was flustered. He asked a few more questions, but I sensed his heart wasn't in it. Part of his mind was still on that scene with Hawthorne and the Venn brothers and I guessed it might be moving in a direction the Venns wouldn't like. He wasn't a stupid man, unfortunately. He marked the end of the interview by asking what my immediate plans were. I hadn't made any but supposed I'd be going back to London. I couldn't do anything useful by staying on here.

'You'll be hearing from us,' he said.

Inquest? Charges? I didn't ask, feeling bone-weary. The inspector opened the door for me and followed me downstairs, a little too closely, as if making sure I didn't pocket anything in passing. Adam Venn was waiting down in the hall, looking as if he were holding the whole family together by sheer force of will. Carol stood just behind him in an open doorway, unobtrusive but supporting. 'We need to speak to your brother,' the inspector told Adam. 'And Mrs Venn, your uncle and the servants. Is there anyone else in the household?'

Silence for a second then Adam said, 'There's Miss Foster, but I'm not sure that she's well enough to . . .'

'Who's Miss Foster?'

'A . . . a friend of the family.' Then Adam decided to take the hurdle after all, cleared it. 'In fact, Miss Foster is my brother's fiancée.'

A decision made for all the family, and not an easy one. He'd have had to take a gamble on whether I'd told the inspector about Daniel's other engagement. I could sense him relaxing just a little when Inspector Bull made no comment.

'Was she in the house when Miss Smith's body was found?'

'Yes, and she's in a bad state of shock. We had to give her a sleeping draught and—'

'Was Daisy Smith a particular friend of hers, then?'

'No, she'd never met her. But Miss Foster is a highly strung young woman and it was naturally very distressing for her.'

Carol Venn said, from the doorway, 'Poor Felicia really is in no condition to be questioned. You can take me next if you like, then Adam can have Uncle Olly and Daniel ready and waiting for you.'

Adam gave her a grateful look. I wondered if Inspector Bull had guessed her reason for volunteering so promptly – that it would give her husband more time to talk sense to Daniel. By the look of the scene outside, he'd need all the time he could get. But if he did guess, there wasn't much he could do about it without rudeness and the Venns were

141

not of the class that police could be rude to without reprisals. He thanked her and they went back upstairs together, Carol walking as confidently as any hostess with any guest.

'Daniel wants to see you,' Adam said. He'd waited until the inspector was out of earshot.

'Why?'

'He won't tell me. Try not to unsettle him if you can.'

Unsettle him from what? Adam was taking it for granted that I'd do it when all I wanted to do was get away from the place to fresh air, clean clothes and sleep.

'Where is he?'

'In the summerhouse last time I saw him.'

I went out of the front door and round the house into the garden. The sun was high now, bees overloaded with pollen blundering around at waist height, smell of bruised geranium leaves heavy in the air. The weeds on the way to the summerhouse were thoroughly trampled, but that could have been any of us. It seemed to me an ill-omened place to have chosen, after Felicia and the gun. Daniel was slumped on a bench in the shade, head bent. The blanket and oil lamp were still there beside him. He jumped up when he heard my steps.

'You wanted to talk to me?'

'What did Harry mean? Is he saying I killed her?'

He looked desperate and scared. I guessed that Daniel had never been unhappy before in his short adult life. Singer and dancer, protected younger brother and indulged nephew, his existence had been as sunny and open as downland with blue butterflies. But then, I might be wrong.

'He didn't say you, in particular. He said "they killed her".'

'It's nonsense.'

He said it not angrily, but in a confused and defeated way, shaking his head. 'What did he mean?'

'Let's sit down.'

He sat down heavily on the bench and I went into the summerhouse and joined him, not too close. There was a smell of old sweat and sour breath coming from him.

'I'm not sure if he knew himself. He seemed very grieved and angry about Daisy Smith. Do you think he might have met her before somewhere?'

Daniel's head came up and he stared at me. 'No. Why should he?'

'I just wondered. You're sure about that?'

'Yes. I just went up to him as soon as we arrived at the camp and told him about Daisy and . . . oh God . . .' His head went down again and he talked at the cobbles of the summerhouse floor. 'Why can't we go back to where we were? You know . . . you get a piece of music or a dance wrong and you can go back to the beginning, do it over again until you get it right. But this, you can't go back. I've been thinking all the things I might have done differently . . .'

'Like leaving Daisy where she was?'

'No. I couldn't have done that.'

I didn't say the obvious – she'd still be alive at least.

'So what else might you have done differently?'

'Last night, everything. I should have told her first, or Felicia first, or . . .'

I said, as gently as possible in the circumstances, 'If you want me to listen to you, could you please tell me what you're talking about?'

'Last night. I . . . you see after I'd spoken to you, I . . .'

'All right. Let's take it from when you spoke to me. I told you about finding Felicia in the summerhouse here, with the revolver. You were on your way down to see Daisy when I met you. Did you go to her?'

'No. I needed more time.'

'So you didn't see Daisy last night?'

143

'No. After what you'd told me I started thinking and . . .' His voice died away. I waited and I suppose he got his mind into some sort of order because after a long time he looked up at me and started talking more or less coherently.

'I couldn't have faced Daisy or anybody else. I just walked round the fields, thinking about her and Felicia. You see, I hadn't realised that she – Felicia, I mean – I just hadn't realised that she, well, *loved* me. I mean, I knew we liked each other a lot, and the family liked her, and it would be quite jolly being married to her and writing music and bringing up children and so on, but I just didn't think I was the sort of man that women felt . . . felt like *that* about. We weren't Tristan and Isolde, if you see what I mean.'

He paused and I murmured that yes, I saw they weren't Tristan and Isolde. Thinking all the time how ironic it was that he'd been right first time. Unless I'd misunderstood Felicia completely, it wasn't love for Daniel himself that had driven her to despair but the prospect of losing the life that had opened out to her with the Venns. Worse than useless to say that now, though.

'So, when I thought about that, I knew the engagement to Felicia had to be on again. After all, Daisy couldn't be in love like that with me, could she? Not after just a few days.'

I thought Daisy had looked too scared and broken in spirit to think of loving anybody for a long time.

'She needed somebody to help her, though,' I said.

'Yes, of course she did. And I'd have gone on helping her. We'd have all helped her. It would have been a lot easier with Felicia and me engaged again. So that was what I worked out, walking round and round the fields in the dark. Get engaged again to Felicia, tell Daisy as gently as possible that we weren't engaged any more but we'd look after her. Lot of humble pie for me then back to the beginning, start again and get it right this time.'

144

'So which of them did you decide to tell first, Felicia or Daisy?'

Daniel ran his hands through his hair. 'Well, neither. That is . . . I decided I'd tell Harry Hawthorne first.'

I just managed to bite back a comment on his habit of talking about his emotional affairs to practically anybody but the women directly involved. Too late now.

'Why Harry Hawthorne?'

'I suppose I saw him as a kind of godfather of my engagement to Daisy. I know you don't have godfathers at engagements, but you know what I mean.'

'No.'

'Well, that night when we were all dancing and making music round the bonfire, it came to me quite suddenly what the answer to the Daisy question was. So I put it to Harry Hawthorne there and then and he was all for it.'

So Max had been right. The combination of romance and defiance to the middle classes had fitted in nicely with Harry's plans.

'Are you sure he didn't suggest it?'

'No. It was definitely my idea. But he thought I should make the announcement there and then. And it seemed like a good idea, so . . .'

'So you decided he had a right to know it was all off. How did he take it?'

'Not well. In fact, he was furious. I'd wanted to get him on his own. He'd gone to bed in the old schoolhouse by then, but I roused him and he came out in the yard and I told him. God, that man can talk. From the way he went on you'd have thought I was some depraved old French count seducing the peasants' daughters.'

'I can imagine. Did you get a chance to put a word in?'

'Eventually. I told him I'd changed my mind because of Felicia trying to kill herself . . .'

145

'You what!'

'Maybe I shouldn't have. But the things he was saying, I thought I had a right to defend myself, show I wasn't entirely heartless.'

'Did it make any difference?'

'I'm not sure he believed me at first. So I remembered I still had the revolver you'd given me in my pocket. I took it out and showed it to him and . . . What did you say?'

I'd groaned. 'Nothing. Go on.'

'I think it convinced him I was telling the truth, because he went quiet. Then he just got up and went inside.'

'Without saying anything?'

'Just a few words over his shoulder about the rottenness of the middle class. Anyway, whether he liked it or not, I'd done what I'd come to do.'

'So what happened then?'

'I couldn't tell Daisy because I thought she'd be sleeping with the rest of the women in the old dairy and I could hardly go in there and get her. So I thought that would have to wait till morning and I'd go back to the house and tell Felicia. But I hadn't realised how late it was. When I got back to the house it was after eleven and she'd gone to bed.'

'So what did you do then?'

'I remembered I'd promised to check the studio door was open for you, so I went and saw to that.'

'So you were in the studio some time after eleven? Did you hear or see anything?'

'I didn't go in. I just checked the door from outside on the terrace. You mean she might have been in there?'

'I think she might have been, yes.'

He shivered. 'Did somebody put her there deliberately, do you think?'

'Deliberately?'

'The Long Lankin story, the woman being killed.'

146

Chapter Twelve

I CAUGHT AN AFTERNOON TRAIN BACK to town. The mechanical harvester was still at work, although I suppose it must have moved on to a new field by then. The steam from it stood out bright and white against a grey sky. By the time we got to Paddington it was drizzling, just enough moisture to turn the dusty pavements greasy, to wilt the feathers on the hats of women waiting with me in the bus queue and paste bits of torn newspaper and wisps of hay into a mushy layer in the gutters. There was an end of summer feel to everything that would have been depressing even without what had happened. When the motor bus came at last the conductor was surly, standing room only, and a child who was told by his mother to be a little gentleman and give up his seat to the lady left a blob of everlasting toffee as a souvenir that lived up to its name by forming what seemed likely to be a lifelong attachment to my skirt. The only piece of good luck was that when I got to Clement's Inn Emmeline was out, not expected back until the morning. I said I wouldn't leave a message, dodged questions about where I'd been and why I looked as if I'd been sleeping under a hedge, and went home to Hampstead. There was a mountain of mail inside the door, all of it dull looking. The milk in the pantry had turned to curds and whey, the bread had grown green mould and a mouse had been at the cheese because I'd left the top off the dish. Too tired to shop, I dined off black tea, Bath

Olivers and raspberry jam, went to bed and slept for ten solid hours.

Next morning, a Wednesday, I gave Emmeline a carefully edited account. She had to know of course that both pictures were still in Oliver Venn's possession, and that a young woman had been shot. A protégée of the Venns, I said, a musical young woman from a poor family. The police were investigating how she died and I would probably have to go to the inquest because I'd been unlucky enough to find her body. I've never been more grateful for Emmeline's ability to ignore distractions and concentrate on the job in hand. A lesser woman might have wasted time expressing regret over the dead girl or even over the shock to my nerves.

'It's all very unfortunate, but in the circumstances we can't press the subject of the picture without risking unwanted publicity,' she said. 'We'll have to wait until the police have finished investigating, then take it up through the lawyers.'

Just what I'd suggested in the first place and it would have saved me a lot of trouble, although I had the sense not to point that out. I didn't mention my burglary attempt, let alone that I'd allowed Lady Fieldfare's daughter to get involved in it, because I was sure Oliver Venn wouldn't dare let the police prosecute me.

With that interview over, all there was left for me to do was get on with my work and wait for the next few days, so that's what I did. I spent a couple of blameless days at home. Finished the bicycle catalogue translations and sent them off with an invoice saying prompt payment would oblige. I was down to my last ten pounds or so in the bank. Shopped, answered mail, cleaned the house up to a point, found the lid of the cheese dish. Considered seriously an offer from a neighbour of two pretty kittens to deal with the mice. On Friday I went back to Clement's Inn, did some proof reading for our newspaper, wrote letters to supporters and was even driven to using the telephone twice – I hate not being able to see people when I talk to them – in connection with a conference of the Women's Trade Union League due to take place in Bath the following week. During one of the proof-reading spells, Bobbie Fieldfare arrived suddenly at my shoulder.

'Hello, Miss Bray. What's happening?'

'Work's happening.' I handed her a damp galley proof. 'Read that to me. Out loud and not too fast.'

It was about the work of women sanitary inspectors. She got through a couple of paragraphs, while I checked from the manuscript copy.

'It's not very interesting, is it? What I wanted to ask you is whether the police—'

'Don't interrupt. Start again from "Statistics for the last five years in Burnley . . ."'

Another few paragraphs, then, 'My mother was awfully curious about where I'd been. I didn't tell her anything.'

'Good, but keep reading. We'll be locking the page up in a few minutes.'

'Talking of locking up, I wondered if—'

'Bobbie, are you in there?' Lady Fieldfare's voice from the corridor.

'Oh dash it. I'd better go.' She let the proof slide to the floor. 'Only I do want to talk to you. I'll see you soon.'

Not if I can help it, I thought as she whisked out of the door. Already, with her instinct for doing the wrong thing, she'd wrenched my mind back to where I didn't want to be. I'd tried hard over the last few days not to think about Daisy, avoided the parts of newspapers that might have carried a paragraph about the death by shooting of a young woman in the Cotswolds, but probably wouldn't because it wasn't significant. Only after Bobbie had gone and we'd got the page locked up did I start wondering why I'd been trying so hard not to think. I said I needed some fresh air, went outside and walked round the streets under dusty and tattered plane trees, dodging children playing hopscotch. Once I let myself think, the answer was clear. I felt guilty.

It took another few turns of the streets to decide what I felt guilty about. Certainly not trying to take the picture. My conscience was as clear about that as it always had been and it was just a pity I'd failed. Lying to the police, then? Well, it wasn't the first time I'd had to do that, unfortunately. Anyway, I hadn't lied in so many words, just left out a few things. All right, more than a few things. Daniel's engagement. Felicia with the revolver. '*I had a gun, didn't I?*' Daniel with the revolver. Bobbie. An impressive list, and yet that wasn't at the heart of my trouble. In the end it came to just one word – Daisy. We'd all of us pulled and pushed her around as it suited us. By Daniel's account her uncle had been prepared to sell her with less care than most men would sell a horse. Even Daniel had started out wanting her for the tunes and dances in her head then cast her as the rescued damsel in his own personal drama. The rest of the Venn family saw her as an embarrassment. True, they'd intended to deal with her honourably enough, a little room of her own in some distant college, a folk-dance teacher's certificate as her stock in trade. But what it amounted to was getting her out of their civilised, socialist, nicely ordered lives. Harry Hawthorne had been right to be angry, but then wasn't he using her for his own purposes just the same? Manoeuvring Daniel into announcing his engagement to her was a way for Harry to embarrass the bourgeoisie, like his noisy grief for Daisy dead. They'd all used her as it suited them, tried to tidy her away when it didn't and now they were trying to tidy away her death. Correction, now *we* were trying to tidy

154

away her death. I didn't like it, but I was as guilty of that as any of the rest of them. So the question was, why was I conspiring with them?

Once I started being honest about it, the answer wasn't complicated. Protecting Bobbie was only a part of it. Naturally I was glad to get her out of the way, but that wouldn't justify keeping things from the police and helping to conceal evidence of murder. The truth was that I was almost sure I knew who had killed Daisy and that the Venns knew it too. The name had been thumping like a terrified heart in the background of that talk in the early hours before Adam could bring himself to go to the police. Fe-lic-i-a, Fe-lic-i-a. As if vibrating through the timbers of the house from the room where she was sleeping a drugged sleep upstairs. She had the motive to kill Daisy Smith. With Philomena's revolver accessible to anybody in the household, she had the means. And I'd almost caught her doing it red-handed, taken the gun from her when it was still warm.

The more I thought about that, the more horribly neatly it fitted. The shot Bobbie and I heard was the one that had killed Daisy. When I found Felicia with the gun, Daisy's body might have been only yards away at the back of the summerhouse or even tumbled into one of the overgrown borders. Perhaps I hadn't been so wrong in thinking that Felicia intended to kill herself: murder, then suicide. (Perhaps she'd even tried. Daniel thought two rounds had been fired from the revolver, although in my memory there'd been only one.) I'd got there in time to stop her and, in taking the gun, unintentionally confused the evidence. She'd recovered enough to talk to Carol more or less normally then pleaded illness and gone upstairs to her room. Late at night, she went down to the garden, picked up Daisy's stiffening body from where it had fallen or been

155

hidden and propped it in the cabinet. Not impossible physically. Daisy was small and thin and Felicia from the look of her a normal healthy young woman. The question why she'd do that could only be answered from a place most of us never go to – the mind of a person who has taken the life of another human being. Outside that, I could only guess. Perhaps it had been remorse – giving Daisy a kind of entombment. Perhaps it was a message to Daniel, blaming him for driving her to it. The strain of carrying the body through the garden into the studio would explain her state when Carol and I found her. If the police knew even a part of what we knew, Felicia would come in for some hard questioning and in that case, I was certain, she'd break down and confess. If she were lucky enough to escape hanging – with a good barrister and a jury sympathetic to her youth, unhappiness and provocation – she'd wither slowly away in a prison cell. Even if that was what she deserved, should I be the one to put her there? On the other hand, by not telling the police what I'd seen and heard I was behaving as if Daisy didn't matter.

I sat on a bench under a tree, watching a pigeon chasing another pigeon in the dust, trying to think a way out of where I'd put myself. Now, if Daisy had been my friend or my sister, Felicia's fate wouldn't have mattered a jot. I'd have wanted justice for Daisy, revenge even. But she hadn't been a friend or, even in the comradely sense, a sister because I hadn't tried to make her one. Apart from comforting her after the nightmare, I'd been content for the Scipian girls to look after her. Now like all the rest of them all I wanted was to keep her out of my life because to do otherwise would mean grief and pain.

'And you know it would, Daisy,' I said to her in my head. 'A lot of grief and pain for everybody. Is that what you'd want?'

The answer was that I had no idea what she'd have wanted because I didn't know her. None of us knew her.

I took the unanswered question home with me, tried to smother it in work over the weekend. A postcard arrived on Saturday about a meeting in Holborn the following evening, protesting about the French military action in Morocco. Still out of sorts and angry with myself I thought there was no point in pretending to worry about whole countries if I couldn't even help one person and decided not to go. Then on Sunday it occurred to me that Max Blume would certainly be there and he was the only person I knew in London who'd actually met Daisy Smith. So I was there at the meeting, noting and deploring along with the rest. Afterwards, I got Max on his own at the back of the hall.

'Have you recovered from all that country air, Nell?'

He was waiting for me to make the first move.

'When did you leave?' I said.

'Wednesday, the day after you. Not before I'd been questioned by the police.'

'You!'

'No personal distinction about it. They questioned everybody left in the Scipian camp – although there were no more than a couple of dozen of us left by then. The main thing they seemed interested in was whether Hawthorne might have been inciting us to tear down the Venns' house.'

'Not about Daisy?'

'Oh, they wanted to know when anybody had last seen her, but they didn't get far.'

There it was again. Even among the Scipians – who were kindly disposed to her – she'd hardly existed in her own right, made no more lasting impression than a shadow on a brick wall.

He gave me a sideways look. 'What's wrong, Nell?'

157

'I don't know. A lot, I think.'

Somebody came round with a petition. Max read it at a glance, then signed. I broke my own rule by signing without reading for once.

'Let me get us something to drink and we'll talk properly,' Max said. 'Coffee or cocoa?'

He collected two mugs from the table by the urn and we settled in two seats in a far corner. The coffee was vile, as it normally is with good causes. Max took a gulp, winced. 'So what do you want to know?' he asked.

'Did the police ask you about Daniel and Daisy?'

'The engagement? No.'

'Did you have the impression they knew about it?'

'I don't see how they could fail to. After all, it was the talk of the camp so I'm sure one of the women will have mentioned it to them. Does that matter?'

'Probably, yes.'

He looked worried. 'Is all this for the sake of Daniel Venn's *beaux yeux*?'

'Not exactly, no.'

'Then what is it?'

'I was the one who found her – found Daisy's body.'

I desperately needed someone to discuss it with and when a friend was really in trouble Max could be relied on to put aside his journalist's instincts. So I told him about the attempt at art theft and how it ended but couldn't tell even him about Felicia. That left a hole in the middle of the story and Max, of course, spotted it.

'Yes, I can see it was bad for you and I'm sorry, but I don't see why you have to stay involved.'

'There'll be an inquest and so on and the police will want to speak to me again.'

'And you'll simply tell them everything you know – won't you?'

I just looked at him.

'Like that, is it?'

'Yes.'

'Nell, if you'll accept some advice from me, don't get too close to the Venns.'

'I'm not close to them. I don't want to be close to them. It's only . . .'

'So it is Daniel?'

'No, of course it isn't. If it's anything, it's Daisy. I hate the way the world's closing over her already as if she never existed. Even when she was alive, she never existed much. None of us can even remember properly when we last saw her.'

'One of the things the police wanted to know was whether anybody had seen her with a stranger from outside the camp.'

'Had anybody?'

'No, but there again, would they have noticed? After all, we were most of us strangers to each other. The camp had only been going for three days and if somebody saw a woman talking to Daisy, they'd simply assume it was a Scipian they didn't happen to recognise.'

'Why a woman?'

'Because she spent most of her time with the women. She was such a timid little thing I think somebody would have noticed if she'd been talking to a man.'

Another point against Felicia. One of the things that had puzzled me was how Daisy came to be on her own in the garden of the Venns' house. Suppose Felicia had gone down to the Scipian camp at some time in the day, found Daisy and delivered a message – a message, say, that Daniel wanted her to come and meet him. If she'd done that and it could be proved against her, at least then I could forget the picture of her spending the rest of her life in prison. That cold premeditation would be enough to hang her. I tried to get

159

that out of my mind and concentrate on what Max was saying.

'Of course, I don't know what Harry Hawthorne said to the police. Most of us were questioned by constables, but they sent an inspector down to see Harry. They were more than an hour together and neither of them looked very happy at the end of it.'

'Inspector Bull, big man with cold grey eyes?'

'That's the one.'

'Do you think Harry Hawthorne might have met Daisy somewhere before? He was up at the Venns' house playing a lament for her soon after the police got there. It was grotesque and yet I'd have sworn he was really mourning Daisy.'

'Perhaps it was guilt.'

'Guilt!' I looked round, making sure nobody was near enough to hear. They were all safely clustered round the urns. 'You're not saying he had something to do with killing Daisy?'

'No. But I do think it's possible he put her into a situation where she got killed. You know what I said to you about trying to embarrass the Venns. Suppose he decided to persuade Daisy to go up to the house and confront them?'

'She wouldn't confront anybody.'

'Not on her own, no. But if he had one of his crazy schemes – oh, I don't know – imagine all the Venns trooping into dinner and Daisy sitting there at the table with Harry hiding behind a curtain, working class come to claim its own from the bourgeoisie. I'm not saying that's what Harry did, but something like that would be in character.'

'But they wouldn't have shot Daisy for that.'

'No. Well, maybe he persuades her to creep in after dark and one of the Venns really does take them for burglars and – like any good middle-class socialist in defence of his property – fires into the dark to scare them off. Only he hits poor Daisy and Hawthorne gets away.'

160

'I just don't believe he'd go off and leave her like that.'

'Perhaps he'd convinced himself she was only injured and it was a real shock when he heard she was dead, hence the guilt.'

'But if he hates the Venns so much, surely he'd tell the police that.'

'No, because he'd be quite sure the police would side with the Venns and put the blame on him. He might even be right about that.'

'Is Hawthorne still at the Scipian camp?'

'No. That broke up after the police came. Nobody had much heart for it. I suppose Harry's back in town. In fact, I thought he might be here tonight but—'

Before he finished speaking, there was a stir by the doorway and Harry Hawthorne walked in with a little group of supporters behind him. By then the meeting had been on the point of breaking up; people had separated into little groups, the caretaker was fidgeting with keys. When he came in there were shouts of welcome, cheerful insults about being late as usual. The petition was produced and Hawthorne scrawled his signature, taking up three lines. I noticed because I was at his shoulder by then. Before I could speak he turned round and saw me.

'You were at the camp. You're a friend of young Daniel Venn's, aren't you?'

At the top of his voice as usual, his beard practically scratching my face. A knot of people had collected round him already and others began to drift in from corners of the room. I started saying I was more of an acquaintance than a friend, but he didn't take any notice.

'Well, did they kill her?' Gasps and questions from all round. He played up to them. 'Rich young man got himself engaged to a working-class girl and the family objected so they shot her, like doing away with a puppy you don't want.'

161

I said, loudly because he seemed to be making a public meeting of it, 'We don't know who did it. Anybody could have shot her.'

'But who'd have wanted to?'

I felt Max's grip on my elbow. He said to Hawthorne, 'I don't think we'll get far like this. Why don't we go and talk outside?'

Surprisingly, Hawthorne obeyed. Max steered the two of us out of a side door into an alleyway. There was a gas lamp on the brick wall above us and by the direct light of it Hawthorne's face looked lined, older. He lit a cigarette that smelt like a cattle shed, his hand shaking, and took a long drag on it.

'Why do you think they killed her?' I said.

'They'd taken a trip to the marriage market and brought him back a nice young woman with a dowry. Then he goes off slumming and comes back with a penniless girl who'll cost them a packet. What would you expect them to do?'

'You're talking as if they were millionaires,' I said. 'You can't describe Daniel as rich, and even if Felicia is going to inherit some money of her own, I'm sure it won't be the sort of fortune people get killed for.'

'What do you know about what people will kill for, girl? I've been in places where I've seen a man murdered for ten bob and that's daylight truth.'

I started saying but this was a different world, but it only played into his hands.

'It's all the same world, girl. Just that some of it has prettier curtains than the rest.'

Max came in on my side. 'That's all very well, Harry, but the Venns aren't stupid. Why would they take a risk like that for a few hundred pounds and some passing social embarrassment? Give them a year or two, they'd have had poor Miss Smith pouring Earl Grey tea and playing Chopin on the piano just like the rest of them.'

162

Hawthorne's laugh was short and bitter. 'Anyone will behave stupidly when he's panicking.'

'And you think the Venns were panicking?' I said.

'Daniel admitted it himself. That Sunday, when he came down to tell me how they'd taken it, he said his brother and his uncle were in a panic about it.'

'They didn't like it, of course,' I said.

'More than that. Daniel had some money in trust from his aunt for when he got married – you knew that?'

'Yes.'

'Well, his uncle's a trustee and his brother knows all about it. Daniel goes to them on the Sunday and says he'd like his money, please, because he's going to marry Daisy and they tell him he can't have it because it's not there.'

'Daniel told you that?'

'He did, and the day after that, the girl's shot. What more do you want? Daniel even had a gun. He showed it to me the night she was killed.'

With only the two of us for audience, his voice was more subdued, almost depressed.

'So you're claiming Daniel himself shot Daisy?' I said.

He shook his head. 'I think there's just a shred more decency in Daniel than the rest of them, just a shred. Showing it to me, he was as good as confessing what his brother and uncle had done.'

'Daniel had the gun because he thought the other girl he was engaged to had used it to try to kill herself. He told you that, didn't he?'

'That was the story at the time, yes.'

'What did he do with the gun? Did he leave it with you?'

'Of course not. Why would he do that? He took it away with him.'

'What happened when he'd gone? Did you try to find Daisy Smith and tell her what he'd said about ending the engagement?'

'No. I thought she'd be asleep with the rest of the women.'

'But she wasn't, was she? When did you notice she was missing?'

'I didn't. By the time I knew, she was dead.'

'Did you suggest she should go up to the house?'

'I might have if I'd talked to her, but I didn't get a chance to talk to her.'

'When did you last see her?'

He took another long drag on his cigarette. 'Some time on Monday, I suppose, probably at Daniel's talk in the morning.'

I looked up and caught Max's eye. He seemed content to let me ask the questions but I knew I wasn't getting far. Hawthorne was keeping something back.

'Why were you so pleased when Daniel announced he was engaged to Daisy Smith?'

He shrugged. 'Nice to see a poor girl getting a chance.'

'There was more to it than that, wasn't there? You knew it would embarrass his family.'

His eyes went to Max. 'Have you been talking to her?'

Max nodded. Hawthorne took another lungful of tobacco smoke, threw the butt down and ground it under his heel until it was no more than a smear on the cobbles.

'All right, he's told you that the Venns owe us money. There was five thousand the old lady wanted the Scipians to have and they haven't got it. So yes, I was showing them that we weren't going to go away quietly and forget about it.'

'But it didn't work, did it?'

He grinned. 'You don't think so? At least it got them talking to me.'

'Daniel, you mean?'

'Daniel's not the one with his hands on the purse strings. No, his brother. Ever since the old lady died he'd refused to meet me, sat in his office sending me letters saying to get my dirty working-class boots off his nice doorstep – in lawyer's language, of course. Then three days after we really turn up on his doorstep, he says let's meet and talk.'

'When?'

'Monday evening. He asked me to be patient about the money his aunt wanted us to have and handed over two hundred pounds in banknotes on account. And if you're wondering what's happened to the money it's duly entered in the Scipian bank balance and will be used for educational purposes just as the old lady wanted. If you don't believe me I'll give you the treasurer's name and you can check with him.'

I believed that at least. Financial greed on his own account was something even his enemies had never attributed to Hawthorne. For the cause, it was another matter. Still, I found it hard to believe that Adam Venn had voluntarily handed over money.

'Where did you meet him?'

'Down in the village at the back of the public house. He drove up in his gig, handed over the money, drove off again.'

'How was the meeting arranged?'

'I got a note from him on Monday morning, telling me to meet him there at seven o'clock.'

I remembered that as Bobbie and I had been carrying the picture up the hill on Monday evening we'd seen Adam driving down it in the gig. 'How did he behave when you met? Was he angry?' I asked.

'Cold and businesslike, typical lawyer. He had a receipt for me to sign and I signed it. He wanted me to agree not to start legal proceedings for the rest and said it would be forthcoming when the estate was settled. I said if the estate wasn't settled, how come we were getting the two hundred? He said his wife had had to sell her jewellery to get it.'

165

'So you took the money, signed the receipt, and then what?'

'He drove off, I walked back to the old schoolhouse. Some time after that, Daniel came to see me and told me about breaking things off with Daisy.'

'Did you tell him about Adam and the money?'

'I didn't get a chance. It wasn't his business anyway.'

Two of Harry's friends appeared at the end of the alley and called to him to hurry up. Even at this hour of the evening, they were going on to another meeting.

'Well,' he said to me, 'I've answered a lot of your questions but you haven't answered mine. Who killed her?'

'I don't know.'

'Some of the girls reckoned it was the other woman, the fancy fiancée, driven mad by love. I told them not to be so stupid. When the middle classes take to killing, it's not for love – it's for money.'

His friends came down to get him. He grabbed a couple of newspapers from the bundle one of them was carrying. 'Latest edition of the *Wrecker*. Hot off the presses. Free to workers, threepence to members of the predatory classes like you two.'

Resignedly, Max and I fumbled in our pockets for coins. The sheets of thin newsprint were tacky with printer's ink. Harry was dragged away by his friends and Max walked with me to the tram stop.

'Well,' he said, 'what do you make of that?'

'Would Adam Venn have handed over two hundred pounds just like that?'

'I don't know why Harry should lie, but it's hardly a lawyer's way of doing business.'

'Philomena's estate was settled weeks ago. If the money's there, why don't Oliver and Adam just hand it over?'

'A big if, perhaps,' Max said.

'You don't mean there's something in what Hawthorne said?'

'That the Venns killed Daisy because she was a poor working-class girl? Of course not. But I think Oliver and Adam are in deep financial trouble. If you want a guess from me, they'd been gambling on the stock market with trust funds. While Philomena was alive, her money kept them going. Now she's bequeathed a lot of it all over the place, there are problems.'

When I thought of our own problem with the picture, that fitted in too. Perhaps Oliver had wanted to keep the Odalisque for her value rather than sentiment: for money, not love. The tram arrived.

'Let me know what happens, Nell,' Max said.

I would, I said.

I slept on it and woke up thinking that I'd got worse than nowhere. I carried the problem with me all that Monday, on a round of offices and chambers of people who sometimes gave me translation work. It was hard going because most of my customers were just back from their summer holidays with minds full of sandy beaches or golf links, reluctant to get back into harness for the long autumn haul. The most I managed was a half-promise of some French legal documents in the next week or two, provided the client didn't decide to settle first.

By mid-afternoon, I'd decided to do nothing. Why should I take up a campaign that would harm a lot of people for the sake of a girl I hardly knew? A dissenting voice in my mind kept arguing – That's right. Sweep her aside again. Why not? Everybody else did. But that voice was in the minority, so would have to get used to being ignored. I made my way to Clement's Inn. Mondays were open days, when members of the public interested in what we did were welcome to walk in so I expected the place to be busy. Still, I was surprised when a friend grabbed me as soon as I'd set foot through the door.

'Nell, where have you been? There's a man been waiting for you for hours and he's in an awful state.'

'Who?'

'I don't know. He says he won't speak to anybody else, it has to be you. We've put him in the back office and given him some tea and newspapers but he keeps popping out and asking if you're here yet.'

From the way she looked at me as I went along the corridor to the office, you'd have thought they'd got some kind of unpredictable beast penned up there. I opened the door, not too worried, then stood rooted in the doorway. Tea on the table, grey and untasted. Newspapers spread all over the floor and table as if he'd been looking for something. On his feet in the middle of it all, face grey, hair sticking out at all angles, whole body quivering with nerves and impatience – Daniel Venn. He didn't give me time to ask a question or even step inside the room, just came straight out with it in a croak of a voice, nothing musical about it.

'They're going to arrest me.'

Chapter Thirteen

I CLOSED THE DOOR.

'Have they said so?'

'Not in so many words, but even Adam thinks so. He said to me last night we should be prepared for the worst.'

'But why? What's happened?'

'They found the gun. It was there on the terrace in one of the big flowerpots. It might have been there all the time. Then they took my fingerprints. Oh God.'

'Sit down,' I said. 'Just get things in order and tell me what there is to tell.'

I felt nearly as rattled as he looked, but tried not to show it. We sat down opposite each other at the table.

'If Adam thinks the police are going to arrest you, there must be a reason. Start from Tuesday when the police questioned you.'

'Was it Tuesday? They've been at me so many times since then.' He took a few deep breaths, staring down at his hands, then started.

'It wasn't so bad the first time. They wanted to know if I knew Daisy and I said yes and where her family lived and so on, and about bringing her to the camp because we were both interested in folk music, and the other girls looking after her. I could tell the inspector didn't approve. Adam had told me not to talk about being engaged to her unless they asked outright and they didn't, so I didn't. Not then.'

'But they heard anyway?'

'From Hawthorne. After the show he put on at the house, they must have gone down to the camp and asked him and the others about Daisy. So of course it all came out and I suppose he made things look as black for me as possible.'

I wondered why, even in a state of shock, we'd ever thought the news wouldn't come out. It had been Adam's initiative and he'd been stupid as intelligent people can be sometimes, underestimating the opposition. I didn't say that to Daniel, just waited for him to go on.

'The same day the police sent . . . a kind of a covered cart to take Daisy away. I asked what would happen to her and they said she'd be going back to her family, in due course, as they put it. It makes me feel sick, the thought of her going back there, even dead.'

He was fighting hard not to break down.

'And the next day,' I asked, 'when the police came back?'

'The inspector was furious with me, with all of us. He accused me of concealing evidence. He asked if I'd been worried that Daisy would bring a breach of promise case against me. I told him that was utter rot. I'm sure Hawthorne put that into his head.'

'Did they talk to Felicia?'

'Yes. They asked her if she knew about the engagement to Daisy and she said she did. Had she met Daisy? No, of course she hadn't. Then the usual things they asked the rest of us, like had she heard or seen anything unusual.'

'She hadn't?'

'No. They were . . . quite gentle with her, Carol said. They let Carol stay with her while they were asking questions.'

The inspector would have had no reason to deal harshly with Felicia. She'd have been wearing, almost for certain, a long-sleeved blouse buttoned at the wrist as any properly dressed girl would. No scratches visible.

'So when did they find the revolver?'

'The same day, the Wednesday. They brought a couple more constables in and one of them found it in one of those big stone pots by the studio door.'

'But it's not evidence against you, is it? Anybody could have left it there.'

'That's what Adam said. Anyway, the next day they came to take our fingerprints, his and mine and even poor Uncle Olly's because the thing belonged to him. Do you know about fingerprints?'

'A bit. Not much.'

'Apparently they can tell if people have handled something, even days afterwards, and metal things are good for showing fingerprints. That's what the inspector told me. I think he was probably trying to scare me.'

I could imagine Inspector Bull's pale grey eyes as he said it.

'And did he succeed?'

The look on Daniel's face answered for him.

'I thought I'd better tell him I'd had the gun. It would have looked worse if they found my fingerprints on it and I hadn't, wouldn't it?'

'I suppose so.'

Meanly, I was thinking that this put me in deeper trouble. I'd actually given him the gun so could expect another and more awkward interview with the inspector. He'd want to know why I hadn't told him before and I couldn't answer that without bringing in Felicia.

'I didn't tell him about Felicia, though,' Daniel said, as if he'd read my thoughts.

'Then how did you explain having the gun?'

'I told him I was carrying it around all afternoon to shoot at squirrels and things. I knew Uncle Olly kept it in his drawer, so I just borrowed it without asking him.'

171

The lurch of relief for myself gave way to horror at the way Daniel was managing to dig himself in deeper all the time.

'And he believed you were wandering round with a Smith and Wesson revolver to shoot squirrels?'

'No, I don't think he did. Not from the way he looked at me.'

'I'm not surprised. And how did you explain its turning up in the flowerpot?'

'I said I supposed I must have dropped it. I'm always carrying a lot of things round in my pockets so I might not have noticed it had gone.'

No need even to ask how the inspector had reacted to that.

'Could you have left it there on the Monday night when you checked the door was unlocked?'

'I suppose so. I've been trying to remember but I can't. Sometimes I can picture myself putting it back in the drawer where Uncle Olly kept it.'

'Ah.'

'But that's no good, because I can picture myself just as clearly putting it down on a bench in the school yard and leaving it there. The more I think about it, the more confused I get.'

'What else did the police ask you?'

'They kept on about where I'd been all afternoon and evening. I don't think I made a lot of sense to them. I'm not good with clock-watching at the best of times, and with Daisy and so on to think about . . .' His voice trailed away.

'Did they ask you when you'd last seen Daisy?'

'Yes. I was sure about that, at any rate. It was the Monday morning when I gave the talk.'

'Did you speak to her that morning?'

'A bit, yes. Asked how she was and if she was getting

enough to eat and so on. I said I was trying to sort things out with my family. I didn't tell her what a row there'd been.'

'How did she seem?'

'Quiet, but then she always was.'

'Did she tell you she'd woken up in the night with a screaming nightmare?'

'No!'

'She was shouting *Don't let him take me*. Who do you think she meant?'

'Fardel. Her uncle.' It came out as something between a snarl and a groan. 'All the time we were coming here she was terrified of him, sure he'd follow us and take her back.'

'Did he try to?'

'No, he was too cowardly for that. Cock of his own little dunghill, that's all.'

'But she was still terrified of him?'

'Of course she was. After the life he'd led her, of course she was. I was going to make it up to her, see she wasn't scared any more. The nightmares would have stopped and . . .'

His head went down into his hands. I waited, conscious of the normal noises of a WSPU At Home going on around us: talk, laughter, doors slamming. They were leaving us tactfully alone.

'So you don't think he followed you?'

'If he had, wouldn't he have come to me for his wretched money? That was all he was interested in. I wish I could say he had.'

'Why?'

'Because then it might have been him who killed her, out of spite.'

'With your aunt's gun in your garden? And why would she have gone to him?'

'He might have dragged her away.'

'With Scipians all over the place? Besides, you're right. If he'd been anywhere near, he'd probably have come looking for you.'

He slumped, all the energy gone out of him. He'd used the last of it in bringing his problem to dump at my feet.

'Did you tell the police you'd arranged to meet Daisy again that evening?'

'Yes, but then I said I'd changed my mind.'

'Did they want to know why?'

'Yes. The inspector kept coming back to that, trying to trip me up. I couldn't tell him.'

'Why not?'

'You know why not.'

'Felicia?'

'Yes. If I told him what you told me – about her having the gun, he might have thought . . .'

He'd been mumbling it to the desk top; now his voice died away altogether.

'Thought that Felicia killed her?'

He nodded.

'Do *you* think so?'

His head jerked up. 'No!' For a moment the light was back in his eyes, then he looked away. 'You don't think so, do you?'

'She had the gun.'

'But . . . but you'd have seen, wouldn't you? You were there.'

'Almost there. I wouldn't necessarily have seen.'

'But you don't think so?'

He said it so pleadingly that part of me wanted to comfort him and say no, no of course not.

'The police must think it's possible. I think you know it's possible too or you wouldn't have told them that lie about having the gun all afternoon.'

174

'No. I only wanted to protect her from being nagged at the way they're nagging at me. She's ill. It would drive her mad.'

(Mad enough to confess. Was that what he meant?)

'What it comes to,' I said, 'is that you're lying to the police and making them suspicious of you to protect Felicia.'

'Don't I owe her that?'

'Perhaps. But you'd better start deciding exactly how much you owe.'

'What do you mean?'

'You think they're going to arrest you. You might even be right. If they've got enough evidence they'll charge you, lock you up, put you on trial and possibly . . .'

I intended to scare him into thinking about what he was doing, but even I couldn't finish the sentence. In any case, he looked scared enough.

'Did you kill her?'

'No!' He was on his feet, sending papers from the table flying everywhere. I thought for a moment he might try to hit me, then he sank back in the chair. 'No. I swear by everything that's ever mattered to me or ever will that I didn't kill her.'

We stared at each other. Feet came and went in the corridor. I asked him if Adam agreed with what he was doing.

'He doesn't have any choice.'

'He does. He could tell the police you're lying about having the gun all afternoon. So could I.'

'You won't, will you?'

'Yes, if I have to. In the last resort, I won't stand by and see you hanged.'

'It won't come to that.'

'Don't rely on it.'

'No, it really won't. All I'm trying to do is gain time so that we can find out who killed her without involving Felicia. That's why I've come to you.'

175

'So that I can produce a handy murderer out of the moss? I'm not a conjurer.'

'If they lock me up, I can't go round asking questions. You can.'

'Oh yes? Have you any suggestions where I start?'

'Yes, as a matter of fact.'

I'd intended sarcasm and was caught off balance to find that he'd taken me seriously.

'Well?'

'You might not like this. He's probably a friend of yours.' Then, after a little silence, 'Harry Hawthorne.'

He watched my expression change and gave an impatient little sigh, as much to say: I was right.

'He's not particularly a friend,' I said. 'But why do you think he has something to do with it?'

'*Long Lankin*. The cabinet. It's not a coincidence, I'm sure it's not. You were there in the workshop when we were talking about it. He and I were even singing it, God help us. He knew the words as well as I did. He might have put her in there as . . . as a kind of symbol. Like Long Lankin getting in and killing the lady.'

'But why?'

'To punish me for breaking off the engagement. The crimes of the middle classes coming back to haunt them.'

'You think he'd kill her for that?'

'I can't believe anybody killed her for anything, but somebody did.'

In other parts of the building doors were still opening and closing, voices saying goodbye. The At Home was nearly over. I asked Daniel what he intended to do next.

'Go back, I suppose. Adam's sending for a friend of his who specialises in . . . in criminal work. Apart from that, he says all we can do is wait.'

'He might be right.'

176

'But how can I? How can I just sit there and wait for them to come and arrest me? I ran out of the house and got the train for London. The family don't even know I'm here.'

'I think you should go back to them. It will look even worse if the police think you've run away.'

'Will you come back with me? Now?'

'I can't just drop everything and rush off like that.'

'So you won't help me?'

'If you think it will help, then I will come back.' I hadn't intended to say that, but the hopeless look on his face would have melted stone. He grabbed my hand.

'You will. Oh thank you, thank you.'

'Only not today. There really are things I have to do and anyway I need time to think. I'll come tomorrow.'

He let go of my hand. 'They may have arrested me by then. They may be waiting to arrest me when I get off the train.'

I didn't say anything to that because I thought it was a possibility at least.

'Thank you anyway,' he said, dejectedly but like a polite boy. I had to take him along the corridor and out, under the curious eyes of friends and colleagues getting the entirely wrong idea. When I shut the door on him and turned round, Bobbie Fieldfare was standing there, eyes wide.

'They're not really going to arrest him, are they?'

'Weren't you told not to listen at doors?'

'No. All they told me was that well-brought-up young ladies don't listen at doors and I'm not one of those. But are they?'

'Miss Fieldfare, I've gone to considerable trouble to keep you out of this and you will kindly stay out of it.'

She apologised but looked about as truly contrite as a boy caught with a stag beetle in his desk.

*   *   *

177

Soon after that I left, avoiding further questions. It was about half-past five with an overcast sky and a used-up feel to the air. I walked up Kingsway towards Oxford Street just for the sake of going somewhere. Should I have done more to talk sense into Daniel? Probably, but what was sense in this situation? I couldn't stand by and see him on trial for murder without telling the police what I'd seen and heard – in which case they'd probably arrest Felicia. The point of his plan, if you could call it a plan, was to buy time to find a murderer who wasn't Felicia. He'd nominated Harry Hawthorne for the role. Hawthorne was trying to steer suspicion towards the Venns, Adam in particular. There was a problem with that theory that I hadn't discussed with Hawthorne because I didn't trust him. As far as I could see, Adam was the only person who couldn't have shot Daisy. Bobbie and I had seen him driving down to the village. Hawthorne himself had confirmed the alibi without intending to, saying the two of them had met in the pub yard. Adam could not possibly have driven back to the house in time to fire the shot in the garden.

So we were back with Felicia again. Wasn't it a sign of Daniel's innocence that he was so anxious to protect her? Or perhaps I was fooling myself out of liking for him, as Max had hinted. There's something in us that makes it hard to believe that anybody we like, or even know, can be guilty of the worst of crimes. No logic in it. Everybody who's ever committed murder had to have some people who knew him, even liked or loved him. Liking is no guarantee – and I had good reason from my past to know that. Still, the instinct to believe that evil must be something that comes from the outside, from people we don't know, is strong. *Except one little window where Long Lankin crept in.* Crept in from the moss with long fingers and a devil's face.

By this point I'd got as far as Oxford Street and was being jostled by crowds of people making for bus stops and underground stations on their way home from work, or just arriving from the suburbs for an evening's entertainment. The smells from a café doorway reminded me that I was hungry, so I went in and ordered poached egg on toast and a pot of tea, wondering while I waited for it why I'd walked nearly to the west end of Oxford Street when it wasn't on my way home. As I made the first cut into the yolk of an especially succulent egg it came to me – the Esperance Club.

If you're not interested in good works or folk-dancing the Esperance Club may need some explaining. It was originally set up by a suffragette friend of mine, Mary Neal, as an evening social club for working girls, especially the ones from the sweatshops of the garment trade around Wigmore Street. Then it had been overtaken by the new craze for folk-dancing, to such an extent that it was now one of the main teaching centres and Esperance girls went all over the country, giving demonstrations and teaching morris dancing. The reason why my feet had carried me most of the way to the Esperance Club without my brain knowing wasn't that my problems had driven me to morris dancing, as Max might have feared. It was because they had more sense than my head and knew I'd been disregarding what might be an important group of witnesses.

Some of the girls at the camp had been Londoners and country dancers, so it was a fair guess that they'd be members of the Esperance Club. Most of them had gone back to town on Sunday evening but there was an outside chance that some might have stayed. If so, an outside chance of an outside chance that they might be able to fill in the blank of Daisy's last hours. As far as I knew, nobody had seen her after four o'clock on Monday afternoon at the latest, nine hours or so

179

between then and when I'd found her body in the cabinet. If Harry Hawthorne, or anybody else for that matter, had encouraged Daisy to go up to the Venns' house, they were the most likely ones to know about it.

I finished my egg on toast, drank another cup of tea and walked on up Portland Place and Albany Street to the club premises in Cumberland Market.

Even from outside, you could hear the piano playing and the sticks clicking. Inside, the pattering of feet and the tinkling of hundreds of ankle bells sounded like an avalanche of icicles. It was obviously a dress rehearsal for one of the club's demonstration teams, for the six women clashing sticks in two dancing lines facing each other were dressed like somebody's idea of country milkmaids. Cotton frocks in bright colours, blues, greens and reds, tight-fitted in the bodice and ending a few inches above the ankle. Over these, white muslin aprons and fichus, topped by big sunbonnets in the same colours as the dresses, trimmed with rows and rows of cotton lace.

As they danced, a tall woman with two long plaits of brown hair stood by the piano, calling out comments. 'Don't stamp, Phyllis. Sally, more height in the hops.' In spite of this, they seemed to be enjoying it, grinning at each other, eyes bright. I found a seat by the wall along with some other spectators and looked round to see if I could recognise anybody from the Scipian camp. A couple at the far end looked familiar, in ordinary working clothes apart from their dancing shoes. When the morris ended in a final clash of sticks and the woman with the pigtails said the dancers could take a ten-minute break, I walked over and reintroduced myself. They knew about Daisy's death and didn't seem to find it surprising that I wanted to know more. But neither had spoken to Daisy, beyond a few kind and casual remarks

about food or blankets, and both of them had left the camp
on Sunday evening. I asked if anybody else there had been
at the camp.

'Sally was.'

One of them nodded at the group of dancers crowded
round the instructor by the piano, probably receiving a
detailed critique. Sally – the one who hadn't been hopping
high enough – was a spectacularly pretty dark-haired girl who
looked around nineteen or twenty. She was wearing a poppy-
red dress with a lovingly tailored bodice that emphasised
every curve, her white fichu knotted over it in a way that
managed to be less demure than the costume designer probably intended. The group broke up as we looked and the
other two beckoned her over. She came across with an easy
walk, almost a swagger, and recognised me.

'Weren't you at that bloody camp?'

Quite friendly, though. The other two tutted at the
language, but Sally wasn't bothered. I said I'd like to talk to
her about Daisy and she glanced towards the door.

'Outside do you all right?'

I followed her, supposing she had something confidential
to tell me but when we got outside she settled on the top
step with her back to the door, flipped up her white apron
and took a packet of cigarettes and a box of matches out of
her dress pocket, both rather crushed from the dancing. She
offered me a cigarette – not taking offence when I said no
thanks – lit one for herself, took a few deep draws on it and
sighed with satisfaction.

'Ufff, that feels better. Florence'd go mad if she knew. She
says cigarettes spoil your wind for dancing.'

'You enjoy morris dancing?'

She made a face. 'Left to myself, I'd as soon be doing
cakewalk, but you get around more with morris and meet a
nicer class of young man.'

'Was that why you went to the Scipian camp?'

'Oh, come on! Waste of time and money, that was. I only went because a friend said did I fancy a cheap few days in the country and when we got there, nothing but miles of grass and cows' doings and blokes from factories without the price of a port and lemon between them going on about bringing down capitalism. I'd have gone straight back to town on the next train, only the girl I share a room with was having a friend in for the weekend and three's a crowd, isn't it?'

She untied her sunbonnet and put it down on the step beside her, stretched out her legs in their blue-grey stockings and crossed her ankles. A passing workman whistled from the street but she took no notice. It turned out that she too had left on Sunday evening.

'And not before time either. I'd had enough country air to last me a long lifetime.'

'Did you see much of Daisy?'

'The one who got killed? Not much, no. The other girls were looking after her and I'm not the sort who goes round adopting strays. I'm not saying I'm hard-hearted, but there's enough problems in life without going out to look for them.'

'Did you notice Mr Hawthorne with her at any time?'

'He the big hairy bloke that did all the talking?'

'Yes.'

She shook her head. 'Shouldn't think she was his type, too skinny. He made a grab at me when we were dancing and quite a few of the other girls too, the old goat. I just let him have it in the ribs, like this.' She demonstrated on me with her elbow, quite painfully.

'Was anybody else talking to her or paying her particular attention?'

'No, apart from the one she was supposed to be engaged

182

to, Daniel Venn. And he wasn't there much of the time either. I suppose he had other business elsewhere.'

There was something about the way she said it and her eyes had narrowed, watching her cigarette smoke float upwards. Also, she remembered the name.

'You noticed Daniel Venn, then?'

She nodded, not at all put out. 'Didn't you? He's a bit of a bantamweight, but if it had been him trying to put a hand where he shouldn't in *A-Nutting We Will Go* he might not have got the elbow quite so fast.'

'He could hardly do that with his fiancée there, could he?' I said, pretending innocence. The conversation wasn't going quite the way I'd expected and I couldn't see how to get it back on track. Her laugh wafted a cloud of smoke in my face.

'You'd be surprised what men will do.'

Again, there was something in her tone and it struck me that she might have heard about Daniel's engagement to Felicia, although I hadn't thought news of that had reached the Scipian camp by Sunday.

'Are you thinking of Daniel Venn in particular?' I said.

She nodded again. 'I don't know why he went and got engaged to that poor little scrap, but I don't reckon it would have lasted even if she hadn't got killed.'

'Why not?'

'Something I overheard.' She was grinning, not maliciously but enjoying the gossip.

'What about?'

'Not about anything in particular. Just heard.'

'Overheard, you said.'

'All right, overheard. And I wasn't creeping round listening deliberately. We just happened to hit on the same cart shed, that's all.'

'Same cart shed as what?' I was floundering, trying to keep up.

'Same as Daniel and the other one. You all right? I mean, you're not part of his family or anything?'

'No. But I'm trying to find out what happened to Daisy.'

'Well, this wasn't anything to do with her, apart from what I'm saying about the engagement not lasting anyway. We just happened to go to the cart shed they were in and heard them talking.'

'We?'

'There was this man I'd met before in London and quite liked. He'd got dragged down to the camp by his friends like I had and he didn't think much of it either. So we were quite pleased to see each other and we decided to go for a walk and get away from the others. So we'd gone a little way and I was fed up of all that grass and the flies and we came to this big shed place with a hay cart and hay, so I said why don't we go and sit inside and have a cigarette?'

'When was this?'

'The day we all got there, the Saturday. It was before suppertime – if you can call the muck they served up supper. Anyway, we started going inside, but before we'd gone more than a step or two we heard somebody else in there on the other side of the hay cart. So we stopped and kept quiet, thinking it might be the farmer or somebody and he might not like it. But there was this woman's voice, saying something about they shouldn't have done it.'

'Shouldn't have done what?'

'Well, it's obvious, if you think about it. You get a man and a woman in a shed full of hay and she's saying they shouldn't have done it, what would you think?'

'How does this connect with Daniel Venn?'

'Well, it didn't at the time because I'd never met him. But we heard this toff's voice, telling her the usual things.'

'Usual things?'

'That it would be all right, she mustn't worry, nobody would guess. You know the sort of things.'

'The woman's voice – was it Daisy's?' I felt angry, remembering Daniel's elaborate concern for Daisy's reputation.

'Good God, no. The woman was a toff as well. That was what made it so funny.'

'Did . . . did you see them?'

'What do you think we are, peeping Toms? No, we got out smartish and they didn't hear us, only later when Daniel Venn was there at the bonfire, as soon as I heard him talking I thought, "So it was you then was it, my lad," and when he got up on his hind legs later and said he was engaged to Daisy, well – it was all I could do not to laugh.'

'You're sure it was Daniel Venn you heard in the barn?'

'Well, there weren't many other toffs round there, were there? We'd been laughing to ourselves all the way back, imitating them.'

'Imitating?'

'Just for the laugh. I put on a voice like the woman's and was saying "Oh, we should never have done it. What if he finds out?" And Jimmy – that's my friend – he puts on this other voice – "Don't worry, Flissie, he won't ever know and—"'

'What was that you said?' I couldn't help it coming out sharply. She looked at me, surprised.

'Just what he was saying. Not to worry, the other man wouldn't know.'

'No, the name he called her.'

'I said, Flissie. That was part of the joke, it was such a silly sort of name.'

From inside the hall the piano thumped out a few emphatic dancing bars. The cry went up, 'Sally. Where's Sally?'

She stood up, stamped out the cigarette butt with her silver-buckled dancing shoe.

185

'Got to go. Nice meeting you. Sorry I haven't been able to help.'

I stayed sitting on the step for quite a while, hearing the music and jingle of bells through the half-open door.

Chapter Fourteen

IN THE END I WALKED ALL the way home, through Chalk
Farm and up Haverstock Hill back to Hampstead. There
was an edge of autumn in the air, with a sharp breeze skittering the first leaves off the plane trees and dusk coming
early. I could have caught a tram most of the way but my
mind works best when I'm walking. Sally was speaking the
truth as she saw and heard it, I'd have bet money on that.
After all, what reason did she have for lying? And yet what
she'd said made nonsense of what I thought I knew.

The toff in the barn, assumed quite reasonably to be Daniel
Venn, had called a woman Flissie. A diminutive, a family pet
name. I'd even heard some of the Venns calling Felicia by
it. All this had happened on Saturday afternoon before
suppertime at the Scipian camp, hours before the dancing by
the bonfire and Daniel's impulsive engagement to Daisy. I'd
met Felicia that afternoon up at the house and she'd been
impatient because Daniel wasn't back. Then later I'd met
Daniel in the camp, supposedly newly returned from Wiltshire
with Daisy in tow, and when I mentioned Felicia he'd asked
after her in a way that suggested he hadn't seen her since he
got back. Which meant that they couldn't have been the
couple Sally and her friend heard in the barn – unless they'd
both been lying to me by implication. And why not, come
to think of it? They didn't owe any duty of truth to me and
if the two of them had a secret tryst in a cart shed, they

wouldn't want the world to know. But if that was what had happened on Saturday evening it made Daniel's decision a few hours later to betray Felicia even worse.

When I got home there were scuttlings of mice diving for their holes as soon as I opened the door and a letter from the bicycle manufacturers saying they'd forgotten to ask me to translate another page about patent battery lamps, enclosed, and could I please do it as soon as possible? No mention of an extra fee, naturally. I sat up half the night to do it, on cups of strong coffee, because in my financial state I couldn't afford to lose customers, even annoying ones. But while most of my mind was on switches and batteries another part of it must have been thinking about Daisy, because in the early hours of the morning there was a nagging question that wouldn't let me sleep until I'd dealt with it. So I went upstairs and rooted around for the few of my father's medical books that I'd kept out of sentiment. One of them had quite a long and comprehensible section on rigor mortis. I read and re-read it.

The feel of Daisy's body as Adam and I lifted her out of the cabinet had been at the back of my mind all the time and wouldn't go away. Now I dropped the mental defences and let it come back to me without resisting – her arms and legs thin and stiff like dry sticks, as if a little pressure would snap them, her neck slewed sideways. She'd bent a little at the waist when we'd lifted her out but that was all. Daniel had noticed it too some time later, appalled by the stiffness of her quick violinist's hands. The book, dating back fifty years or so, was cautious about the time rigor mortis would take to set in after death. This would be affected by various factors like air temperature or body weight. The first onset of it in hands and feet might be noticed as early as two hours after death. It could take anything between six and twelve hours for stiffness to spread to the whole body. So Daisy was six hours dead at least when we found her. I hadn't checked the exact time, but thought it was probably around an hour past midnight. In that case, it would fit well enough with the shot Bobbie and I heard around seven o'clock, just before it got dark.

Almost beyond doubt, Daniel hadn't killed her and neither had Hawthorne. For several hours from around seven o'clock the gun had been in my possession. About ten o'clock, probably, I'd given it to Daniel. Some time after that he'd shown it to Hawthorne then mislaid it. But if Daisy had been shot after ten o'clock, her body wouldn't have been almost completely stiff a mere three hours or so later. I wondered briefly if there were two guns involved and decided against it. The inspector would know more about guns than I did and he was obviously concentrating on Philomena's revolver. Besides, this was the Cotswolds not the American West – hardly bristling with revolvers. Except there was something I was missing. It was late, my mind was muzzy. I looked again at the passage in the book – between six and twelve hours for rigor to spread to the entire body. Forget the shortest time for a while and look at the longest. Assuming twelve hours, Daisy might have been shot as early as one o'clock in the afternoon – but I knew she hadn't been, for she'd been scraping carrots at the Scipian camp as late as three or even four. It might have been at any time after that. Which meant . . .

My mind was creaking like the timbers of an old ship in a gale, both from tiredness and from having to go where it didn't want to go. Daniel had told the police that he'd taken his aunt's revolver, had it with him all afternoon. I'd assumed it was a lie to save Felicia but suppose it had happened? And it had been Daniel after all who left the blanket in the summerhouse for me, as I'd asked him. Was I intended to find the gun under it much later and add another layer of confusion to the evidence? If so, Daniel had been the cold and calculating one and Felicia's unlikely story of happening to find it under the blanket might even be true.

Up to that point I'd still believed in Felicia's guilt. Now the picture had shifted and I liked what I saw even less. Daniel and Felicia were lovers, they'd been together in the cart shed. Daisy was a regrettable mistake and must be disposed of. And I was the worst fool in the world for thinking that a person I'd instinctively liked couldn't be guilty of murder. Inspector Bull, without that emotional disadvantage, must have got there before me. For all I knew, knowledge of rigor mortis might have improved since my father's student days so that the police could judge the time of death more precisely. But come to think of it, in that respect at least Inspector Bull was at a disadvantage. It was daylight by the time he arrived on the Tuesday morning, around five o'clock, say. Four hours for the body to stiffen completely, with no way of telling how long it had been like that. It would annoy him when he thought about it, and he'd had time to think by now. Why hadn't we called the police earlier? Why hadn't we done the normal thing and sent somebody running down to the village policeman? The decision not to had been Adam's. A questionable decision by an intelligent man – unless he'd known more than he admitted about when Daisy died. I put the book back on the shelf and got to bed at last for a few hours' sleep.

In the morning I packed a carpet bag with a change of clothes, put a note through my neighbour's door saying yes please to the kittens when I got back and went to Clement's Inn to break the news that I'd be away for a couple of days. It wasn't as easy as that, of course, because there were half a dozen things that had to be settled before I went. I was sitting in the main office, working through a series of memoranda about speakers' out-of-town expenses ('*Is it too much to expect that the hosts should provide a meat tea?*') and being distracted by a friend at the other end of the table who was trying to talk to me while dealing with incoming telephone calls.

'. . . so I told her, if all they could do was quarrel about who was going to ride the horse they might as well give up there and then. The trouble with processions . . . Hello, yes, this is Holborn 2724. No, should she be? No, I don't think so. If you'll hold on a minute I'll go and look.' She left the phone off its hook and disappeared, leaving me in peace for a while. 'No, I'm sorry Lady Fieldfare, nobody here's seen her today. Well, of course we will. I hope you find her.'

She hooked the phone back. 'Lady Fieldfare, worrying about her daughter.'

'Why worrying?'

'She was supposed to be somewhere or other this morning and she hasn't turned up. From what I've seen of that young woman, that's not unusual.'

Probably not. I scrawled a hasty memorandum of my own to add to the out-of-town expenses saga, put on my hat and picked up my bag.

'Off already, Nell? Are you coming back for the meeting this afternoon?'

I told her no and please give them my apologies. I was already heading for the door. At Paddington I sprinted for a train, caught it as the guard's whistle was blowing and by mid-afternoon was getting out at the all too familiar halt.

Somewhere to stay the night was a priority. I didn't intend to live under the Venns' roof. I enquired at the village store and post office and was told that Mrs Penny sometimes took in hikers, opposite the Crown with geranium pots outside. Her cottage was a sliver of honey-coloured limestone wedged between two taller houses and looked approximately one and a half storeys high, with the overhang of the ragged thatch coming halfway down the small upstairs windows. Mrs Penny herself was in proportion to her cottage, less than five feet tall from her black boots to her grey topknot. She looked me down and up on her doorstep, tilting her head right back as a protest at my height.

'You a hiker then, miss?'

'Yes.' I quieted my conscience with the thought that I'd probably do plenty of walking.

'I only take hikers in the summer.'

'But it's only just September. Couldn't you stretch a point?'

'Hiking on your own?' She made it sound like a suspicious act in itself. Why did I have to work so hard round here to persuade my way into an uncomfortable bed? 'I usually have gentlemen.'

I assured her my habits were civilised. She still looked doubtful.

'I had a lady here for her health once. A teacher, she was. The doctor said if she stayed in Birmingham with her chest he wouldn't be answerable.'

The meaning was clear. Ill health was acceptable. Lone females gadding around for selfish pleasure were not.

'I'm sure the country air would do my chest a world of good too,' I said.

Her eyes gleamed, bright as a robin's sighting a worm. 'So it's for your health, then?'

'I hope so.'

I doubted it, but it was enough to get me over the threshold and up the stairs to a wedge-shaped room with a slanting ceiling. Even in the high part of the room I couldn't have stood upright, and anyway that was taken up with the brass bedstead. In the lower part all I could do was crouch by the window with a view of the village street and the yard of the public house.

192

'Tea's at six o'clock,' she said. 'Cold beef and pickles.'

'Could you possibly make it later? I've got a call to make first.'

The look in her eyes told me she'd never have let me in if she'd known I was going to be a nuisance, but the thing was done now.

'You don't want to be out late, not with your chest. But no later than nine o'clock, because some of us need our sleep.'

I washed dust and train smuts off my face in the cracked basin on the toilet table, was shown the hiding place of the key – under a pot of geraniums by the front doorstep – and turned up the street towards the open road, aware of Mrs Penny's eyes on me as I went. I'd almost certainly taken up lodgings with the village gossip, but nothing to be done about that. The road between the fields to the Venns' house was empty of people or carts, and shining in watery sun after a shower. By five o'clock I was walking up the steps to the front door.

Annie answered it, a scared look on her face, eyes puffy and red-rimmed. Before she could say anything, Carol appeared on the stairs.

'Daniel said you'd be coming.'

Her pale skin was drum-tight over her cheekbones, her eyes hot and bright. She led the way through to the room where we'd had our meeting.

'Adam's gone to the junction to collect Mr Galway.'

'Galway?'

'He's a friend of Adam's, another solicitor. Adam asked him to come down in case . . .'

'In case they arrest Daniel?'

She bit her lip, then nodded. 'You see what he's doing, trying to protect her?'

'Has he told you so?'

'I guessed. Daniel's an open book.'

193

'Did you try to talk him out of it?'

'Yes, but it was a waste of breath. Daniel may act like a madcap some of the time, but there's so much determination there, even as a boy. He was only ten when I got engaged to Adam and . . . oh, I'm sorry, I'm rambling. I don't know what to do.'

I said, 'If it comes to it, I may have to take the choice away from you. You realise I couldn't let Daniel stand trial for murder without telling the police what I saw.'

'Felicia?'

'Yes. How is she?'

'She's hardly been out of bed since she spoke to the police. The inspector was quite gentle with her, all things considered, but it didn't help. The doctor's seen her twice. Nervous prostration, he says. Keep her quiet and give her time.'

'From what Daniel said to me, he's trying to buy us all time,' I said. 'Time to find out who killed her.'

'Yes.'

'He believes somebody left her body in the cabinet to put the blame on the family.' I didn't mention Hawthorne's name, not sure how much Daniel had discussed with her.

'Do you think that?'

'I don't know. Would many people know the cabinet was here?'

'The whole village, I suppose. Mr Bestley the carter brought it up on Monday morning and he's the biggest gossip in the district.'

'What about when it was in the workshop. Did anybody show any special interest in it?'

'I'm not sure.'

'Would you mind if I went there tomorrow and asked Mr Sutton?'

She looked worried. 'Do you really need to do that?'

'You don't want me to?'

'It's just that you might not get a lot of sense out of Mr Sutton at the moment. His wife Janie's left him, just up and taken the baby without saying a word. He can't think or talk about anything else.'

'Why did she go?'

'He doesn't know. Oh God, everything's such a mess.'

She seemed so brittle with worry and tiredness that I didn't press the point.

'Where's Daniel? Can I talk to him?' I said.

'In the music room. He says there's something he wants to finish before . . . you know.'

She got up, led the way across the hall and tapped on a door. 'Daniel, Miss Bray.'

She left me at the door. Daniel opened it. The top of the upright piano behind him was scattered with sheets of music. He had a pen in his hand, ink blots on his fingers.

'Do you think I'm heartless, trying to work? Not that it's any good anyway.'

He plumped himself back on the piano stool, leaving me to take a seat by the table. It was a small room, very much a musician's workshop, with an upright piano, a guitar, and a concertina on the table. Music stands and a cello case were pushed against the wall.

'Did Carol tell you the inspector was waiting for me when I got back last night? Wanted to know where I'd been. I didn't tell him I'd been up to see you but he asked about you anyway.'

'What?'

'Had I spoken to you since last Tuesday? I said it was none of his business. But I got the impression he wants to talk to you again. He seems to be in a pretty savage temper with all of us.'

That was predictable, but bad news all the same.

195

'What else did he ask you?'

'More about where I'd been on Monday afternoon. In here, I said, trying to work or out strolling around because I couldn't work. When? Had anybody seen me? How am I supposed to know who saw me or who didn't?'

So I'd been right. Inspector Bull had done the same sums as I had, probably more accurately.

'Did he ask you about the gun again?'

'How many squirrels I'd bagged – very sarcastic.'

'And you stuck to the story that you'd had it with you all afternoon?'

'Yes.'

'Tell me, did you put it under the blanket in the summer-house?'

He brought his fist crashing down on the piano keys.

'For heaven's sake, don't you start. Haven't I had enough of it from the police? You're supposed to be on my side.'

'If I'm on anybody's side, it's Daisy's.'

'Too late for her.'

'I know. But you can't rely on my being on your side or anybody else's side. If you want me here, you're going to have to put up with my questions.'

He sighed, loud and exasperated, like a child giving in reluctantly.

'Ask, then.'

'I've asked. Did you put the revolver under the blanket?'

'No.'

'Had you seen it or handled it that day, before I gave it to you down at the camp?'

'If I answer that, are you going to tell the police?'

'I reserve the right to, yes.'

'Then I reserve the right not to answer.'

'Very well, when I gave it to you, you said you thought two rounds had been fired. Do you remember that?'

'Yes.' Reluctantly.

'Looking back, do you still think so?'

He frowned down at the piano keys. 'It's difficult, but yes.'

'Why did you notice that in particular?'

'I don't know.'

'Think, then. Wasn't it an odd thing to notice in the circumstances?'

'Habit, I suppose. You know Aunt Philly used to have shooting competitions with Adam and me? The game was, you'd have five shots each at the bottles. Then when you'd fired your five and the chamber was empty you had to pass the gun on to the next one, to reload. As a kid, I always enjoyed breaking open the gun.'

'I heard one shot in the garden,' I said. 'If that wasn't the one that killed Daisy, there must have been another earlier.'

'I suppose so.'

I didn't tell him about my researches into rigor mortis.

'There's something else I want to ask you,' I said. 'In the ordinary way it would be none of my business but you brought me into this, after all.'

'Go on.'

'You remember that Saturday, when we first met at the camp? I had a strong impression that at that point you hadn't seen Felicia since you'd got back.'

He wrinkled his forehead, as if it were too far back to think about. 'Wasn't that when I'd just got back here with Daisy? No, I didn't see Felicia until the next day, when I told her the engagement was off.'

'Are you sure?'

'Yes. I wouldn't forget a thing like that, would I?'

'I ask because somebody is sure they heard you and Felicia talking together in a cart shed near the camp, some time before it got dark on the Saturday evening.'

'Who?' He twisted round on the piano stool. 'It's just not true. Who have you been talking to?'

'That doesn't matter. The point is, what the person thinks she—'

'So it's a she, is it, this gossip?'

'That doesn't matter either. She heard a man she believed to be you talking to a woman with what she described as a toff's voice. She didn't see either of them. The woman said "We should never have done it. What if they find out?" The man comforted her and said they wouldn't know. He called her Flissie.'

'He called her *what?*' Daniel jumped up. His face was so close to my own that I could feel the heat of his breath and he looked furious. 'I'm supposed to have been in a cart shed with Felicia and called her Flissie?'

'Were you?'

'Listen, this is important. If I'd never told the truth before in my life I'd be telling it now. I've never, as it happens, on any occasion been in any cart shed with Felicia. More than that, I'm totally and utterly incapable of calling her *Flissie.*'

The depth of loathing he put into the last two syllables spattered my face. He apologised and took a step back, but still looked furious.

'Why not?'

'Just think about it. I'm a musician. What I do best is setting words to music. That means you have to like words, hear the music in them. About the first thing I said to Felicia was that she had a beautiful name. It practically sings itself.' He sat down again, played and sang 'Fel-ic-i-a', the four syllables clear and high as a blackbird's song. 'Then I'm supposed to have called her Flissie. *Fliss-ee.* Listen to it. Like a coster-monger whistling to his dog. I hate it when the others call her that. I tell you, I may be guilty of all kinds of stupidity,

I may even be guilty of murder if you like, but I could never, ever be capable of uttering an atrocity like *Flissie*.'

He took a deep breath and sagged with his head just above the keys. The ridiculous thing was that I believed him. But then I'd believed Sally too and, looking back, I still did.

I left him there, let myself quietly out of the front door and went back down the road to the village. The key to Mrs Penny's cottage was under the geraniums as promised. There was no sign of her but a fat marmalade cat kept me company and cadged scraps while I ate cold beef with home-made piccalilli and drank very stewed tea at the kitchen table. Afterwards I went upstairs and after a long struggle managed to persuade the old oil lamp on the washstand to give out just enough light to read by. I'd brought a pile of papers and magazines from London with me and one of them happened to be Hawthorne's publication the *Wrecker*. I sat down on the bed with it, turning pages idly until I came to something that made me sit up. It had a panel to itself and was headed, in bold black type, A TALE OF MODERN TIMES. I read on, fearing the worst, and got it.

> *Once upon a week ago in a not far away county – let us call it Oxfordshire – a handsome young prince went looking for a bride. His princely choice fell on a beautiful girl with long red hair – let us call her Daisy – who played the violin and sang and danced better than anybody else in the kingdom. So the handsome young prince took her away from her friends and said to his family, 'This is the princess I am going to marry.' But his family were proud and wealthy. They said, 'She is no princess, for all that she sings and plays the violin and dances better than anyone in the kingdom. She is born of the working classes and has no money.' So they killed the red-haired girl, and the young*

199

prince was sad for a while, but soon found himself another bride who was not beautiful and could not sing or dance or play the violin but was born of the upper classes and had a lot of money. This is a true story, gentle reader, but you will not find it in any of your other so-called newspapers, because if they were to print it people might ask questions which would anger other people in high places – such as whether it is right that girls should be killed because they come from the working classes and have no money or what the police in Oxfordshire – led by a wise and kindly Inspector with a name something like Ox – are doing to put the murderers of the girl in prison. But then, if you think our brave boys in blue will ever defend the rights of the working classes against the taking classes, then you really do believe in fairy tales.

If anything had been needed to make matters worse, this was it. Hawthorne's total disregard for the laws of libel was notorious and had already caused two or three publications to sink under him, but this was beyond his worst. If Inspector Bull had read it – and I wouldn't put it past Hawthorne to have posted a copy to him – it explained the bad temper Daniel had noticed.

Soon after that the little supply of oil in the lamp gave out so I got undressed in the dark and dozed. It was an uneasy doze because my room was just opposite the public house. Although the village was quiet by day, the pub in the evening seemed to be a magnet for men from miles around. Heavy boots tramped up and down the street, voices called out cheerful insults in local accents to friends leaving or arriving. As the evening went on there was some singing, all of it music hall songs, nothing to excite the folk-song collectors. Even though the noise stopped me from sleeping it was pleasant enough in its way and I half listened to the comings and

200

goings to stop my mind tramping round in the familiar circles about Daisy. All of a sudden something very different from the rest of the noise jolted me into full wakefulness. One pair of heavy boots marching, like the rest, up the street towards the pub. A man singing as he came, already sounding as if he'd had a drink or three. But it was what he was singing that set my heart thumping: 'A varmer he lived in the West Countree, And he had daughters one, two and three.'

I made a jump for the window, but by the time I got there the singing had stopped and all I could see was the back of a man silhouetted against the yellow lamplight from the pub doorway. Then the door closed on him. I started getting into my clothes, scrabbling in the dark for skirt and blouse, with no plan in my mind except to see the man and talk to him. A woman hurtling into the public bar would scandalise the village but there was no help for it. Buttons done up skew-whiff, not bothering with stockings, I dived under the bed, looking for my second shoe.

It was while I was under there that the fighting started. I heard the pub door opening, a roar of protest, a shout of, 'I told you to get out and stay out!' The crash of my head against the bed frame drowned the next few words and by the time I'd stopped seeing stars and shuffled over to the window the fight was down to ground level, with what looked like two or three men wrestling on the pub doorstep and others standing round shouting. Presumably one of the fighters was my singer, but there was nothing to distinguish him in a writhing mass of arms, legs and backs. A cry went up 'Police! Police coming.' The writhing mass became vertical and a man tore himself away from it and ran heavily down the street. Within a few strides he'd gone beyond the light from the pub doorway and into dark-ness. I found my shoe, went downstairs as quickly as I could in the dark and let myself out on to the street. There was still a lot of excitement round the pub doorway, but no sign of a policeman, so that had probably been somebody's bright idea to break things up.

'. . . told him last night I didn't want him in here.'

'Not us owes him money, any road.'

'Bit me. Bugger tried to bite my ear off.'

I ran past them, down the street in the direction the man had gone, but the time it had taken me to find my shoe and get downstairs had given him two minutes' or so start. Soon I was through the village and on a country road with hedges both sides, nothing but darkness beyond. He could be anywhere, in a ditch not far from where I was standing or out in the fields, and much though I wanted to speak to him it made no sense to track a violent man across country on my own.

More slowly I went back up the street to the pub. Men were still standing and talking outside and by this time they'd recovered enough from the excitement to notice me. When I came into the light and they saw I was a stranger they stopped talking, startled rather than hostile.

'Good evening, miss,' one of them said. He looked like the landlord, a big plump man with a brown apron over his clothes.

'I'm lodging with Mrs Penny,' I said. 'I heard a noise so I thought I'd better come down and see what was happening.'

They relaxed, relieved I was accounted for.

'I'm sorry you've had your sleep broken, miss,' the landlord said, 'but there's nothing for you to worry about. Just a ruffian trying to push himself in where he's not wanted.'

'A local man?'

A general shaking of heads. I was being nosy, but perhaps they were used to that from hikers and cyclists. They didn't seem to resent it.

'Was he by any chance a big tall man with a beard?'

'Why, are you looking for one of they?'

That from a man in the doorway who seemed more drunk than the rest. They shushed him.

'No,' the landlord said. 'Broad in the shoulder but not big out of the common and no beard. Stubble, but no beard.'

Not Harry Hawthorne, then. Even if he'd shaved off his beard he couldn't change his size. I asked what he'd done to get banned from the pub.

'He's got a nasty temper,' the landlord said. It set off a chorus from the others.

'And he keeps trying to cadge drinks off people.'

'Stole me drink once, he did, nearly whole pint left there was.'

'That's right, pinches people's pints off the bar when he thinks they're not looking, then starts a fight when you pick him up on it.'

'And keeps on about people owing him money.'

More to keep the conversation going than anything, I picked up on the last remark. 'One of these men owed a fortune, is he?' I asked.

'Don't know about a fortune, miss. Time I heard it, it was twenty pounds.'

The others chorused that was right, supposed to be twenty pounds. They were fidgeting now, night air cold and bladders full probably, wanting the conversation to end. I wished them good night and they drifted away up and down the street. The landlord hoped I'd sleep better now all that was over and went back inside. I let myself into the house opposite and locked the door behind me. Mrs Penny was still snoring in her room. With luck, she might not know about my nocturnal gallivanting, but villages being villages I couldn't depend on that. Anyway, there was something else bothering me more. The man had been quite specific, several times over, about the amount he was owed – twenty pounds.

203

Consistency was unusual in a violent drunk. The sum was unusual too. If a man of that kind thinks he's owed money it's either a modest shilling for the next drink or untold thousands he should have inherited and didn't. Twenty pounds was either too big or too small for the pattern. I undressed again, got under the sheets and blankets, and slept.

Some time later, while it was still dark, I was suddenly broad awake again because I'd remembered when I'd last heard of somebody wanting twenty pounds. Daniel Venn had told me: '. . . *he said I could have her for twenty pounds*'. The price of Daisy.

Chapter Fifteen

'SERVE HIM RIGHT,' MRS PENNY SAID when I told her I'd heard a man being thrown out of the Crown. 'Tramp, probably. We get more of those than a dog has fleas.'

I hadn't slept much and was up and dressed by six, but she and her cat were in the kitchen before me. She poured me a cup of tea, spread a hunk of farmhouse loaf with butter and put an egg on to boil.

'There's no bacon on account of Bestley's foot. Swollen up purple and yellow.' She went into a lot of medical details involving the probability of gangrene, delirium and amputation.

I ate my egg and walked out to the village street. It was a fine morning, a smell of fresh bread and ripe apples over everything, swallows twittering around and getting ready to migrate. I spoke to a couple of farm labourers on their way to work, a woman scrubbing her front step, a man delivering bread from a pony cart. They'd all of them seen tramps around over the past few weeks, but there was nothing unusual about that. A lot of them had their familiar rounds, going from workhouse to workhouse, picking up the occasional odd job or piece of charity in between. But they hadn't noticed anything unusual in the way of tramps in the last day or two and my description – broad shoulders, stubble, average build – could have applied to almost any of them. Later, when the shop-cum-post-office opened I took my place in the queue. It was only the size of a small parlour and with half of it taken up by the counter and a woman and man in front of me I could just about wedge into the corner beside the broom handles and scrubbing boards.

The woman at the counter was weighing out two ounces of tea, carefully and slowly, for an old dear who was saying that girls who got killed probably did something to deserve it. The man gave his opinion that it was probably some of them anthiests from Manchester. It took me a while to realise he was talking about the Scipian camp, presumably merging atheists and anarchists in general suspicion. He'd come to collect some boots that had gone to town for mending, but was disappointed. Bestley's foot again. It seemed to be having a disastrous effect on the village economy. The name struck a chord and I remembered that Mr Bestley was the village carter who'd taken the cabinet up to the Venns' house. When it came to my turn I bought a pair of bootlaces and a packet of chocolate. As it seemed to be the local custom I enquired after Bestley's foot and was told he'd dropped a hammer on it last week. After more chat about the weather and hiking I mentioned that I was staying with Mrs Penny and there'd been a bit of trouble outside the Crown last night. The shop-keeper was inclined to resent it at first as a slur on the village. (Murder, it seemed, was acceptable but public house fights might lower the tone of a place.)

'I think the troublemaker was an outsider,' I said. 'He didn't sound like a local man.'

'We've had a lot of those around in the past couple of weeks.'

I hadn't understood till then how the Scipian camp had been resented. The rumours of what was going on up there had been bad enough, but entertaining at least. The worst of it was that the Scipians had spent very little money in the village at the shop, pub or bakery. So, as the village saw it, the Scipians got all the sin and the locals got none of the profits. I might have explained that the camp, from what I'd seen of it, had been as virtuous as a Sunday school outing and if the Scipians hadn't spent money it was because they hadn't got much. But I just said the man hadn't sounded like one of those to me.

'There are tramps about,' the woman behind the counter said. 'One of them got a chicken of ours two nights ago. Johnson tried to make out it was a fox. I said, don't you give me fox. What fox you ever heard of could unlatch a coop and take a hen out of it without fuss or feathers?'

This sounded more promising. If Fardel had been in the area nine or ten days without money, he'd have to eat.

'Is Mr Johnson your husband?'

She made a derisive noise. 'No, thank God. Constable Johnson at the police house.'

Inspector Bull had brought his own constable with him from outside. There'd been no mention of a Constable Johnson. I paid for my things and asked where the police house was.

'The other side of the school. You'll know it from the dahlias.'

She was right. The lower floor of the little stone cottage was almost hidden by a breaking wave of reds and yellows and purples. Above the front door, just visible, a new stone plaque with the county arms was the only sign that this was the law's residence. Among the flowers, a red-faced man in his fifties straightened up and looked at me. He was in waist-coat and shirtsleeves and holding a flowerpot stuffed with straw. I wished him good afternoon and said I was staying in the village, a friend of the Venn family. His face clouded.

'I'm sorry for what's happened to them, miss. Mrs Venn's always been good to the village.'

'The old Mrs Venn or the young one?'

207

'Both, miss.'

My guess that the village policeman had little if anything to do with the murder investigation seemed right. I admired his dahlias and he invited me in through the gate to see them. Earwigs were a pest, he said. His big red fist jerked the straw out of the flowerpot into a bucket of water on the path. Earwigs burst out of it into the water, rowing uselessly with hundreds of legs. Again, I mentioned the trouble outside the Crown. He'd heard about it, no more. As for tramps, he knew most of the regulars in his area and thought them harmless on the whole. No new ones had come to his notice over the past couple of weeks.

'The woman at the shop thinks a tramp stole one of her chickens,' I said.

His expression showed what he thought of the woman at the shop. His big hand hovered over a yellow explosion of bloom, delicately twitched off a single petal, earwig-nibbled.

'Drive you mad it would, sometimes. I retire with a pension this time next year and it can't come a day too soon for me. They all want you to find their dogs or their chickens or their wives and it's you they blame if you can't, not whoever it is who went off with their wives or their dogs or their chickens in the first place.'

'You count wives along with the rest of the livestock?' I was annoyed but luckily he didn't realise that.

'You don't, that's what I have to explain to them. A chicken or a dog or a horse, that's your possession and if somebody takes it, he's committed an offence. It's not the same with a wife. Like it or not, she's a free person in law and if she decides to take herself off of her own free will or go off with somebody else, you can't send a policeman to fetch her back. You might not like it, but that's the law.'

From the way he said it, I guessed he'd made that little speech recently to somebody else. Come to think of it, I'd heard a bit of gossip recently about a man's wife leaving him.

'Mr Sutton the woodworker?'

Carol Venn had mentioned it. He nodded and turned back to his flowers, dutifully unwilling to talk about a particular case. I thanked him, said I hoped the frost would come late this year for the sake of his dahlias and went back to the main street to go on with the discouraging search. I went up and down in the morning sun, talking to women standing at open doors, old men gossiping by the pump. One man had seen a dark figure slinking into a copse around twilight about a week ago – but he couldn't remember when exactly, only saw him from a field away and thought he was probably a poacher. Apart from that, nothing.

I went on to the end of the street and stopped outside the furniture workshop. A lad was out in the yard, stacking pieces of seasoned oak. Through a window open to the street I could see Mr Sutton leaning over, planing something. I hesitated to bother him but although he had his back to me he must have sensed that I was there. He whirled round with such a look of hope on his face that I thought he must be seeing somebody behind me. But there was nobody. The hope died away and his face crumpled like a kicked paper lantern. The plane clattered to the floor. By the time I got inside he was kneeling down in the pale wood shavings, head bent, forehead against the wood he'd been planing.

'I'm sorry,' I said. 'I wasn't meaning to spy on you.'

There was nobody else in the workshop.

'Janie,' he said, to the wood, not to me. It came out as the kind of groan tree branches make, rubbing against each other in a gale. 'Every time there's someone there, I think it's Janie.' He levered himself upright and sat down on a block of wood. 'She's been gone more than a week now.'

'I'm sorry.'

He looked at me, as if he couldn't get me or anything else into focus. 'You're Mrs Venn's friend, aren't you? You were there that day it started.'

'What started?'

'That cabinet. I've never liked black oak, never liked it. Poor Janie was so scared of it. You saw that?'

She'd been scared, no doubt about it, but looking back I wasn't sure if it had been of the cabinet itself. But I said nothing because he was in such a tightly stretched state of nerves it looked as if even the slightest extra strain would spring him apart. He looked as if he hadn't slept for days and his hands were shaking so much it was surprising he could operate the plane.

'And then the two of them singing that song, about a baby being tormented and a woman killed. How could anybody sing a song like that? There was a curse on the thing. I should never have let it in the workshop. I'd have burned it to ashes in the yard if I'd known, damn whether it was valuable or not.'

'A curse on the cabinet?'

'Why not? You can build love into a piece of furniture, I know that because I've done it. If you can build love in you can build hate as well. Somebody carved that thing with hate in his hands. If I had him here . . .'

He jumped up, grabbed a chisel from a bench and started tearing jagged runnels into the piece of wood he'd been planing, ugly and random. The torn wood looked terribly like flesh drawing back from the edges of a wound. Tears were running down his face. 'They say the poor girl was in it, actually inside it. Is that true?'

I nodded. He stared at the slashes in the wood as if somebody else had made them and came back to sit down.

'At least her family knows what's become of her. I might never know what's happened to Janie or the baby. Just gone off, that fool of a policeman says. Women just go off and you can't do anything about it. Janie wasn't like that. Where would she go? Who would she go to?'

'Can you think of any reason why she'd go?'

He looked away, going red. 'Are people gossiping then?'

'If they are, I haven't heard any.'

'I'd done no harm to her. She was happy with the baby and we had a good roof over our heads. Mrs Venn had set us up nicely so I could do the work I always wanted to do. We had everything to look forward to, then like a fool I let that black oak in my shop.'

'When did she go?'

'The Monday. She got me my breakfast as usual. I had to get that damned – excuse me – the cabinet up to the house, then go on over Chadlington way to see a customer. When I got back in the afternoon, she'd gone.'

Monday. The day Daisy died.

'Did she leave a note?'

'No note. She'd taken a shawl and a blanket and some clothes for the baby and left a couple of slices of bread and cheese on a plate with a cloth over them for my lunch. Why did she think I'd eat lunch with her and the baby gone?'

'If she took the shawl and things . . .'

'That's what Constable Johnson says. If she took the things with her, that shows she wasn't forced away against her will. It's all very well for him to talk. I know Janie and he doesn't.'

I supposed but didn't say that every husband ever deserted thought he knew his wife. But it was undeniable that on the Saturday afternoon, something had scared Janie very much.

'Was she all right on the Sunday?'

'Thinking back, she was a bit on the quiet side but she gets tired with the baby so I didn't think much to it. In the

211

afternoon Mrs Venn called and the two of them went for a bit of a walk together.'

'Janie and Carol.'

'Mrs Venn's always been very kind to Janie. They go out together sometimes to pick leaves and flowers for Mrs Venn to paint. Anyway, she came back still a bit pale and quiet and I said she should go upstairs and rest, so she did.'

'And no mention to you of being worried about anything?'

'Never a word. But I think she was still brooding about that black oak and the song.'

He was calmer now, so I risked the question.

'So what do you think happened to her?'

'What do I think? I think she's been killed by whatever monster killed that other poor girl, that's what I think.'

We stayed there in silence, he sitting with arms hanging and head bent. Then a woman's voice called softly from outside the window, 'Your dinner, Mr Sutton.'

She was a kindly plump woman carrying a white soup plate with another one upside down on top of it. She put them down on a bench with sorrowful care, like a person placing a wreath on a tomb. 'Any news?' she asked him.

'No news.'

The lad was still stacking wood in the yard. I asked him where Mr Bestley the carter lived and he pointed up a lane beside the forge. There was just the shadow of an idea in my mind and I wanted to test it. It was around midday and the blacksmith was taking a rest.

'Going up to old Bestley?' Then, when I said I was, 'If you want any civility out of him, you might try taking a bit of baccy.'

So I went back to the shop again, bought an ounce of shag tobacco and took it past the forge and along the lane. There were two deep parallel wheel ruts all along it, already

getting overgrown with grass and pineapple weed. The ruts
ended in a yard with an empty stable on one side of it and
a lean-to on the other with the carter's wagon inside. A
cottage closed off the third side of the yard, a little worse
for wear with pennycress growing from gaps in the rough
stone walls. Some stone tiles missing from the roof had been
replaced with tin cans hammered flat. I knocked on the door.
There was a sound of somebody moving about inside then,
'Who's that?'

'A visitor,' I said. Then, blessing the smith's foresight, 'I've
brought you some tobacco.'

I heard a dragging sound and a voice moaning to itself.
The door opened into a dim space like a ship's cabin. Possibly
at one time it had been a normal-sized cottage room, but
all sides of it were stacked from floor to ceiling with empty
boxes and packing cases with just two spaces for a small
window in one wall and a fireplace in another. In the middle
of the room was a nest of blankets and old curtains that
might possibly have a chair somewhere underneath, with an
elderly dog on the carpet beside it, peering at me suspiciously
from filmy eyes. Mr Bestley stood leaning against the doorframe, stick in hand, right foot so swaddled in dirty cloth it
looked three times its normal size.

'I'm staying with Mrs Penny,' I said. 'I heard you'd been
hurt.'

Luckily, he seemed to take the interest as no more than
his due.

'I can't stand up for long. If you want to talk you'll have
to come in and sit down.'

I held the tobacco in its twist of paper so that he could
see it, but didn't hand it over. The lure of it and the chance
to talk about his bad luck to a new audience were irresistible.
Slowly he went over and settled into the nest-like chair, indi-
cating that I should draw up a packing case and sit down. I

handed the tobacco over. He tipped some of it into the palm of a hand that looked as tough as saddle leather, stirred it with his finger and sniffed mournfully, as if to say it wasn't much good but the best that life was likely to put his way.

'Staying with her, are you? I might have married her myself only she liked another man better. She's been widowed ten years any road.'

He said it with gloomy satisfaction. Even before the accident he probably hadn't been one of the cheery whistling types of carter.

'I'm a friend of the Venns,' I told him. (I wasn't sure about that, but he'd need some explanation.) 'I believe you delivered the black oak cabinet to them last Monday week.'

'That dratted thing. There's a curse on it. First the poor gal gets killed, then Sutton's wife takes herself off, then it's my poor foot.'

'But I thought you dropped a hammer on your foot.'

'I did, but it happened the day after we carted that bleeding cabinet and if I hadn't been weakened from the weight of it I might not have dropped the hammer.'

He took a short-stemmed clay pipe out of his pocket, filled and lit it. Blue smoke drifted up to a ceiling kipper-coloured from years of nicotine. The dog put its head on his knee and he stroked it.

'Blind as a bat and deaf as a post. Fine pair, him and me.'

After a few long drags on the pipe he told his story. He'd taken the cob down to the forge for shoeing the day after they delivered the cabinet to the Venns' house, tried to help the smith by handing him a hammer and dropped it on his foot. No bones broken and – in spite of Mrs Penny's gloating predictions – no signs of gangrene or delirium. But enough to keep him off work for several weeks.

'And you think it's because the black cabinet brought bad luck?'

'Well, for certain it didn't bring anybody good luck, did it? Is it true they found the poor gal's body inside it?'

'Yes.'

No surprise that the story had got round the village.

'It had a hanged man on it. Saw it myself.'

'Did you look inside when you moved it?'

'I know what you're thinking. You're thinking was the gal inside it when we moved it out of Sutton's place. Everybody wants to know that. Well, she wasn't. I looked inside because the door came open when we were trying to shift it and it was as empty as a pauper's stomach.'

'Did the police ask you about that?'

'Police? What would the police be wanting with me? All I did was help shift it and that isn't a job I'd do again in a hurry.'

'Yes, it looked heavy.'

'Heavy! It was as much as the three of us could do to get it into the house. Up the steps to the front door and then Mrs Venn wants it taken all the way through the house and—'

'Three of you? That's you and Mr Sutton and who else?'

'Bloke I took on for the day. I knew we were in for a bit of heavy work, and he was hanging round by the forge, so I said did he want to earn himself a couple of bob. She'd pay all right, I knew that. Without him, we'd still be there trying to shift it now.'

'This other man, was he from the village?'

'No. Never seen him before or since.'

'A tramp?'

'Not what you'd call a tramp exactly. You get a lot of casual workers coming in for the harvest and I took him for one of them. All the same to me if he could do the job.'

'And he did?'

'Oh yes, strong enough.'

'Then what?'

215

'What do you mean, then what?'

'This man, he helped you carry the cabinet inside.'

'Yes, that was the whole point of it. I said to Mrs Venn I'd had to promise him a couple of bob, and she gave me a half-crown to give to him. I gave it to him when we'd finished and off he went.'

'You didn't see where?'

'Didn't care either. He'd done his job and we were in a hurry to get off. I had something to collect from Chadlington and Walter Sutton was getting a ride with me, so the two of us went off and that was that.'

'This other man, what did he look like?'

He thought and smoked for a while.

'Ordinary sort of fellow.'

'Dark? Fair? How old?'

'Dark, definitely dark. Not young and not old either. Maybe thirtyish. Not what you'd call respectable looking, needed a shave and a change of shirt, but not ragged. Bit down in the mouth.'

'What about his voice?'

'Didn't say much. He wasn't from round here.'

It wasn't much of a description, but I was certain all the same. I said goodbye to him and practically ran up the street. Long Lankin, the demon figure from the song, was now flesh and blood. I had no proof that the man thrown out of the Crown was Daisy's uncle, Fardel. No proof either that he was one and the same as the dark-haired man who'd helped carry the cabinet. But I'd have bet my last shilling on it. He'd actually set foot in the Venns' house, handled the cabinet where Daisy's body was found. If I'd analysed the reason for my excitement – which I didn't – it would have been that we were all off the hook, no more doubts and dilemmas. Something evil had walked in on our lives, killed and walked out again.

216

I was making for the Venns' house to tell Daniel and didn't intend to waste time by calling in at Mrs Penny's. But as I walked past her cottage there was a sharp tap-tapping from inside her window. She was looking out at me, waving a letter. Reluctantly I stopped and she opened the window and put her head out.

'Looking all over the place for you, he was. Said it was urgent.'

'Who?'

'Mr Venn's driver.'

She gave me the letter. Inside the envelope was a single sheet of paper and two lines in black ink, not with Daniel's signature as I'd expected, but Adam's.

'*Police arrested Daniel early this morning. Please come as soon as you can.*'

Chapter Sixteen

A S I TURNED IN AT THE Venns' drive their gig overtook me, with Adam driving it at a fast trot and the roan horse hot and sweaty. A tall man was sitting beside him; both of them wore dark suits and bowler hats. Carol was waiting at the front door. The tall man got down and shook hands with her. Adam said something I didn't hear, turned the gig and drove it away down the side of the house, probably to the stable yard.

When I got to the door Carol introduced the thin man as Timothy Galway, the solicitor friend from London who knew about criminal work. I liked the look of him. He was in his thirties, calm and measured in the way he moved but with observant eyes. I imagined him as a fly-fisherman, standing long hours beside a river, then the sudden silver dash of a trout pulled into the air. His hair was brown with a hint of red to it, enough for interest but not so much as to startle the customers.

'Mr Galway wants to talk to all of us.'

She was trying hard to be calm, but looked as tight-stretched as the paper over a circus hoop. I waited in the dining room while Carol took Galway upstairs. There was dust on the walnut surface of the table and the posy of white rosebuds in the middle had dried out and hardened like flowers in an undertaker's window. After a while Adam came in, smelling of horse sweat and saddle soap.

'Thank you for coming.'

'Have they charged him?'

It was all very well to decide I should keep my distance from the Venns, but it was impossible to be in the same house with them and not share the worry. Worse than worry now. It was something like cold panic, as if all our attempts to keep this thing in control had failed and we were sitting in a carriage with the reins snapped and the cliff edge just in front of us.

'Not yet, but Galway thinks we should be prepared for it later today.'

'There's something I've just found out. It may help.'

I was starting to tell him about Fardel when Oliver Venn came in, shuffling in embroidered slippers. The veins on his forehead showed blue through skin as thin and dry as slivers of birch bark. Carol and Timothy Galway came in behind him and we all sat down at the table. Galway glanced at Adam, who nodded to him to go ahead.

'The position is that Daniel has not yet been charged with anything, but they are holding him for questioning in connection with Miss Smith's killing. He will probably be kept in a police cell overnight and if they do decide to charge him they'll have to bring him before the magistrates for a remand in custody.'

Oliver said, 'Keep him locked up? They can't do that, can they?'

Adam told him quietly that yes, they could. I asked how Daniel was.

'Reasonably composed in the circumstances,' Galway said.

'He's dazed,' Oliver said. 'You could see from his face when they took him away this morning. The poor boy just doesn't know what's happening to him.'

His hand on the table was clenched and trembling. Carol laid her hand over it, trying to calm him. Galway waited, then went on in the same level voice.

'Adam has asked me, quite reasonably, what we can do to help Daniel. I've already told the inspector that I don't think he's justified in arresting him, but on the facts as I know them so far it wasn't an easy argument for me.'

Oliver opened his mouth to protest but Carol gave a little shake of her head and he closed it.

Galway went on, 'The first thing to say is that Daniel firmly and consistently denies killing Miss Smith, both to the police and to me. Unfortunately some things the police have discovered and the way they've come to light makes them believe they have a case.'

Adam said, looking straight ahead and sounding as if the words came painfully, 'The fact is, Timothy believes we've all made some bad mistakes already, me especially.'

'I'm not blaming you, Adam,' Galway said. 'Goodness knows, I probably wouldn't have done any better if it had been my brother. But not to put too fine a point on it, the inspector believes you're all in a conspiracy to protect Daniel – you too, I'm afraid, Miss Bray – and it's not going to be easy to convince him otherwise.' He looked round the table at each of us in turn, taking his time. 'For a start, there's the matter of the revolver.'

Oliver heaved a deep sigh. Galway turned to him.

'I believe you confirmed, Mr Venn, that the revolver the police found in the flowerpot was the property of your late wife?'

Oliver nodded.

'And it was kept in a place where anybody in the household might have access to it?'

Another nod, more reluctant.

'Daniel has told the police that he had it with him on the day Miss Smith was killed because he thought he might want to shoot squirrels. The police find that hard to believe and frankly, so do I.'

Nobody said anything to that. He went on: 'The gun is a type with a revolving magazine which contains five rounds. When the police found the gun, two rounds had been fired. Miss Smith was killed with a single shot to the head from a bullet of the type and calibre fired from that gun. Daniel denies having fired the gun but he does admit to having it with him all afternoon until he mislaid it somewhere in the late evening. I wonder if anybody can cast any light on that?'

I glanced at Adam and his eyes said no, don't tell him. Adam knew that whatever we told Galway he'd have to pass on to the police. A solicitor can't withhold evidence. I wasn't necessarily going to do what Adam wanted, but wasn't ready either to take the decision that might get Daniel out of prison at the cost of putting Felicia in it.

'There's another factor,' I said to Galway. 'It might make all of this irrelevant.'

I told them everything that had happened from the whistling tramp outside the barn onwards. It was a relief to be able to tell a story straightforwardly, hiding nothing apart from Bobbie's presence. Galway listened, chin on hand, making an occasional note. At the end he glanced at his notes, then at me.

'Have you ever knowingly met this man, Fardel?'

'No.'

'I gather you didn't see the face of the man thrown out of the public house last night.'

'No, I didn't.'

'And you weren't able to find out his name?'

'No.'

'Or where he comes from?'

'No.'

'And you didn't see the face of the person whistling outside the barn that night?'

'No.'

'And you have only the carter's description of the man who helped to deliver the cabinet here?'

'Yes.'

'So your supposition that the whistling tramp, the man in the fight, the furniture deliverer and Fardel are one and the same is based on a snatch of folk-song and a mention – gathered by hearsay, not directly – of a twenty-pound debt?'

'Yes.'

I tried not to resent it. His business was to consider whether a story like that might influence a jury in a murder trial. Looked at in that light it wasn't impressive. He turned to Carol.

'Mrs Venn, were you at home when the cabinet was delivered?'

'Yes, I was.'

She sounded shaken, probably from the idea of the man being so close.

'Do you remember the men who delivered it?'

'Mr Sutton, of course, and the carter Mr Bestley. I took them into the studio and showed them where I wanted them to put it.'

'Was there a third man?'

'Yes, I know there was because Mr Bestley was moaning about it being heavy. He said he'd had to promise another man two shillings to help them. I gave him the money but I didn't see the other man. I supposed he was outside with the cart.'

'And you didn't see them carrying the cabinet in?'

'No. With Mr Sutton in charge, I didn't need to.'

I said to Galway, 'At least that supports the story Mr Bestley told me. He was quite specific about asking Mrs Venn for two shillings.'

'Yes, but that only proves there was a third man involved in the delivery, not that it was Fardel. And we'd still have the question of how he got his hands on the gun – unless we're assuming that he'd somehow acquired a similar revolver, and I wouldn't like to have to argue that.'

'I agree,' I said. 'But the gun was just in a drawer, not locked up. If he'd gone upstairs, say, to try to steal the twenty pounds he thought he was owed . . .'

'Except that we have no proof he did any such thing, even if we accept it was Fardel.' I must have looked downcast, because he apologised. 'I'm sorry, it's a very interesting line of enquiry and of course you must tell Inspector Bull about it. Only I'd advise you to expect a rather sceptical reaction. Now, may we please come back to the question of the revolver?'

Sighs all round the table. He looked at Adam. 'I've told you that, frankly, I don't believe your brother. The question is, if he's not telling the truth, why?'

Adam said, 'If your assumption's right, Daniel's made a decision for reasons that seem good to him. Shouldn't we respect that?'

'How long?'

The question came unexpectedly from Carol. We all turned to look at her. Her face was white, and her hands clasped so tightly together that it hurt to look at them. 'How long do we go on respecting it? Until he's charged? Until he's on trial. Until he's . . .' She stopped, swallowed, then said, 'Until he's hanged?'

Oliver let out a little cry of distress.

'It won't come to that,' Adam said.

'How do we know that? We never thought he'd be arrested. If we leave it to him he'll go on protecting her out of guilt and chivalry until it's too late.'

'Carol, please . . .'

Adam, sitting next to her, tried to take her hands. She pushed him away.

223

'I agree with Mrs Venn.' Galway's voice was calm and reassuring, difficult families being part of his work. 'If Daniel, for whatever reason, is telling less than the truth to protect somebody else, then it's not only a dangerous thing to do, but I can assure you it won't work and the sooner we make him realise that the better. If you—'

'What's happening? What's dangerous?'

None of us had heard footsteps or the door opening. Felicia was standing there, asking questions. She'd appeared suddenly like a ghost and got much the same reaction, startled and unwelcoming. There was still a look of the sickroom about her, skin milky pale and eyes too bright. The smell of rosewater came off her in clouds, her hair had been put up hastily in a net and she'd missed one of the buttons on the bodice of her lilac dress so that it didn't meet properly at the neck. When she saw Galway she instinctively raised a hand to cover it. Fingertips, nibbled to the quick of the nails, flared like fire coral against her pale hands. Adam and Carol were on their feet, trying to persuade her to go back to bed, promising to tell her later. She disregarded them and took a few steps into the room.

Galway stood up and pulled out a chair for her at the table. She glanced round, frowned when she saw me, but sat down. 'You're talking about Daniel?' she said.

'Felicia, if you'll just go back upstairs, we'll tell you when—'

Adam, still standing, touched her shoulder. She jerked away from him. 'No, I've had enough of being upstairs and waiting. Something's happening, isn't it? Why is Annie crying?'

Adam looked to Carol for help but she was sitting down, hands to her forehead. So he sat down as well, choosing a chair on the opposite side of the table from Felicia. He looked scared.

Galway asked him 'Miss Foster?' and got a nod. As none

224

of the rest of us seemed ready to break the news, he did it.

'The police have arrested Daniel. They think he killed Daisy Smith.'

'Oh.' There wasn't a lot you could tell from the way she said it. Although she hadn't wanted Adam to touch her, she was looking at him as if trying to pick up her cue. He didn't meet her eyes.

'Why?'

'Mainly because they think he's not telling them the truth about something.'

'About what?'

Her voice was sane and level. The only odd thing about it was its total lack of expression.

'I don't think we should go on with this,' Adam said to Galway. 'Miss Foster has been suffering from a serious nervous collapse. The doctor says she must avoid strain at all costs.'

'At all costs?' Galway's rebuke to his friend was so softly spoken you might have missed it, but it was clear Adam hadn't. The two of them stood up, Galway asked us to excuse him and they went off to the other end of the room and murmured together, Galway doing most of the talking. I caught the words '. . . my client' and '. . . no choice'. Meanwhile the four of us sat round the table, not talking. They came back and took their seats, Adam looking even more miserable.

'Miss Foster,' Galway said, very careful and polite, 'it might be helpful to us if you are able to stay, but if this becomes intolerably painful, you must say so. You understand that?' She nodded. He turned to the rest of us.

'My position is that I don't believe Daniel when he says he had the revolver in his possession most of the afternoon and for part of the evening. If any of you knows anything to challenge or support that, I'd strongly advise you to say it now rather than later.'

I made my decision and opened my mouth, but Felicia got there first.

'The revolver in the summerhouse? The one I fired?'

Galway's calm fisherman's eyes didn't change but his shoulders sagged like a man who'd taken on a heavier burden than he'd expected.

'You fired a revolver? When?'

'The day . . . the day it happened. Some time in the evening.' She turned to me, looking simply relieved to have somebody to back up her story. 'Miss Bray can tell you more. She took it from me.'

So I told him everything I knew about the gun, hearing the shot, taking it from Felicia and the rest. None of it was new to the Venns because we'd been through it in the few hours after we'd found Daisy, but they didn't admit that with Galway there. At the end of it, he looked at me for a long time.

'And you haven't told the police this?'

'No.'

'Nor you, Miss Foster?'

She shook her head.

'Why not?'

He put the question to me. I looked at Felicia. She rested her bitten fingertips against her cheek and nodded to me. I'd no idea what the nod meant. That she trusted me? That she knew what I was going to say? If there'd been some way of signalling that I was giving her no promises, I'd have done it. As it was, I answered Galway's question.

'I thought she might have been trying to kill herself.'

'Because Daniel had jilted me, wasn't that it?' Felicia put the question to me, ignoring the others. Her voice was shaky. She tried to cover it by putting in a little laugh at the end.

226

'Felicia,' Adam said. 'Felicia, please . . .'

'Is that true?' Galway said to me.

'True of what I thought at the time, yes.'

'Only she was wrong,' Felicia said. 'I moved the blanket and the gun fell out. I picked it up and it went off. I didn't know it was there. That's all. I didn't even think of shooting myself. Not myself.'

She tried the laugh again. It ended in a kind of hiccup. Adam was on his feet, pushing his chair back so violently it fell over. He put a hand on Galway's arm.

'That's quite enough. You can see she isn't in any state to be questioned.'

Hardly fair to his friend, seeing that Felicia herself had taken the initiative. Carol sighed and stood up too.

'Flissie, I'll see you upstairs. I promise we'll tell you if anything happens.'

'Will you, I wonder?' The question was wistful rather than rude. The nervous energy that had driven Felicia so far was draining away and she let Carol guide her towards the door. But when she got to the doorway it flared up again. She turned to Galway, who was standing to see her out.

'If I'd thought of shooting anybody, it would have been Daisy. You can tell the police that if you think it will help Daniel.'

The door closed behind them. Adam picked up the chair and lowered himself into it. Even Galway looked shaken. Oliver was trembling and repeating to himself 'Poor girl. Oh the poor girl.' I wasn't sure how much he'd taken in.

'You see our problem?' Adam said to Galway. Then, more firmly, 'I must insist that you don't pass on what she's just said to the police.'

'The last thing she said, no. It's not relevant. But I'll be telling them about the gun. We've now got two witnesses saying much the same thing and it proves Daniel didn't have the gun all afternoon. Miss Bray will have to give them a second statement and I'm afraid they will want to talk to Miss Foster again.'

'But will it help?' I said. They both looked at me. 'All it proves is that the gun was in the summerhouse round about seven o'clock. I can honestly state that it was in my possession from then until I handed it over to Daniel at about ten. But Daisy might have been dead before it got to the summerhouse.'

And probably was, I thought but didn't add, not wanting a detailed discussion on rigor mortis.

'As far as that goes, I quite agree with you.' Galway didn't try to patronise me. 'But it does cast considerable doubt on Daniel's own statement.'

'Yes, but once the police know for sure he's been lying to them, they'll ask why,' I said.

Adam's eyes went to the closed door.

'No,' Galway said, picking up his thought. 'I've said I won't pass on her remark about Daisy. But when the police question her, we can't guarantee that she won't repeat it.' He turned to me. 'You realise that I shall pass what you've told me to the police?'

'I understand, yes.' It was a relief in its way.

'I'm afraid there's a possibility that they may charge you with concealing evidence.'

'Yes.'

We'd all been guilty of that, though the Venns weren't rushing to admit it.

'It will help Daniel, though, won't it?' Carol said.

'We have to hope so.' Galway hesitated, looking more unhappy than was professionally necessary. 'There are two drawbacks. As Miss Bray has pointed out, we don't know when Miss Smith was shot. The police have almost certainly got their own ideas on the subject, but at this stage they have no obligation to tell us. The second, well . . .' He paused. 'The second is that they might not believe Miss Bray.'

If he was waiting for protests, he didn't get them. In the circumstances, I wouldn't have believed myself.

He went on, sounding apologetic. 'The fact is, rightly or wrongly, Inspector Bull has already got it into his head that his job is deliberately being made difficult. Unfortunately, there's been a certain amount of gossip and press comment in London that has given the case more prominence than it had originally.'

'Hawthorne,' Adam said, making it sound like a swear word.

'Yes, it hasn't improved matters,' Galway said.

He'd have sounded even more depressed if he knew I was still concealing something – Felicia's collapse after the body was discovered; the scratches on her arms.

Feeling weary, I said I'd better go and see Inspector Bull and get it over. It was around four o'clock by then and I supposed I'd be able to catch a train to Chipping Norton. But Galway said the inspector had been called back to Oxford for the afternoon – probably to discuss the case with higher authority – and I should wait for his return in the morning rather than go through the whole thing with a constable. He and Adam would have to be in Chipping Norton early in case the police decided to charge Daniel, and I could travel with them. But he'd forgotten there was only room for two in the gig. In the end we settled that I'd go independently by train. Carol came downstairs and walked with me to the front door.

'How's Felicia?'

'Drowsy. I hope she'll sleep.'

More of Uncle Olly's drops? If so, they couldn't keep her sedated for ever.

At the front door Carol said she'd walk with me along the drive because she needed some air.

229

'Thank you for what you're doing,' she said.

'I'm not sure I'm doing anything useful.'

'Daniel thinks you are. He said . . .' She hesitated.

'Said what?'

'That he thought you might have been involved in something like this before. Was he right?'

'Yes.' We took a few more steps. 'As for being useful, I might be if I could find Fardel. You know, there's one problem with my theory that Mr Galway didn't point out.'

'What?'

'If he'd taken the trouble to follow Daniel and Daisy here to get his twenty pounds, you'd have expected him to approach Daniel as soon as he got the chance, even come to the house. Did Daniel say anything to you about that?'

'Not a word.'

'Or about seeing him?'

'No. I'm sorry.'

'Do you think if it had happened he might have kept it secret?'

'Not from me. Daniel's brought his troubles to me since he was ten years old. I'm the problem solver.'

I thought suddenly: *Suppose Carol's in love with him* . . . Then decided I was wrong and her tone was more like an elder sister's than a lover's. I changed the subject and said I'd been to see Mr Sutton in his workshop.

'Oh, what a mess it all is. We told him Janie must have gone of her own accord or she wouldn't have taken the things for the baby – but to find out this way . . .'

'Do you know why she went? He says everything was perfectly happy.'

'What does anybody know about other people's marriages? They seemed happy enough, yes, but there were worries. I'm afraid I was part of that.'

'How?'

230

'I'd had to tell him I might not be able to go on financing the workshop beyond Christmas. I suppose it's no secret to anybody that we've had money problems since Philomena died and it was costing more money than I have. I was naïve, I suppose. I thought if you loved what you were doing and made honest, beautiful things the money side of it would work itself out. But if it's love against money, money always seems to win, doesn't it?'

'Mr Sutton says you went out for a walk with Janie the day before she disappeared. Did she say anything then that suggested she might go?'

She had to think about it.

'That was the Sunday before . . . ?'

'Yes. The day after Daniel announced that he was engaged to Miss Smith.'

'Oh yes. You can imagine the atmosphere in the house. Towards the end of the afternoon I had to get away from it for a while so I went down to the village and called in on the workshop. I did notice Janie looked pale and strained so I suggested we should go out for a little walk while he kept an eye on the baby. We didn't talk much. I suppose I was too wrapped up in what was happening about Daniel to let her tell me her troubles.'

I said goodbye to Carol at the end of the drive and walked back down to the village.

Chapter Seventeen

I'D LIKE TO HAVE AVOIDED HIGH tea at Mrs Penny's because I knew she'd want to gossip, but there was nowhere else to eat in the village. I dealt with the usual cold beef and pickles and her questions as briskly as I could and escaped with about an hour of daylight left, taking hat, coat and bicycle lamp with me. If Fardel was out there somewhere, he moved by night. It had been well after dark when he tried to get into the Crown, probably after dark too when the postmistress's chicken was grabbed from its coop. The man had to eat and wanted to drink, so if I walked the lanes and footpaths at twilight and beyond, I'd have a chance of seeing him. No more than seeing him. I wasn't stupid enough to think of tackling him: if I could find where he slept and cooked his stolen meals, Inspector Bull would have to carry on from there.

I turned off the main street and walked up a steep lane beside the churchyard. Once past the church it became a narrower track with a small oak wood on the left. From higher up the lane there was a view of the village with lamplight already glowing from a few windows, the street deserted. To the west, low hills sloped away into the valley of the Evenlode and the sun was setting in ragged pink streaks against dark grey cloud. On the other side of the hedge was an orchard, old neglected trees that might once have belonged to a cottage that didn't exist any more. Still, one of them near the hedge had managed to produce an early crop of apples that glowed temptingly in the pink light. I stretched to pick one and started munching, looking out at the view. Something rustled behind the hedge. I jumped round, saw a pair of human eyes glinting at me and nearly choked. After the first shock I saw a man: small, shorter than I was, sixty or so and the front of his head where his cap was pushed back as bald and shiny as a hazelnut. Although I'd come out to find Fardel, I could almost have hugged the man for not being him.

'I'm sorry. Are they your apples?'

Standing close up against the hedge, he had probably been watching me for some time. He was carrying a small oil lamp, the sort with a shutter that can be pushed round to hide the light.

'Reckon you and me are at the same game, miss.'

He pushed through a gap in the hedge. There were wire loops and wooden pegs hanging from his belt. He was right: poachers, the pair of us.

'Only I'm wasting my time,' he said. 'Summat's got here before me.' I saw a snare in the hedge, between two hazel branches. The peg had been pulled out of the ground and bits of rabbit fur were scattered all round it. A late-working fly buzzed round fragments of bright pink flesh the same colour as the sunset.

'A fox?' I said.

He shook his head, an odd look on his face like a man who both wanted to talk and didn't at the same time.

'Foxes carry knives where you come from, miss?'

'Knives?'

He picked up a fur-covered hind leg and stretched it out between his blood and earth-stained hands. 'See that? Bin cut, it has.' And then, seeing I still didn't understand, 'Reckon he cut it up and ate it raw.'

233

'Who?'

'I don't know who, but he must have bin desperate hungry.'

Coincidence, of course, but the birds seemed to have stopped singing; the night had come suddenly.

'Have you seen him?' I said. 'Was he a dark-haired man with broad shoulders?'

'Might have been Old Nick for all I know.'

'But have you seen him?'

He shook his head. 'Reckon I've seen his lair, though.'

'Where?'

He pointed back down the lane towards the little oak wood. 'Old quarry up at the top there. Somebody had a fire in it a day or two ago.'

He merged back into the hedge and I followed the track back down to the coppice. Dusk was thick under the trees, the ground matted with brambles. I scrambled over the fence and went uphill, dry branches cracking underfoot, leaves swishing. If he were in there he'd hear me from half a mile away. After a while the ground levelled to a quarry floor with a rock face looming over it, about thirty feet high. It was only a small quarry, probably the source of stone for a cottage long ago. I hadn't used the cycle lamp until then because there wasn't much in the battery but I switched it on and found I was standing in a circle of grey ash. Bronze chicken feathers were scattered round, a clenched claw, bones. For one evening at any rate he hadn't eaten his stolen meat raw. But if it had been his lair, it looked abandoned now. The ashes were cold, several days old and a few dry leaves had shifted over them. Oak leaves. Shrivelled brown oak leaves.

I suddenly felt shivery and wondered why. Of course there were dead oak leaves, this was a whole coppice of them. But I was seeing other leaves in my mind – dead leaves clinging to thick woollen stockings and red hair, the memory of them bringing back the metallic smell of blood so that I felt sick with it. The leaves on Daisy's body had been dead oak leaves, like these. Why not? I tried to talk sense to myself, stop the shivering. After all, I'd already guessed that her body had been lying outside somewhere before it was put in the cabinet, possibly in the Venns' garden. Only there weren't any oak trees in or near the garden. The more I thought about it, the more sure I was. Yews, elms, hazels, but no oaks. Anyway it wasn't the sort of garden where leaves were raked in tidy piles. The leaves that had fallen last autumn would have been smothered by now in a summer's unchecked growth. It was only in woodlands that they'd still be thick on the ground. So Daisy's body had at some time been in this wood, or in a wood like it. From here to the Venns' house would be a good mile across country. Surely Felicia couldn't have carried her body all that way. It would have taken a strong man. And if Daisy had been shot in the garden, as I'd thought, why move her body at all? The logic must be that Daisy was shot here in this place, or a place like it, and Fardel had been here.

I switched off the lamp and got myself out of the coppice. For the next few hours as the stars came out I covered miles of track and footpath, just able to see dark shapes of hedges or individual trees for guidance. The aim was to draw a rough circle round the village, assuming that Fardel would stay within walking distance of it. Every now and then I'd stop for some time and listen, but the countryside is a noisy place at night with sheep fidgeting behind hedges, badgers crashing and snuffling in the undergrowth, dogs barking from farms. Fardel could have been a dozen steps behind me and I might not have known it. I remembered a line from the song. *Said my lord to my lady, as he mounted his horse: Beware of Long Lankin that lives in the moss.* I wished my mind didn't keep going back to it. Being nervous makes you tired, and by the time the church clock struck ten I'd had enough. I crossed a couple of fields, scrambled over a gate and got back to the road. The nearest buildings were the forge on one side of the road and the furniture workshop, both in darkness. I was looking towards the forge when I saw from the corner of my eye a flicker of movement across the road, towards the workshop. When I turned, whatever it was had gone. It had been too big for a dog or fox, too quick-moving for a lost cow. A human being, crossing the road. The hunting instinct stirred again. It had come and gone so quickly that it didn't seem likely to be up to anything good. The workshop yard, crowded with piles of maturing timber, might look like a good hiding place, even somewhere to sleep for a man without a roof over his head.

Quietly I stepped off the road and into the yard, holding my breath, telling myself that at least Mr Sutton was within yelling distance if things went wrong. Total quiet and almost total dark. The man might have been crouching within arm's reach of me, or away over the yard wall in a dark mass of bushes on the far side. If so, he'd moved remarkably quickly and quietly for a broad-shouldered drunkard. I waited, beginning to think I must be wrong about seeing a person at all. Then I heard a sound, not from where I expected it, but from inside the workshop. Footsteps, like somebody moving on tiptoe. The workshop door was on the far side of the building from me. I started moving towards it, then tripped over a wigwam of small planks. They fell with a noise like twenty school desk tops clattering and I went sprawling. As I fell, I heard the door on the other side slamming open, footsteps running up the street. A window opened overhead. Mr Sutton's voice: 'What's going on?'

I reintroduced myself from my supine position among the planks. 'Somebody's just been in your workshop,' I said.

By the time I'd picked myself up and got round to the door he was down in the workshop in trousers and jacket, shirtless underneath it.

'What's happened? Where's he gone?'

'Away up the street. Is anything missing?'

It could have been any thief, not my man necessarily. While Mr Sutton was getting an oil lamp alight my heartbeat and breathing slowed down.

'Not disturbed much anyway,' Mr Sutton said.

The workshop was much as I'd seen it a few hours before, the plate of congealed stew on the bench. A little painted chest stood in the corner, its lid open.

'I never left it like that.' Mr Sutton went over to it. Then, 'The money's gone.'

'How much money?'

'Fourteen pounds.'

A large sum, worth probably around two months' wages for him, but he sounded hurt and puzzled rather than angry.

'Shall I run and get the policeman?' I said.

I'd no high hopes of Constable Johnson, but it was what you did when you were burgled, after all. Sutton shook his head, staring at the empty chest. I went over to look. It was neatly fitted out with a removable top tray, probably for sewing materials or a child's toy soldiers. He pointed to a little gap between the tray and the back of the chest.

'We kept it there. Sometimes there'd be a delivery of wood, expensive wood like good walnut or mahogany, and the carrier would want paying for it. You'd have to know it was there.'

'Who knew?'

'Just the three of us. Mrs Venn, of course, because it was her money, me and . . .'

237

He couldn't say it.

'Your wife? Janie?'

He nodded. His face was a painful mixture of hope and hurt. 'But why would she do it? If she wanted money she could have every farthing in the place. Why would she sneak in and take it and not even talk to me?'

When I thought about it, the quickness of the figure flickering across the road, its quiet-footedness in the workshop, went with a woman more than a man. But I couldn't answer his question. He stopped by a workbench, staring down at it.

'My knife's gone too, my favourite. You can see the gap where it was. She'd never have taken that from me, not of her own free will.'

A row of knives of various sizes, glinting frost sharp in the lamplight. He was right about the gap. He sat down heavily on a chest.

'I'm going out to look for her,' he said and disappeared upstairs. I waited until he came down again, fully dressed, and got his boots on, then walked out with him.

'At least let me tell the constable.'

'Waste of time.'

The two of us walked around the village for another hour or more, around outbuildings, up and down lanes. After midnight he said, sounding more dead than alive, 'What I think, he must have made her tell him about the money first before he killed them. I'll never see her again.'

I watched his dark shape fading back down the street, stumbling from tiredness. The village was quiet by then, the Crown long shut and all the lamps out. Under the stars it looked such a small huddle of life, the woods and fields round it steep and threatening in a way they weren't by day. I got myself upstairs and huddled shivering under blankets and eiderdown.

Chapter Eighteen

ICAUGHT AN EARLY TRAIN IN the morning a few stops along the line to Chipping Norton. It was Thursday, a misty start to the day, elm leaves turning yellow, bright flares of rosehips along the embankments. The two women in my compartment were talking about making chutney before frost got the green tomatoes. Chipping Norton was a neat and busy little station. Across some fields a big woollen mill built of yellow brick and looking more like a mansion than a factory billowed clouds of steam from its ornate chimney. I asked directions to the police station in London Road and when I got there found Timothy Galway waiting outside. He raised his bowler to me, looking serious.

'What's happening?'

'I'm sorry to tell you they've decided to charge Daniel. They're bringing him in front of the magistrates in about an hour for a remand in custody. We shall ask for bail, of course, but frankly I don't think we'll get it.'

It turned out that the magistrates' court was in the same building as the police station. Also in that same building, presumably, was some cell where Daniel was locked, all his bounding energy turned to a prisoner's passivity. Adam had gone to leave the gig at a stables, Galway told me. He and I wished each other luck without any conviction that we'd get it. I went inside, gave my name to the duty officer and asked to see Inspector Bull. After a long wait a constable escorted me to a cramped room at the end of a corridor.

'Well, Miss Bray?' The inspector was on his own. He looked tired and harassed. The masthead of the *Wrecker* was poking out from a pile of papers on his desk.

'There's something I want to add to my statement. It's about the revolver.'

If that surprised him, he gave no sign of it. I told him about hearing the shot and finding Felicia in the summer-house with the gun, including my belief that she'd been trying to kill herself. All I left out was the presence of Bobbie.

'Why didn't you tell us this at once?'

'Attempted suicide is a crime.'

'Murder's a worse one. You do agree with that, I suppose.'

'Of course.'

'So what made you change your mind, Miss Bray? What made you decide to take us into your confidence now?'

'I suppose I've had a chance to think about it. People are naturally shocked when something like that happens.'

'People may be, but when we first spoke to you, you seemed pretty cool. I seem to remember you even raised the question of rigor mortis. Why was that?'

'Because I'd noticed most of her body was stiff when we took her out of the cabinet.'

'Yes. So you were already calculating, weren't you? I wonder why. Did you come to any conclusions?'

'I'm no expert.'

'But . . . ?'

'I'd guess she'd already been dead at least six hours then, probably more. And there's something else. I've remembered that there were some dead oak leaves on her clothes when we took her out of the cabinet. Only a few of them. They might have fallen off by the time you saw her.'

'Quite a lot of things might have happened before we saw her. What significance am I supposed to find in dead oak leaves?'

'There are none anywhere near the Venns' garden. I think she might have been shot some distance away.'

'And put in the chest where you say you found her?'

'Where I did find her, yes. I don't know why, but I think that's what happened.'

His expression gave me no idea whether my guess was right.

'I dare say you know now that your friend Daniel Venn has admitted to walking around all afternoon with a revolver in his pocket.'

'He's not my friend particularly. Two weeks ago I hadn't even met him.'

'Answer my question.'

'I wasn't aware you'd asked one.'

'Are you aware that he says he had the revolver in his pocket all afternoon? Yes or no.'

'Yes.'

'So once he's arrested and charged you suddenly decide it might be useful to spread a little confusion about when he did or didn't have his hands on the gun and when and where Miss Smith might have been shot.'

'Since I don't know when or where she was shot, how could I know if it was useful?'

'You've been trying to guess, though. You've been thinking about all this?'

'Yes, of course I've been thinking about it.'

I think he was one of those people who use anger like a good rider uses his horse's energy, reining it in then letting it go when it suits him. It suited him now.

'Well, I've been thinking about it too. It's what I'm paid to do, and I'm paid to do it on behalf of everybody. I do mean everybody. Not just people who happen to have money or powerful friends or nice table manners, or young women who've been to college and think that means they can pick or choose what laws it suits them to obey, or artistic young men who think they've got a licence to do what they like provided you can paint it or sing it or write poetry about it. I can assure you that I'm sick and fed up with the whole pack of you, and if I had my way you'd be standing down there in the dock alongside young Mr Venn for conspiracy to obstruct the course of justice.'

He paused for breath. There wasn't a thing I could say in reply because I agreed with every word. He took a deep breath.

'You realise you're going to have to make a second statement about this?'

'Yes.'

'And you understand that you might be facing a charge of withholding evidence?'

'Yes.'

'Are there any more things that you happened to be too shocked to tell me at the time?'

'There is something else, but I couldn't tell you before because it only happened over the last two nights.'

I told him my theory about Fardel, starting without much confidence that he'd take it seriously, ending with none at all. He asked much the same questions as Galway, then a few more of his own.

'Even if it were Miss Smith's uncle, are you suggesting he's connected in some way with her murder?'

'I'm suggesting it's worth looking at, especially if it's the same man who was at the barn late on the Monday night.'

'So a woman who's already admitted to committing two offences is trying to teach me how to do my duty?'

'I'm assuming you wouldn't want to see a man convicted of murder if there's any doubt about it.'

'Oh, I'm sure you'll make sure there's plenty of doubt about it. There are probably things you're still hiding.'

Which was quite true. If I kept trying to stand on the high moral ground, there'd be a landslide. I tried to sound properly humble. 'At least would you agree that it's worth trying to find the man?'

'Perhaps, if I had a dozen spare constables to go round half of Oxfordshire looking for a badly shaven, dark-haired, broad-shouldered tramp who whistles folk-songs.'

There was a knock on the door and a voice from the corridor.

'Magistrates are here, sir.'

He stood up and picked up his cap from the top of a filing cabinet.

'I shouldn't be long, Miss Bray. We'll take your latest statement when I get back.'

He went, shutting the door firmly behind him. He didn't lock it, but he might as well have done. Unless I wanted trouble, I should stay where I was. So I stayed and heard doors opening and closing along the corridor, footsteps on stairs and the occasional male voice giving sharp orders to go there, do that. The whole building seemed to be in a state of excitement. It isn't every day a police court in a small country town sees a man remanded on a murder charge. Somewhere one or two floors below where I was sitting Daniel would be brought up from a cell, taken to the dock. Three magistrates more used to dealing with pub brawls and rural theft would decide that he should be kept in custody until such time as the case could be heard at the assizes. Daniel Venn would leave the dock not belonging to himself or his family any more but to the law. And his story would be the property of the public. On the whole, I was glad not to be there to see it.

The window of my room looked down on a side street. No sign of excitement there at any rate, just a two-wheeled dogcart with a boy on foot beside it and a bay horse eating from a nosebag, a mongrel sniffing in the gutter, a man in a panama hat pushing a bicycle. But when I opened the window and leaned out I could hear vehicles coming and going from the front of the building, wheels, a horse whinnying, even the cough and splutter of a motor car.

Half an hour passed. In that time the mongrel had a fight with a whippet, the man wheeling the bicycle stopped and held a long conversation with another man carrying a new zinc bucket, the horse went on eating and pigeons scuffled in the dust for the few bits of grain that dropped from the nosebag. Then a groom came running down the street, gave a coin to the boy, whipped off the nosebag and drove the dogcart away to the front of the building. Magistrate going home, I thought, job done. There were a lot of footsteps in the corridor, people coming up stairs, but it was another twenty minutes before the inspector came back. He had a constable with him, not the same one as before.

'Right, Miss Bray, your new statement. Start it by saying you are now making an additional statement to the one of Tuesday 27 August.'

It took an age. I don't know whether he'd deliberately chosen the slowest-writing constable available, but I wouldn't have put it past him. At last we finished it. I read, signed, then felt entitled to ask a question.

'Was Mr Venn remanded?'

He nodded.

'Am I free to go now?'

Another nod, but he stayed sitting at the table.

'I had a talk with Mr Daniel Venn before he was taken back to his cell. I put it to him that in the light of new information, we had reason to believe that his story about taking his aunt's gun to shoot squirrels was a fabrication and there was another reason for having it in his possession.'

A heavy pause. I thought Daniel would have guessed where

the new information came from and probably wouldn't be pleased about it but he'd have to get used to other people making decisions for him.

'He totally and utterly denies it,' the inspector said.

I thought: He's still trying to protect her.

He picked up my statement from the table and handed it to the constable as if it needed disinfecting. 'File that with the other one, please.' Then, to me, 'So one of you must be lying. Are you going to tell me which?'

I said I had nothing to add to my statement. It was all I could say.

'Well, I look forward to meeting you again, Miss Bray, when you've decided what else to tell us. Good morning.'

I got myself downstairs and out. If there had been a crowd at the front of the building it had gone by now and there was no sign of Adam or Galway. I was desperate to talk to them and started walking fast towards the station.

'Cooee. Miss Bray.'

A yell from the other side of the street. I turned and saw a young woman in a brown check riding costume and rakish brown bowler bounding up and down like a boy in a music hall gallery, waving a silver-mounted riding crop at me. For two pins – even two of those that sprang out of her hair as she bounced – I'd have ignored her and walked on but she came running at me across the road, dodging a delivery cart.

'Miss Bray, where've you been? They've just sent a poor man to prison for murdering that girl.'

At the top of her voice, with several people turning to watch. No escape. I took her to a bench under a tree, made her sit down and, while she got her breath back, explained the difference between a remand in custody by magistrates and a murder trial. I might have saved myself the trouble.

'But he's still in prison, isn't he, and they think he did it?'

'Yes.'

'But he didn't, did he?'

'Oh? And on what do you base that opinion?'

'He's so young and nice looking. He doesn't look like a murderer.'

'So if he'd been sixty years old and covered in warts he'd be guilty, would he?'

But she was babbling on. 'I was there in court. I looked for you but you weren't there. I can tell you all about it.'

'What are you doing here, anyway? The last I heard was your mother worrying because you'd missed an appointment in London.'

'Oh don't worry about that.' She waved Mother and missed appointments away with a twirl of her riding crop. 'I remembered I had an old schoolfriend not far from here. I've sent Mummy a telegram to say I'm staying with her.'

'Why here?'

'Because I wanted to know what happened. Anyway, it's just as well I am here because we can work together.'

'In what way, precisely?'

'To stop them hanging him, find out who really killed the girl.'

To hear her, you'd think it was as easy as putting up a string of flags. I was about to tell her to go back to her old schoolfriend and keep out of it until it struck me that there was one small detail on which she might be of some use.

'You remember when you and Bessie Broadbeam were waiting for me in the barn. You said a tramp tried to come in.'

'Yes, and I said—' Her mouth dropped open. 'Is that it? Was it my whistling tramp who killed her?'

'There's no proof whatsoever of that. I just wondered if you'd noticed anything else about him. For instance—'

'That shot, the shot we heard in the garden.' Her eyes

were shining, her body vibrating with excitement like a puppy seeing a rabbit. 'Was that when he killed her?'

'Probably not.'

'*Probably* not. You mean it might have been? While we were taking Bessie through the garden he was lurking there and—'

'Will you please listen. We don't need any more theories, we've got more than enough of those. What I want to know is if there's anything else you can remember about the tramp you didn't tell me at the time.'

At least that silenced her for the second or two it took her to think.

'Well, as I said, I didn't see him properly.'

'He said something but you couldn't make it out. What was his voice like? Old? Young?'

'About halfway, I think.'

'What he was saying – could it have had anything to do with money?'

'Well, I suppose he might have been asking for money like they mostly do. Mummy says you should never give it to them because they only drink it, but—'

'He didn't mention any particular sum of money?'

'Like tuppence for a cup of tea? Well, if he did I didn't understand him.'

I tried a few more questions but all that did was to make her more curious about why I wanted to know.

'Anyway, if you want we'll look for him together. My friend's father could lend you quite a decent hack.'

'No, we will not look for him together. You will kindly go back to your old schoolfriend . . .'

Then the idea that I was to regret so much struck me. Even at the time I knew it was probably a mistake, but there was something about Bobbie's puppyish enthusiasm that made it hard to push her away. There were good reasons

247

too. If I had any chance of finding Fardel I needed help, and as Bobbie had access to a horse she could cover much more country than I could.

'Where does your friend live?'

'About an hour's ride that way.' She gestured vaguely in the direction of Banbury.

'When you're out riding, you might ask around to see if anybody's noticed a tramp or vagrant they haven't seen before. He's in his thirties, dark-haired, broad-shouldered, probably needs a shave and speaks with a Wiltshire accent. His name's Luke Fardel but he might not be using it. He steals chickens from coops and rabbits out of snares.'

'And he's our man?' Her eyes were bright.

'The police want to speak to him, at least. But listen, this is very important.' She was showing signs of wanting to jump up and start the search straight away. 'If you do get word of him, you're on no account to try to approach him yourself. I want you to let me know, nothing else. Understand?'

She nodded. I told her where I was staying and made her repeat it – cottage opposite the Crown, with geraniums. Then, with another wave of her riding crop, she was up and away.

Chapter Nineteen

I WENT BACK TO THE STATION. I supposed I'd have to compare notes with Adam Venn and Galway but I was in no hurry about it. The inspector's words had stung and I wasn't feeling pleased with myself. There was no train due for some time so I bought a newspaper and sat on a bench in the sun, relieved to have time to myself for a while. A porter moved packing cases from one end of the platform to another, a man with a walking cane and a derby hat was idling on the opposite side.

We had the little station to ourselves, apart from a girl on the bridge. It was the passenger bridge over the rails, with latticed metal sides. I didn't notice her at first because I wasn't looking that way and when I did it was only to wonder idly what she was doing there. She might be looking along the line for a train, in which case she had a long wait because there wasn't one due in either direction. When I looked up again some time later she was still there. She was wearing a neat navy blue costume over a white blouse, a small white and navy hat on her dark hair. This time I realised that she wasn't watching for a train at all, she was staring at me. Another moment and I recognised her as Felicia Foster.

I must have given some signal, although I was too surprised to think about it, because she turned and walked slowly down the steps towards me. It was worse than surprise, I was downright alarmed. It had been unexpected that she'd left her sickbed and come down to join our conference the day before; almost unbelievable that she'd organised herself to get this far on her own. But she was walking along the platform towards me looking quite composed, though pale. Fardel went out of my head. I thought: She's going to confess to me after all, and then what do I do? Why she should have chosen me, practically a stranger, I didn't know – unless that was the reason. I started making up the speech for the defence in my head. '*The prisoner before the court has pleaded guilty to the most serious of charges. In considering the sentence, I ask you to remember her state of mind when the act was committed. Her life, as she saw it, was already in ruins. The man she loved and was to marry within a few short weeks had suddenly and callously announced his engagement to another young woman . . .*'

'I hoped I'd find you here,' she said. 'What happened?'

'Daniel was remanded in custody.'

'I see.' Almost expressionless. White gloves covered her fiery bitten fingertips. 'So what happens now?'

'Unless any evidence turns up to clear him, he'll go on trial, probably in a month or two. Why did you hope you'd find me?'

'I want to speak to you, away from the rest of them.'

She sat down on the bench beside me.

'Before you tell me anything,' I said, 'please understand that I won't guarantee to keep it between the two of us.'

'Yes, I understand. It's more asking than telling. I feel as if I'm in a boat in the fog and I don't know where land is . . . or even if land *is* any more – it's as if it's stopped existing. Am I making sense?'

'Yes.'

'It's the medicine, partly. You know the doctor prescribed something to keep me calm? I was taking it until yesterday, then I thought "What is there to be calm about?" So I

250

stopped taking it and started trying to think, only I'm going round and round in circles and I can't talk to anybody at home.'

She was staring as if she wanted to drag what she needed out of me by hypnotism. Her eyes were bright and feverish.

'What do you want to know?'

'Have you told the police you took the gun from me?'

'Yes, but I'm not sure they believed me. Daniel's still insisting he had it all the time.'

'I could go and tell them that you're telling the truth and he isn't.'

'Yes, but if you do that they might ask you a lot of other questions as well. Are you ready for that?'

'What sort of questions?'

'Like where you were through that afternoon and evening.'

She looked down at the toes of her neat navy shoes.

'At home. In my room mostly.'

'All the time? I'm not saying you have to tell me, but that would be the sort of question the police would ask you.'

She said nothing for a long time, then, 'You think Daniel's doing this to protect me?'

'What other reason could there be?'

'But why?'

'Because he feels guilty, I suppose. For bringing Daisy here.'

'That means he really thinks I killed her, doesn't it?'

'Yes, probably.'

'He's not so far wrong, you know. If I'd had the gun and her in front of me, I think I'd have done it. That's why it went off. I really did find it the way I told you, hidden under the blanket. But once I'd got it in my hand I thought "I could find her and kill her". And I must have squeezed very hard on it because it went off and it scared me – as if I really had been firing at her.'

251

'Why did you hate her so much?'

'Because she was taking away from me the only thing in the world I wanted.'

'Not Daniel?'

She shook her head slowly. 'No, not Daniel. How did you guess? Or perhaps Carol told you. I think she's known from the start and decided not to say anything.'

'No, Carol's said nothing.'

'So what made you guess? Is there a look in the eye we have, or a way we walk? A smell, perhaps. Is it a smell?'

'What do you mean?'

'Bad women. She put a hand to her mouth. When she took it away there was an arc of tooth marks on her white glove.

'You mean, how did I guess that you and Adam Venn are lovers?'

'Were. Yes, that's what I mean. How did you guess?'

'Somebody heard you in the cart shed the day Daniel came home.'

She flinched. Her hand went back to her mouth.

'I'm sorry,' I said. 'I didn't mean to find it out and I haven't told anybody else. The person who heard it thought it was you and Daniel. Only he never calls you Flissie, does he?'

'No. He hates it. Poor Daniel. I suppose you think I've betrayed him . . .'

'I'm not making judgements.'

'. . . only there was nothing there to betray. I liked Daniel, but as soon as I came to the house and met Adam I knew I loved him. I wished with all my heart that he was the one I was marrying. Daniel seemed such a boy in comparison. But Adam was Carol's so I knew there was nothing to be done about it. At least if I married Daniel, Adam and I would be able to go on seeing each other all our lives.'

252

'As lovers?'

'No. I'm not that vile – or at least I wasn't. I'd be a good wife to Daniel and Adam would go on being a good husband to Carol, but at least we'd be living in the same house, seeing each other, talking to each other. I couldn't see the harm in that. I still don't, if it had stayed like that.'

I didn't contradict her. Given the accommodations that people come to in marriage, she might be right.

'Did Daniel know about this?'

'No. There was nothing to know at first. I didn't even guess that Adam felt the same way about me as I felt about him. He was always kind, of course. Then gradually I saw how things were and felt so sorry for him.'

'Why?'

'Carol neglected him. Honestly, I think she thought more about her chairs and wardrobes than she did about Adam. She'd spend all hours at the workshop and even when she was home she'd be doing her sketches or writing letters to customers. And it's never made a profit. It costs hundreds of pounds every year to keep up and they can't afford it but she gets angry if he even hints she should give it up. I could see he was worried and hurt. And then, you see, Daniel was away such a lot with his song collecting. So Adam and I were on our own a lot of the time – apart from Uncle Olly who never notices anything – and . . . well, it happened.'

'And you think Carol guessed?'

'Yes, but as long as she had the workshop, she wouldn't care.'

'So if it hadn't been for Daisy you'd have married Daniel and gone on . . . ?'

Her mouth twisted in a bleak little smile. 'That's what's ironic. I'd decided to end it. I knew what we'd been doing was wrong, but it would be even more wrong when I was married to Daniel. That's what I was telling Adam in the barn when you overheard us.'

'I told you, I wasn't the one who overheard you.'

But it made no difference. She went on pouring it out as if her survival depended on it.

'Before Daniel went away, he said we should set a new date for the wedding when he got back. So I had to think what we were going to do. I met Adam in the barn and told him I'd made up my mind and it must stop. I'd marry Daniel and we'd be just sister and brother-in-law, no more than that. Only it wasn't as calm as I'm making it sound. I was scared Daniel would find out. I told Adam it was his fault and we should never have done it. That wasn't true. It was me just as much as him.'

'Did Adam accept that it had to end?'

'Yes. It was either that or I'd have to break the engagement with Daniel and go away and Adam and I would never see each other again. We couldn't stand that. Anything was better than that.'

'And then Daniel broke the engagement anyway.'

'Yes. I was . . . frozen with fury.'

'But he wasn't the one you loved.'

'But it meant I'd have to go away, never see Adam again. That's why if I'd had the gun and her in front of me I might have done it.'

'That night when we found her body – you had scratches all over your arms, leaves on your clothes.'

'Of course I did. I'd been behind a hedge, looking for her. For Daisy.'

'When?'

'After it got dark. I went down to the camp to try to see her, just see her. I didn't believe you when you said she wasn't as pretty as me. I thought anybody who was hurting me so much must be amazing in some way – an angel or a devil. I thought she'd stand out from the others, and even by firelight I'd know her, or hear her playing her violin at least. But there was no firelight that night, no music. I couldn't see anything, so I just came back.'

I remembered the footsteps that had scared Bobbie and me, the person we'd taken for a maid coming home late.

'Which way did you come in?'

Our person had come by the back stairs.

'Through . . . through the door to the studio.'

She'd started trembling.

'And went to bed?'

'Yes. I was tired.'

'You weren't tired. When Carol and I found you in bed you were terrified, practically senseless with terror. And you say you came in through the studio?'

She nodded.

'You saw something, didn't you? Somebody putting her in the cabinet?'

Her eyes had gone wide and terrified.

'No. Her foot, the foot sticking out.'

'You couldn't know it was hers.'

'I knew it was dead, a woman dead. I'd wanted her dead. I'd told him I wished she was dead.'

'Told who?'

'Adam.'

'What did you do?'

'I ran back outside . . . to the terrace, I didn't know what to do. I couldn't go through the studio again, so I went up the back stairs and . . .' She mimed pulling covers over her head and stayed with her shoulders bent and eyes staring up at me, as if she really were looking out from under a blanket.

'Why didn't you raise the alarm? Why didn't you tell somebody?'

She didn't answer, but the look in her eyes told me.

'Because you guessed who she was and thought you knew who'd killed her.'

'No!'

But it wasn't a denial, more an appeal to me not to say it.

'So that's the problem,' I said. 'Which brother you save and which you let go.'

Probably Carol's problem too. She was quite intelligent enough to have drawn her own conclusions. I thought of what she'd said to me the day before: *What does anybody know about other people's marriages?* We'd been talking about the Suttons, but surely it was her own marriage she meant. If I was right, she had her own choice to make too and her heart might not go the same way as Felicia's. The platform began to fill up with people. Felicia sat up and dried her eyes.

'What am I going to do?' she asked.

'If you take my advice, nothing for the moment.'

A trail of smoke appeared from the Banbury direction. The rails started to vibrate. I helped her into the compartment and we sat together on the journey back with a little space between us. Felicia turned towards the glass and the window reflected her tear-smudged face over green fields and hedges. I thought Fardel could be out there somewhere and how much we all needed him. Long Lankin, come and save us.

Chapter Twenty

W HEN WE GOT BACK TO THE village Felicia said she felt
well enough to walk home on her own. I was in no
hurry to meet Adam Venn after what she'd told me, so I
took her at her word and watched her out of sight along the
road. She moved slowly and vaguely between the hedges
thick with berries so that if you'd seen her without knowing
you'd have thought she was any girl with any girl's daydreams.
That left me with most of the afternoon and evening. What
I wanted to do with it was look for Fardel, but results hadn't
been encouraging so far.

The thought of the woodworker's wife Janie was nagging
at me. Although I didn't share Sutton's idea that she was a
victim of the man who'd killed Daisy there was a puzzle there
and it might or might not have a connection with the black
cabinet. After all, the cabinet was there when Daniel and I
arrived and at first Janie had struck me as quite normal. A
little shy and very wrapped up in the baby, but that was all.
She'd become distressed as the conversation went on. While
I was there, watching and listening, something had been said
or done to scare her.

I walked on down the street to the workshop and looked
in at the open door. A man and a lad were fitting a door to
a sideboard, another lad carving a Tudor rose into a block
of wood. When they turned to see who was at the door their
faces were guarded, expecting trouble. I asked the man where

Mr Sutton was and he nodded towards the darker area at the back of the workshop. I found him sorting out lengths of wood but he couldn't have been able to see much of them in the shadows and he was moving like a man underwater.

'Any news?'

He shook his head. The hope that had flared up when he found the money missing had died away.

'No. Janie wouldn't creep in here and take the money and not even let me know she and the baby were alive. She hadn't got it in her to be as cruel as that. No, Janie's dead and all there is left for me to do is break the neck of the man who did it and save the hangman a job.'

He turned his head away. From his voice I knew he was crying. Nothing I said or did could make things worse.

'Carol said you were working in Swindon. Did you meet Janie there?'

He nodded. It was in my mind that Swindon wasn't so far from the Marlborough Downs.

'Did her family come from round there?'

'She was an orphan. She was all the family I wanted, so it didn't matter.'

Last night he'd hoped. Today she was in the past tense. I waited a while then said I must go and I hoped he'd let me know if anything happened.

'You'll hear about it when I find him,' he said.

I went to the shop and bought a couple of wizened oranges that looked as if they'd been waiting since Christmas and a small bag of broken biscuits and had an early lunch sitting on a grassy bank by the road just outside the village. On the Saturday afternoon something had scared Janie Sutton, and yet she didn't leave home until after midday on Monday. So either she'd been brooding about whatever it was all Sunday, or something worse happened on Monday to make her leave.

And on Monday, Daisy Smith died. Mr Sutton had convinced himself that his wife was dead but I doubted it. Somebody had been in the workshop last night and I still thought the person had moved more like a woman than a man. If so, Janie was not only alive but somewhere in the area. I'd been looking unsuccessfully for a man, but a young woman with a baby should be easier to find. Some time between midday and five o'clock on a Monday afternoon she'd dutifully left out her husband's lunch, picked up some things for the baby and disappeared. Even ten days later, it shouldn't be impossible to pick up the trail. Her husband had tried hard, but he was too desperate to think clearly. Even so, he'd done one very useful thing and that was to eliminate a large part of the village from the search.

The workshop was at the far end of the village, with the railway halt about a mile away at the other end. To get to it, Janie would have to carry the baby past the shop and post office, the church, school, policeman's cottage, public house and the front windows of a dozen or so Mrs Pennys and other gossips in broad daylight on a late summer afternoon. She'd struck me as a quiet little thing, so it was just on the bounds of possibility that nobody had noticed her – but allow for the baby and there was simply no possibility at all. Having a baby makes a woman public property, particularly as far as other women are concerned. Even if she'd wanted to, Janie simply wouldn't have been allowed to walk that mile with a baby in her arms without somebody stopping her to tickle it under the chin, go goo-goo at it or ask if it had any teeth yet. But nobody had seen her, therefore Janie had not walked up the street to the railway halt. That meant she'd either cut across the fields – unlikely because she'd have to negotiate stiles and gates with baby, shawl and other paraphernalia – or walked out of the village in the other direction. If so, that would have taken her past where I was sitting now.

I crumbled what was left of the biscuits for the birds, brushed crumbs off my skirt and started walking. I made myself walk more slowly than usual, as if weighed down by baby and belongings. It had looked quite a heavy baby. If it had been Janie who took the money, she must have found shelter for the baby and herself not far away. In the first mile, nothing. There were barns but they were stuffed with hay and close to farmyards, not the kind of place where anyone would hide. Buildings of any sort were few and far between and all of them neat and lived-in, no ruins. Once I looked over a wall and saw a mother and baby playing in a garden, but the woman was nothing like Janie. We spoke and she was friendly enough, but had no memory of a woman and baby passing a week ago last Monday.

Another half an hour later I'd covered at least two miles and my confidence was beginning to wane. If Janie had found a hiding place that far out, had she left the baby on its own while she went to get money? Two miles out, two miles back and a robbery in between. Say two hours' absence at least, at night, leaving a baby on its own in a barn or under a hedge? That was even less likely than setting out to commit the robbery with baby in arms. I was simply walking for the sake of it, not getting anywhere, but since the alternative was going back to the village and thinking about Adam and Felicia, I kept going.

Soon afterwards I came to a T-junction, no signposts and no particular reason to choose left or right. When I climbed on top of a stile I saw that the road on the left went over a humpbacked bridge across a railway line. I'd forgotten to bring the map with me and tried to remember it. This couldn't be the local Chipping Norton line because that was behind me, so it must be the main Great Western from Cheltenham to Oxford, with Chipping Norton Junction up the line to the north. Where there are bridges over railways there are often halts as well, where expresses stop sometimes, unpredictably. I walked down to the line and found there was a halt, much like the one back at the village – an empty wooden platform, a bicycle, a corrugated iron shelter with a pagoda-shaped roof, its paint faded from the summer sun. If I'd walked this far carrying a heavy baby I'd have been tired and thirsty. I sat down in the shelter, wondering what I'd do next. A place this small had no railway staff or station-master's house but there were three terraced brick cottages on the other side of the line, probably workmen's cottages when the line was built. I went over the bridge and found a grey-haired woman in one of the small front gardens, picking runner beans. We said good afternoon to each other and she told me there'd be a down-train towards Oxford in forty minutes and it would have to stop because it was putting off a parcel for one of her neighbours.

'Did you happen to see a young woman with a baby some-time in the afternoon on Monday week?'

Instant concern. 'Oh the poor girl. Did she get home all right?'

'Home?'

'To Swindon. The poor thing didn't know where she was – half fainting from tiredness and the baby crying because it was hungry. I let her into my front room so she could feed it decently and got her some tea. I said wouldn't her husband and family be worrying about her and she said she'd been staying with friends and had lost her way and had to get home to Swindon.'

'Lost her way?'

'Well, I thought that was strange. How do you lose your way to the back end of nowhere like here, with a baby? She seemed quite respectable, so I thought she and her husband had quarrelled and she'd tried to run away and thought better of it. So I said he'd be glad to have her back and if the train stopped we'd get her on it to Oxford, then she could change for Swindon and be back home by the time the baby needed feeding again.'

'And the train stopped?'

'Yes, it stopped. I knew the guard so I had a quick word with him and said to keep an eye on her and make sure she got on the Swindon train. You know her, then?'

'Yes.'

'And did she get home all right?'

She was sensing something wrong.

'I'm sorry, she didn't. Her home's in this part of the world. Swindon's where she used to live.'

She put down the colander full of beans in the middle of a flowerbed.

'Oh dear, did I do wrong?'

'Nothing but kindness. It isn't your fault. Did she say anything else about where she was going?'

She hadn't. The woman invited me to drink tea in the same little parlour where Janie had waited. Sitting there among the plush and best china I decided I couldn't go back to Janie's husband with this half-news.

'Will it be the same guard on the train today?'

She had to think, but only for a moment. Her mind was probably as well stocked with timetables and staff rotas as any foreman's.

'Thursday. Yes, it should be Mr Wills.'

The train arrived on time. The woman came to the platform with me and had a word with the guard while he was unloading the parcel for her neighbour. When the train started I bought my ticket to Swindon and asked for all the details he could remember about the young woman and baby.

'She got on and bought her ticket just like you have, miss. She was worried whether she'd have enough money for it but she did. The baby was crying and she said it was frightened because it had never been in a train before. I don't think she'd been in trains much either because she was so worried about how she'd know the right train for Swindon.'

'Do you know if she found it?'

'Yes I do, miss, because I leave this train at Oxford. I told her when the connection was and saw her to the waiting room on the right platform myself. Couldn't go wrong.'

So at Oxford I did exactly what Janie had done and waited for the Swindon connection. When the train arrived I got on it. It was evening by then, quite crowded and no point in asking if anybody had seen a woman and baby ten days ago. Swindon's a big and busy station, full of steam and clanging and hot metal smells from the railway works alongside. The other passengers who got out hurried away along the platform but I lingered, wondering how it would look to an unhappy and tired young woman with a baby and not much money. Terrifying, was the answer. In Janie's place, I'd have sat down on a bench and cried. There was no need to go that far in putting myself into her shoes, but at least it gave me an idea of what to do next. I found my way to the stationmaster's office and said I wanted to see him. After a short wait in an outer office I got not the man himself but somebody who was probably a senior clerk. He had the resigned air of a man used to dealing with complaints from the travelling public. My question made him blink.

'A young woman with a baby, sitting on a bench and crying? I'm sure if it were drawn to our attention we should act with proper humanity.'

'Yes, but how exactly?'

'That would depend on the circumstances. If, for instance, the lady was distressed because she'd missed her train, we'd calm her and ascertain the time of the next one.'

'But if she'd just arrived and didn't know where to go?'

'In that case, we should probably enquire in what part of the town her friends or relatives lived and show her to an omnibus stop or cab rank as appropriate.'

'And if she had no friends or relatives?'

His look and tone turned a shade colder. 'Are we talking about a vagrant, madam?'

'We're talking about a distressed young mother without relatives or money. If one of your staff had found her, would there be a record of it?'

'What date did you say?'

'Monday 26 August, about this time of day.'

He went away, came back shaking his head. 'We have no record of any such event, madam.'

'Supposing she had asked somebody for help, what do you think he'd have advised?'

'That would depend. He might suggest that she go to the police station, but vagrants usually aren't very eager to do that.'

'So what else?'

'Perhaps one of the churches. There's one in particular that runs a mission for railway vagrants.'

I asked directions to it. A short walk from the station, past brick terraces grimed with railway smoke; even the privet hedges were so grey their leaves might have been made from metal. About five minutes away the clerk had said, but probably three times that for a woman weighed down with a baby, her world fallen apart.

The main door of the church was locked but a side one was open. I found two women carefully polishing a brass eagle lectern. They didn't seem surprised when I enquired about a woman and baby, though neither of them had any knowledge of her. The curate would know, they said.

'Where can I find the curate?'

'He's in the house at the back, but he's having his tea.'

264

They made it sound as if it were some kind of religious ceremony. I went round to the back and interrupted the curate at his tea. He was a young man but slow in speech and movement, as if dazed by the problems of the world.

'Yes, there was an unfortunate young woman. I'm not sure which day it was, but certainly about this time of day some time last week.'

'What happened to her?'

'I gave her a cup of tea and escorted her to Lady Mary Bentley.'

'Who?'

'Its full title is the Lady Mary Bentley Memorial Home for Distressed Women, though not many of us use it. Use the name, I mean. The home as well, of course . . . that is to say . . .'

His embarrassment made it clear what sort of home it was. I asked directions. Three or four more grey terraces, men in grimy overalls and heavy boots marching homewards from their work in the locomotive factories now the sun was setting. Janie would have taken that same walk, with the self-conscious curate beside her and the baby in her arms leaving no doubt at all where she was heading. It was a substantial brick house at the end of a road, set a little apart from its neighbours, the sort of place where the railway owners might have lived before they used their profits to move to healthier places. I walked up the steps to the black-painted front door and knocked.

After some time a harassed woman in a dress the colour of the sooty privet leaves opened it. She didn't give me a chance to speak.

'No visitors after four o'clock.'

From somewhere behind her, unseen, a small chorus of babies cried.

'I just want to enquire if a friend of mine named—'

'All enquiries between office hours of nine-thirty and three-thirty, or in writing to the trustees.'

'But can't you even tell me if—?'

She shut the door on me. I was tempted to hammer until she opened it again but guessed it wouldn't help.

The trail had come temporarily to an end against that door and I was doomed to a night in Swindon. I spent it at a decent kind of lodging house for the poorer sort of railway traveller near the station, a necessary economy because my money, like Janie's, was running low. Lamb chop, beans and mashed potato for supper, then bed in a partitioned-off piece of a room so narrow that if you happened to stand with hands on hips your elbows grazed the walls on either side. The bedding was clean but the mattress lumpy. Not that it mattered because sleep was unlikely anyway, with noise from the trains going on most of the night and the locomotive works in full cry by six in the morning. At nine-thirty on the dot I was back on the doorstep of the Lady Mary Bentley Memorial Home.

The same woman in the same dress opened the door and pretended she'd never set eyes on me before. I restated my business and she grudgingly allowed me into a small office with a desk, a cupboard and two hard chairs and left me there for a quarter of an hour or so without another word. The place smelt of cheap polish and carbolic disinfectant, with a stubborn undertone of sour milk and misery. When the woman returned she asked me yet again the name of my friend, managing to say the word 'friend' as if it were something that had to be picked up with tweezers.

'We have nobody of that name here.'

'Then she must have given a different name. The young woman I'm looking for was brought here by a curate on the evening of the Monday before last.'

266

'Are you the young woman's employer?'

'No, I'm a friend of her husband's.'

That caught her by surprise at least. She went to the cupboard and brought out a thick ledger with cloth covers and a leather spine. When she opened it on the table I saw long columns in copperplate writing.

'A young woman and a male infant were admitted that evening. She gave her name as Brown.'

'May I speak to her, please?'

'She is carrying out her domestic duties at present.'

I stood up and leaned across the table so that she had to look at me.

'Her husband's frantic with worry. He has no idea where she is. Whatever she's doing can't matter as much as this.'

She stared, then went to the door, opened it and shouted into the passage, 'Send Brown Three to the office. She's in the laundry room.'

'Brown Three?'

'They nearly all say they're called Brown or Smith or Jones.'

Silence in the room, broken at last by footsteps on the linoleum in the passage. The door opened.

'You wanted to see me?'

Janie, in grey dress, soiled apron and white cap with a few damp strands of hair straggling out from it, hands bright pink and wrinkled. A smell of boiled towelling followed her into the room. Her eyes were downcast and she didn't see me. I stood up to let her sit down, but the woman gave me a look that said it was against the rules.

'Mrs Sutton,' I said.

Her head jerked up. She recognised me and looked terrified.

'Walter? Has something happened to Walter?'

'No, he's quite safe – only very worried about you.'

She seemed frozen.

'Can we talk on our own, do you think?' I said to the woman, but got a shake of the head.

'Mrs Sutton, Janie, if there's anything he did to make you leave I promise you there's never been a man more sorry. He wants you and the baby back.'

'It wasn't him did anything.'

She said it in a whisper to the floor, her sodden pink hands twisting against the apron as if still wringing out wet nappies.

'Who, then? What happened?'

She didn't answer. I didn't blame her, with the woman listening.

'Will you come back home with me now? Whatever it is that scared you, I promise we'll protect you.'

The woman answered for her. 'They're not allowed to leave unless with an employer or close relative.'

I could have argued with that. Legally I was sure Janie had the right to take the baby and go, but it had to be of her own free will and she looked incapable of even getting out of the room without being told to. I made sure that I spoke to her rather than the woman.

'Well then, I'll go straight back home and tell Mr Sutton where you are. If there's time, I'm sure he'll be back here by this evening. If not, it will be tomorrow. Will you be all right till then?'

She managed to look at me and say yes.

'They'll be needing you back in the laundry, Mrs Sutton.'

There was just a touch more kindness in the woman's voice, now Janie had a Mrs to her name. When the door closed behind Janie, she almost managed an apology.

'How are we to know? Most of them say they're deserted wives or widows.'

'Does it matter?'

I went without saying thank you or goodbye. Afterwards I thought I was hard on the woman who, after all, had to live with the sour milk and boiled nappy smells as well. At the time, I was simply angry. Angry for Janie and the other girls. Even more angry because, after all the trouble of finding her, I was no nearer knowing what had made her run away.

Chapter Twenty-One

IT DIDN'T HELP MY MOOD THAT I missed a connection on the way back so it was mid-afternoon by the time I walked into the workshop.

'I've found Janie. They're all right.'

I had to say it again before he let himself believe it, then he staggered and would have fallen if he hadn't hung on to my arm. At first he thought I'd found her somewhere in the village and it took a long time to make him understand about Swindon and the home for distressed women.

'Why did she go to a place like that?'

'She was running away from something and I still don't know what it is. She's still scared, but she'll come back with you. She can't stay where she is.'

Once he'd gathered that she was waiting for him he rushed upstairs to change and collect money for the journey. I called up to remind him that the three of them would probably have to stay in Swindon overnight and he'd better take their marriage lines with him or the place might not let her out. The train wasn't due for some time but he insisted on going straight away in case of missing it. I went with him and he almost ran up the street. When people looked at him he shouted, 'She's all right! I'm going to fetch them home,' and went hurrying on.

'So it wasn't Janie who took the money from the chest,' I said, trying to keep pace with him.

It hardly registered with him, he was so intent on getting to her. I tried a couple of times more and, still unsuccessful, wished him luck and left him on the platform, staring along the line as if he could make the train come earlier by sheer force of will.

I went up to the Venns' house and asked to see Carol. She was in the studio, Annie said. The maid always had a scared look on her face when she opened the door these days, as if expecting more trouble. She was probably right.

It was the first time I'd been in the studio since finding Daisy's body. The black oak cabinet had gone and at first glance the room was back to normal, but it wasn't the harmonious place it had been just two weeks before. All the fine pieces of furniture seemed to have lost their glow, even though the curtains were drawn back and afternoon sun was coming in through the windows. A light fur of dust had collected, probably because Annie couldn't be expected to come in and clean after what had happened.

At first I couldn't see anybody in the room and stopped, as on my first visit, to look at the woman in the tapestry with her crinkly hair, her remote smile and long white feet among carefully disordered grass blades. Then there was some small sound and I turned to find Carol on her knees by the far wall, paintbrush in hand.

'I'm sorry,' I said.

'Don't worry, admire her while you can.'

She was wearing a dark dress with a painter's smock over it. I went closer and saw she was painting a wooden fire-screen with a design of two swans facing each other, necks entwined. She dipped her brush and drew a long white stroke.

'They're beautiful.'

Her sad smile made her look even more like the woman in the tapestry.

'A commission. You know the way fire fenders are shaped, like swans' necks?' She put down her brush and used both hands to draw complementary curves in the air. 'A client wants to follow it through with this and two log boxes. I haven't been able to work on it but . . . but what do you do after all when things are falling apart round you?'

'It's not all bad news,' I said. 'I've found Janie Sutton.'

She listened to the story, still kneeling by the firescreen.

'But what possessed her to run away to that?'

'I didn't have a chance to ask. We might find out tomorrow when her husband brings her back.'

She picked up a fine brush, loaded it with black and gave the swans eyes. If the news had raised her spirits, there was no sign of it.

'At least he'll be able to work again,' I said.

'At what? The wreck's total, you know. Everything's going: the house, the workshop. That hairy communist friend of yours . . .'

'Not really my friend.'

'Well, he's right. It isn't economic, making furniture the way we do. The world's not built that way and it's no use fighting it.'

'So what will happen to them?'

'Back to the railway carriages, I suppose.'

'What caused the wreck? Was it what Hawthorne wrote?'

'It didn't help, but I can't blame him for all of it. Poor Philomena didn't leave us as well off as we'd hoped and we've been . . . been trying to juggle things I suppose since she died. Only we didn't juggle well enough. You get tired in the end.'

'So what will happen to you?' I said.

'We've already had an offer for the house. A brewer from Birmingham. Quite good taste, as it happens. He'll take it furniture and all.'

A gesture with her brush round the studio. One of the reasons why it looked odd and abandoned already was the space at the heart of it where the dark oak cabinet had stood. Some of the other furniture must have been pushed back to make room for it and the whole arrangement had lost its balance.

'It's gone back to my friends,' she said, guessing what I was thinking. 'Goodness knows what they'll do with it. The police did their measurements and took photographs before it went.'

'There's another little mystery about Janie,' I said.

'Oh God, aren't there enough of them?'

'Her husband was sure she took that money from the chest on Wednesday night. It can't have been her, though. She was at that awful place in Swindon by then.'

She said nothing, sitting back on her heels and staring at the swans.

'And he was certain too that only you, he and Janie knew the money was there.'

'Well, he was wrong about one thing, so maybe he was wrong about the other.'

She got to her feet in one supple movement, not using her hands. 'Thank you for finding poor Janie. Was there anything else you wanted to ask?'

'I don't think so.'

She put her head on one side and looked at me.

'You're not sure, are you? Or rather you are sure, but you don't want to say it. Is it to do with that talk you had with poor Flissie?'

'How did you know about that?'

'She didn't confide in me, but I guessed where she was going. She needed to tell somebody. If I'd encouraged her at all I think she'd have even told me.'

'That she and Adam . . .'

273

'Were lovers? Yes, I knew.'

'And didn't mind?'

Her eyes looked as sad as something left out in the rain but she only shrugged – if you could call the little rippling of her shoulders anything as vulgar as a shrug.

'What I felt didn't matter. Some people make too much fuss about their feelings. The important thing was what was to be done about it – or rather, not done.'

'Not leave him, you mean?'

Divorce was difficult, even for the moneyed classes. The already precarious finances of the Venns would be pulled apart by it, Carol's workshop and her dreams for a village of craftsmen put aside for a lonely room somewhere. A lot of women I knew were forced to make those sorts of bargains.

She shook her head. 'Daniel not finding out.'

'But if he was going to marry her, didn't he have a right?'

'Right? A virgin bride, is that what you mean?'

'No. Trust between him and Felicia.'

'And no trust ever again between him and Adam? I know they've quarrelled now but that's only politics. It doesn't matter. Daniel will stop thinking he's a revolutionary and settle down.'

'And never know?'

'You don't understand how close they are, deep down. Daniel was only four when their parents got killed. Adam was father and elder brother to him in one. I don't want Daniel to lose all that over bedroom business.'

The last two words came out almost explosively.

'And what about Felicia?'

'Oh, don't worry about Felicia. She's tougher than you think. You know the kind of perfectly ordinary woman who comes through earthquakes with a child or a puppy in her arms and not a hair out of place? Felicia will be one of those.'

A touch of contempt in her voice, but I couldn't help smiling at the picture. She smiled too.

274

'But seriously, you're not going to tell Daniel, are you?'

'No. Felicia told me in confidence.'

'Thank you.'

He'd know some time though, I thought. Not many secrets last a lifetime. She knelt down again and made a small adjustment to a swan's eye.

'Are you still looking for Daisy's uncle?'

'Yes. I'm hoping Janie might be able to tell me something when they get back tomorrow.'

'Why Janie?'

'Something scared her. It may be nothing to do with him, but if I'm right he was actually inside the workshop helping to move that cabinet the day she ran away.'

'You may be right. I expect you're usually right. Are you?'

A touch of bitterness in her voice. She didn't look at me.

'Very far from it,' I said.

When I looked back from the door she was still staring at the firescreen. Such a nice civilised family, with so very much to hide. They'd all of them – Oliver, Adam, Carol, even Daniel – behaved as if the survival of the Venns mattered enough to the world to justify financial deceit and lying. And yet it was all coming apart in any case. The Birmingham brewer would enjoy the beautiful rooms and tidy up the garden, the lawyers would pick through the financial wreckage and any money that was left afterwards might go to Philomena's good causes. Mr Sutton would be back fitting precisely similar pieces of wood to lines and lines of precisely similar railway carriages. Daisy's body would rot in some unvisited grave in a remote Wiltshire churchyard. And Felicia, if Carol was right, would walk out of the earthquake with a puppy or a baby in her arms. I doubted it.

I went back to Mrs Penny's for tea and some one-sided gossip on the woodworker's runaway wife. Naturally the news that

275

he'd gone to fetch her back was all round the village and since he'd been seen in my company she knew I had something to do with it but I didn't enlighten her. It was a sore point too that I'd spent a night away without warning her. When she realised she was getting nowhere, she changed tack.

'Did your friend find you?'

'What friend?'

'Girl on a horse. She was round here this morning looking for you. I said you hadn't come home all night and goodness knows where you were.'

'Did she leave a message?'

'Something about seeing somebody and then losing him but not to worry because she'd find him again and let you know.'

I felt like howling with frustration. For once Bobbie had done exactly as instructed and brought word to me, only I hadn't been there so I'd no idea what she'd take it into her head to do now.

'Did she say when she'd be coming back?'

'No. She wanted to know when you'd be here. I said you hadn't been back yesterday so there was no telling if you'd be back today.'

'Did she say where she was going next?'

'I didn't ask her. I had an apple pie in the oven and the crust was burnt black as it was from talking to her. I didn't see the going of her.'

When I'd finished my tea I waited impatiently in my room under the thatch, listening for hooves in the street, cursing myself for not finding out exactly where Bobbie's friends lived. By the time it was getting dusk with no sign of her I knew she wouldn't be coming back that day. All I could hope was that if she was really on the track of Fardel she'd remember my orders not to approach him, but taking orders didn't seem to be one of her talents.

With no news from Bobbie, and Janie still presumably in Swindon, all I could do was go on with my own hunt for Fardel. Experience so far suggested that there wasn't a lot to be gained from wandering the countryside at random. I tried instead to look for a pattern in what I knew – a few shillings earned moving a piece of furniture, the fight outside the Crown, the chicken stolen and cooked, the rabbit eaten raw from the snare. For all I knew, they might involve four separate people. But if I stuck to my hunch that they all involved Fardel, he must have a hiding place in or near the village. If so, he'd been there for over a week. If it were simply a barn or an outhouse, somebody would have come across him by now and turfed him out. Even Constable Johnson might have heard about it.

While I thought about it, I got out my cycle lamp to put in a new battery I'd bought in Swindon. That made me think of the village shop and the woman behind the counter explaining the way shopping was organised in the village. If you wanted anything not stocked in the shop you had to ask Mr Bestley to bring it for you from town, Tuesdays and Fridays, and if the carter happened to be laid up with a bad foot you didn't get it at all. For more than a week the carter hadn't been able to move so neither had his cart. It was a long shot, but worth trying before going back to blundering around footpaths in the dark.

I went downstairs and let myself out, passed the lamplit windows and cheerful men's voices at the Crown and went down the dark and deserted main street. There was nobody at the forge, just the glow of the smith's fire dying down and the lingering smell of singed horse hoof from a day of shoeing. In the carter's yard one window of his cottage glowed faintly but the door was tight shut. He'd be inside there with his sore foot and his old deaf dog, neither of them in any state to be curious about what was happening outside.

277

I took out my bicycle lamp and shone it round the yard on weeds and pieces of rusting agricultural machinery. The wagon in the lean-to with its domed top looming out of the darkness seemed almost as big as the cottage itself. I went closer, stumbled and almost fell over one of its downward angled shafts and the thing gave a creak and shudder.

'Grrrm.'

The sound that came from inside was just recognisable as human, but had too the quality of a large animal half awake, perhaps a bear hibernating, and protesting at being disturbed. I froze, then switched off the lamp and took a few steps back from the shafts. Whether the thumping of my heart was fear or triumph I didn't know. I'd wanted him and I'd found him, but now I had found him I was scared. It was the figure from all our nightmares in there and – for some minutes of panic – it wasn't enough to say that it was human after all, could be faced like any other part of humanity. The carter's cottage was only a few steps away, the blacksmith's house a short run down the track. I could have made for either of them – the blacksmith's probably, because the carter wouldn't be much help – and yet in nightmares if you run away from things they only follow you. Perhaps it was the dread of being followed that kept me there in the dark, listening.

After that first sound there was silence for a while. Then a creaking sound as the body of the cart shifted on its axles. Somebody was moving around inside, slow and heavy-footed. At first I thought he might be coming out to see what had disturbed him, but the movements weren't abrupt enough for that, more like somebody waking up, slowly getting his bearings. It wasn't stupid, whatever was inside there. Needing a roof over its head it had found somewhere better than bushes or a ruined barn – comfortable and convenient for the village and unexpectedly available. It knew how to seize chances, to find the little unregarded niche – *one little window*

278

where Long Lankin crept in. If it settled down and went back to sleep, I'd go away and bring the village policeman here to earn his living. But the noises didn't settle down. There were grunting sounds then heavy footsteps on the wooden boards of the cart. He'd got his boots on. He was coming out. The question was, which way? Out at the front over the driver's seat or the back? If he came out at the back and turned left he'd find me; right, and I'd be screened by the wagon.

He came out of the front. One moment there was just the shape of the driver's platform, then it changed as if some dark fungus had suddenly sprouted from it, a man's head and shoulders. The wagon rocked as he scrambled down. I could hear his breathing now, laboured and resentful as if waking up had taken more energy than he could spare. For a while he just stood, then there was a long pattering on to the weeds, a deeper sigh of unburdening. A relief for me too. If he'd just come out for that purpose he might go back inside without looking round to see what had woken him. But after a while that was probably taken up by rebuttoning he gave another sigh and moved away from the wagon. Three steps would have brought him to where I was standing.

I froze, not breathing. He went in the other direction, towards the forge and the street. For a moment he showed as a silhouette against the red glow from the forge embers, a broad-shouldered man, shoulders a little bent, head thrusting forwards. He walked slowly and surprisingly lightly. Then he moved out of the light and merged into darkness where the track met the street. I guessed he'd gone out to find his food, another chicken from its roosting pole or rabbit from a snare. It wasn't part of my plan to follow him. Now I'd found out where he lived I'd done my part and it was up to the law to do the rest. If nothing else, Fardel had a stolen chicken to account for. But that would mean, perhaps, a night in a police cell and a five-shilling fine – a long way from facing questioning for suspected murder. If, as I was certain now, the man proved to be Daisy's uncle that should be enough to get Inspector Bull's interest, especially as he'd handled the black oak cabinet, been inside the Venns' house. But that still didn't prove murder and the inspector was a sceptical man, especially of any attempt to draw suspicion away from the Venns.

It would take Fardel half an hour at the very least to forage for his supper, probably much longer. The urge to have a look in the wagon on the faint chance there might be something in there to help was stronger than the childish fear of being found by the beast inside its lair. I switched on the lamp and followed the cone of light in at the front of the wagon, over the driver's seat and into the blackness inside.

My feet landed on soft hay. He'd made himself a nest there backing on to the driver's seat and, from the size of the dip in the middle, slept curled up. There was a warm and musty scent about the place – faintly piggish. The wooden floor of the cart was littered with food oddments: a charred chicken leg, a crust of bread erupting with white and green rosettes of mould, apple cores scored with the tracks of broad teeth. No sign of a weapon unless you counted a rusty shovel blade with a splintered handle or a single hobnailed boot, the kind of thing he might have picked up in a ditch. There was a fragment of tarpaulin too that he might have used as a bedcover, thrown aside in a corner. Cautiously I moved it and saw something glinting underneath it. Something silver. I picked it up, thinking it might be an object he'd stolen. It was a riding crop with a horn handle on one end, a thick silver band round it, not too heavy – the kind of thing a lady might carry.

I played the lamp beam on it, certain I'd seen it before.

The lamp beam went zigzagging round the wagon walls, scaring me more until I realised that it was my own hand jolting it. When I last set eyes on the silver-mounted crop, Bobbie Fieldfare had been twirling it. The memory was like a concussion blow that leaves you walking and talking although the conscious mind has given up control. I slithered over the driver's seat, fell to the ground, picked myself up and started running.

The dahlia-fancying constable might as well have existed in a different universe. I didn't think of him or anybody else. My stupidity had brought Bobbie into contact with this man and all I wanted in the world was to get my hands on him and shake out of him what he'd done to her. Nothing ever would or could take away my blame but that was something for the rest of my life. All that existed was the thought that he was out there somewhere, perhaps no more than ten minutes or so ahead of me, half a mile away at the very most.

When I came out of the track by the forge I turned left without thinking. That was the way to the village shop with the hen coop in its garden or, further on, the lane to the old orchard where the poacher set his snares. Animals hunting food go to the places where they've found it before. I ran as far as the shop and looked over the wall into the garden. A dog yapped, sharp and threatening, but there was none of the squawking and clucking there'd have been from the hen coop if somebody had just lifted a chicken out of it. The yapping went on. A voice from inside the cottage called out to ask who was there. I ran on, not wanting to explain, past the school and up the lane by the churchyard. It was steep and rutted. I stumbled and dropped the cycle lamp. It went out and when I found it in the grass and picked it up it made a rattling sound and wouldn't turn on. That bothered me less than it should have done. He was a creature of the darkness so it seemed right to look for him in darkness. After that I made myself slow down. No point in twisting an ankle and having to crawl after him.

After a while the oak trees of the coppice were rustling on my left. He'd had a lair there but it had been days old, probably only used once for cooking the chicken before caution and hunger made him turn to raw meat. The thought of meeting him in the woods scared me more than the open fields. Whether it was that fear or logic that made me ignore the woods and keep moving up the track I don't know. I was gambling on the snares, hoping to find him bending over one of them or standing in the hedge, gnawing on raw rabbit flesh. The woods fell away and there were only hedges right and left. When I looked back down on the village only a few lights glowed and they seemed a long way off. From then on, I counted strides and stopped after every fifty, pressed in against the hedge, to listen to any noises from up the track ahead of me. Nothing but the natural ones – sheep moving around on the other side of the hedge, an owl hooting. A hoarse cough from a few feet away made my heart thump louder, but that was a sheep as well. It took a long time to get to the old orchard where the snares had been. Nothing.

Nothing but miles of dark fields and the knowledge that if I'd got it wrong he could be two miles away by now in another direction altogether. My rage to get him was still as strong, but the uphill walk had left me breathless. That, and fear. Sitting down and waiting was the hardest thing to do, but the right one. If he was going round the snares to find his supper it might be a long business. So I sat on a bank with my feet in a dry ditch and my back to the hazel hedge. Down in the village the church clock struck ten in cracked notes. Wait there till eleven, then, if I'd heard nothing, I'd go back down to the wagon and wait for him to come home. Come home with his mouth wet with rabbit blood. Older blood too, perhaps, on his hands.

The boughs of a twisted apple tree were just visible against the darkness. Not total dark, then. I couldn't see a moon but perhaps it would give oblique light, enough to see him by if he came. The grass in the ditch quivered and went still again. Fieldmouse or frog, too small for a rabbit.

Then the scream.

Chapter Twenty-Two

RABBITS IN SNARES SCREAM. MATING FOXES, injured weasels. But the instant it came, I knew it wasn't one of those. The worst sounds have an instant of silence before them, as if something has punched a hole in the air to let them through. Even before it got into ears or brain I was on my feet in the ditch, wanting to run but not knowing where. It was short, not drawn out or repeated as a trapped animal's would be. Not even loud, perhaps, if you'd heard it by day. Just a second or two of human pain and protest, then the rattle sound of a disturbed pheasant, then silence.

It had come from below me, down between me and the village and probably off to the right, although it had been so short it was hard to tell. The coppice and his lair.

Progress down the track was one long stumble. I fell several times, caught my foot in my skirt and heard a ripping sound from the waistband, gathered up trailing handfuls of material and kilted them round my waist as I went. The trees of the coppice came up as a dark wall on my right. No point in looking for a keeper's stile. I tried a gate vault, head down, over the fence rail, landed on my back in rustling leaves. Dead oak leaves for certain, like the ones that had clung to Daisy's body.

'Bobbie!'

I shouted it as soon as I'd got some breath back. It came out quavering like the call of a sick owl. No response. When

I stood still, the silence on the edge of the wood had a different quality from the open, a swallowing silence. I went slowly through looping brambles and dead branches. Often it was a matter of pushing off from one rough tree trunk and falling in the dark against the next. No point in trying to be cautious now, in fact the more noise the better. He might think there were several people coming at him through the wood. I was trying to work my way uphill to the old quarry but it took an achingly long time. Once when I fell brambles netted themselves round me so tightly that I had to kick and punch my way out, with tearing sounds that might have been clothes, might have been skin, I was past caring. At last the ground levelled out and scraps of dark sky were visible through the more solid dark of tree branches. Then suddenly the face of the old quarry was above me and the smell of old scuffed ash from a bonfire all round.

'Bobbie?'

More quietly this time. No answer. Cursing the loss of the bicycle lamp I got down on my knees and shuffled around patting the ground, looking for anything that hadn't been there on my last visit. Hopeless. If there were anything I couldn't hear or see it. But at least not what I dreaded. No dark bundle. No smell of blood, only the old fire and rotting leaves.

'Anybody?'

No answer. I'd been so sure of finding what I was looking for here that I didn't know what to do. Even in my insane mood I realised that searching the rest of the coppice in the dark was beyond me. Besides, there was no guarantee the scream had come from there.

More slowly now, I got myself back to the lane, down past the churchyard to the village. The dahlias in the police constable's garden were grey and black in the starlight, like fires burned out. It took a lot of battering on the door to get a

285

response and then a lamp went on upstairs, a window opened in the thatch and the constable looked out.

I called up, 'I think somebody's been badly hurt.'

'Where? What's going on? Who are you?'

Reasonable questions from a man dragged from sleep. I told him who I was, reminded him we'd spoken about the tramp.

'I found him. My friend's riding crop was there and I'm afraid he's done something terrible. Would you come down, please?'

It took him a long time to get on his uniform and come to the door but perhaps that was just as well because it gave me a chance to calm down and get my story in some sort of order. Even so, when he did open the door at last he seemed so thunderstruck seeing me at close quarters – and I suppose I was a sight with face and arms scratched and rags of clothes hanging off at all angles – that he wouldn't listen. He assumed I was the one who'd been attacked by a tramp and took a lot of convincing otherwise. Eventually, though, I managed to tell him what had happened, from the carter's wagon onwards. He listened, but still didn't look as disturbed as he should have been.

'This friend of yours, where does she live?'

'In London, but she's staying with friends in this part of the world.'

'What friends?'

'I don't know their name, but they're well-off, not far away and they own horses.'

Hopeless. That could apply to dozens of households. If only I'd taken Bobbie seriously I'd have asked her more questions.

'So have they reported her missing?'

'They may not know she's missing. But she was helping me look for the man, it was her crop in his wagon, she's out there somewhere and I heard a scream.' Then, when he started saying something about rabbits and foxes – 'A human scream. I'm sure of that. He's already killed one woman, now I'm afraid he's killed her too.'

'One woman?'

'Daisy Smith. The girl at the Venns' house.'

I should have pitied the man. Thinking about it much later, I did. All he wanted to do was earn a quiet living policing the small crises and criminalities of the village and make war on earwigs. Murders, screams in the dark, half-naked women outside his door at the dead of night weren't part of his scheme of things. Worse, he was a constable on his own, no colleague within miles, no vehicle except possibly a bicycle, no weapon but a truncheon, no telephone and not even – as it turned out – a battery flashlight. I thought about all this much later but at the time I was half mad with frustration, wanting him to summon up men for a search. He did his best, but I didn't appreciate it.

'Well, miss, the first thing is to get you safe home to Mrs Penny's and—'

'No. If necessary, I'll steal a horse or a bicycle, ride to Chipping Norton and throw stones at the police station window until somebody does something.'

I meant it, and luckily he saw I did. He sighed, went inside and came out after long minutes carrying his helmet in one hand and a lighted oil lamp in the other.

'If you say he's been sleeping in Bestley's wagon, chances are he's gone back there.'

After that scream, I doubted it. Still, it was possible. We hurried together down the street, past the forge and the carter's cottage. The inside of the wagon was just as I'd left it, Bobbie's crop included, the nest in the hay undisturbed. At least the evidence that somebody had been sleeping there made the constable more ready to believe me.

'Tell you what I'll do, miss. I'll wake up a few people and we'll go out and see what we can find.'

So we did, going round the village like a party of carol singers, stopping at the forge first then other places on each side of the street. Probably a routine the village had followed before, looking for lost children or sheep thieves. It took an achingly long time – the knock on the door, the opening of upstairs windows, the constable's long and none too comprehensible explanation about a tramp and a young lady. Then the wait while the man got on his clothes and came sleepy-eyed to the front door, lamp and stick in hand. As the clock struck one there were half a dozen of us standing by the churchyard wall.

'Right,' the constable said. 'The lady thinks she heard the scream from somewhere near Church Coppice but it might have been on the other side. Anyhow, it's not as far up as Fowler's piece. Two of us have a look round the churchyard in case, two in the coppice, two on the other side of the lane.

'He'll be long gone,' someone said. 'Whatever he's done, he won't wait around.'

I agreed. It was in my mind that somebody should run to the Venns and get the horse and gig out, but that might have to wait until daylight. I followed the main party up the lane. When I looked back, two lamps were moving slowly round the churchyard like ghosts. 'Give a shout if you find anything,' the constable had said. Nobody shouted. At the first gateway two more men went off to the right. That left three of us for the coppice. Over the keeper's stile this time, by lamplight, the constable and a man I recognised as the shopkeeper's husband carefully turning their heads away from my tattered skirt and exposed knees. All the time we were searching, above the swish of feet in dead leaves, I was listening for a shout from one of the other searchers. After a while the two from the churchyard joined us, so there were four lamps moving through the coppice.

Around five o'clock the light started coming back, oak leaves showing outlined against a grey sky. Our search party reassembled in the lane, the men looking weary. They had their day jobs to go to in an hour or two, had willingly given up their night's sleep on what might have been a freak of mine. I hoped I thanked them but I'm not sure. Instead of reassuring me, the long night without trace of Fardel or Bobbie had turned the fear to near certainty.

'What I'll do . . .' the constable said. 'What I'll do is ride my bicycle over to Charlbury and report. If you can get in touch with somebody and find out where your friend is staying, we can go there and see if she's at home.'

Yes, I could do that, I said. Somebody in this part of the world must have a telephone, probably at the rail junction. I'd have to ring the office, find out Lady Fieldfare's number. Keep it calm. *I wonder if you could kindly tell me where your daughter's staying. Something's happened and . . .*' And perhaps I'd go there and find Bobbie alive and laughing, nothing to do with a scream in the night. Or perhaps not. '*. . . and your daughter may have been killed and it's my fault*'.

Still two hours to go before the earliest bird would be in at the office. The six men were ready to go off down the lane, waiting for me.

'I'll stay for a while,' I said. 'I'll leave a message at the police house as soon as I know anything.'

They went away, moving with the heaviness that comes to you when you've been up all night. I knelt down, soaked my hands in cold dew from the grass and wiped them over my face. Not much help. The stile was a few steps away. I climbed over it, back into the coppice. The blackbirds were awake now, clattering their warning calls every few steps. My memory from the confused night was that we'd spent most of our time in the middle and upper part where the trees grew thickest. Down the slope they thinned into a tangle of smaller trees with trunks not much bigger than broom handles and coppiced hazels sprouting leafy growth looped with tough stems of honeysuckle. At the bottom you could see through the trees to pasture land with a track running diagonally through it from the road to the bottom corner of the coppice. A path for cattle to go and drink, so probably a pond down there. We hadn't searched a pond.

Down through the hazels, I slid on moss and after a while saw a glint of sunlight on water. No more than a glint because most of the surface I could see was covered with bright green duckweed. Further down, more of the pond was visible. Three cows in the meadow beside it looked as if they'd come for their first drink of the day, only they weren't drinking, just standing staring.

Cows stare at anything, of course they do. Cows stare at anything or nothing. But while I was telling myself that, I was sliding down on the moss and as I slid I saw what they were staring at. Something black and white, near the edge of the pond, black and white and waterlogged. From my side the ground above the pool ended in a steep bank that tipped me down knee-deep into mud and rushes. The mud sucked at my feet as if it wanted to stop me getting there, sucked shoes off and came up between my toes like something cold and fleshy. The cows wheeled and galloped away, tails up.

She was lying head down in the deeper water, face submerged, feet at the muddy edge. The mud was stained mahogany colour. I splashed out waist-deep, lifted up head and shoulders and turned her over, knowing it was no use. She slipped away and her head flopped forward, nape showing very white against the crinkly hair that hadn't lost its tidiness even after hours in the water.

Carol Venn.

Chapter Twenty-Three

WHEN I GOT DOWN TO THE road, Constable Johnson was just coming along on his bicycle. I ran in front of him.

'She's dead. In the pond.'

Naturally he thought, as I'd thought when I'd first seen her, that I meant my missing friend. Even when I managed to get control of myself and tell him, it took a long time for him to understand. He laid his bicycle down on the grass verge and came back with me up the pasture.

She was just as I'd left her except her head and shoulders were lower in the water, the stain on the mud more fresh and red because she'd bled when I'd moved her. He waded in, lifted her. The slash across her throat gurgled out air and water. More blood was coming from cuts in her chest. They looked like deep stab wounds, ripped through the fabric of her blouse and jacket. When her right arm flopped back there were deep slashes across the palm of her hand.

'The devil,' the constable kept saying. 'Oh the devil.'

He let me help him with her out of the water, laid her on the bank and took off his cycling cape to cover her face. You could see him working out what to do next.

'What I'll do . . .' It was a kind of formula, to steady himself. 'What I'll do is get somebody to stay here with her, then I'll ride to the junction and telegraph.'

'We should start looking for Fardel,' I said. 'But he'll be miles away.'

He'd had a whole night from the time I'd heard the scream. He could even have got as far as one of the railway lines and be in a train by now, on his way to lose himself in any city.

'And the husband's got to be told.'

Constable Johnson looked sick at the thought of it, but I couldn't face Adam Venn yet.

'I'll stay here with her while you get somebody,' I said. 'Then I'll take your bicycle and telegraph if you want.'

Constable Johnson went back down the field leaving a broad green track in the silver of the dew-covered grass. I sat down on the bank a little way from her, not touching. The cows came back to drink, avoiding the patch of red-stained mud, uneasy. The church clock struck six. Soon after that the constable came back with another man who'd helped in the search and we left him keeping watch. On the road, the constable surrendered his heavy official bicycle with some reluctance. I raced it the three miles or so to the junction, woke up the telegraph operator and, as instructed, sent a message to Inspector Bull. The stationmaster at the junction had seen no sign of a man who might have been Fardel.

I rode back more slowly, tiredness setting in, and delivered the bicycle back to the constable's door. There was no sign of him – presumably he was still up at the house with the Venns – but the news had spread now and the whole village was stunned. People were out on their steps or clustered round the pump and the village shop, angry or scared in a way they hadn't been over Daisy's death. Soon after that a brake arrived at a smart trot, trailing plumes of dust, with a policeman in the driving seat and two bay cobs between the shafts. It halted in the yard of the Crown and I watched from a distance as Inspector Bull and two more constables climbed down from the back, making sure they didn't see me. I knew I'd have to talk to the inspector but I wasn't ready for it yet. There was another arrival I was watching for.

It happened, with no dust or fuss, an hour or so later. Walter and Janie Sutton came walking down the street from the station, so wrapped up in each other that they didn't notice the groups of people gossiping about what had happened. He had a dazed look of relief on his face and was carrying the baby, she had a brown paper parcel tucked under her arm. I went to meet them, knowing I had to break the news before they heard it more casually. When he saw me he started talking about how grateful they were and she gave me a scared smile.

'I'm sorry,' I said, 'I've got some bad news. Can we go inside?'

The craftsman and the two apprentices were in the workshop and, from the look of them, had been talking about the death.

'Come upstairs,' he said to me.

I followed them up the steep stairs to their living quarters, full of sturdy and simple furniture and bright colours. He made Janie sit down with the baby on her lap. She looked better than in the home, but her eyes were still scared.

'I'm afraid Mrs Venn's dead,' I said. 'She was killed last night.'

Janie gave a thin scream that set the baby crying. My eyes were on her, so all I heard was a thump behind me where Walter Sutton had been standing. He'd slipped down on his knees, head bent on the edge of the baby's cradle. When Janie saw that, she looked terrified.

'Was it . . . was it who I think?' The words came thickly from him; his face was still hidden.

'Yes,' I said. 'The police are looking for him.'

'Who?' Janie said. 'Who does he mean?'

'A man named Luke Fardel.'

She gave another little cry. Walter Sutton got shakily to his feet and went behind her, so that he could put his arm round her without letting her see his face.

'Don't cry, love. You're home. He can't hurt you. Don't cry.' He did quite a good job of keeping his voice calm for her, but the eyes that met mine over her bent head were terrified. I knew there'd never be a good time to do what had to be done next. For the sake of everyone, I thought, get it over with.

'Do you think Janie and I could talk to each other alone?' I asked him.

'What do you want to tell her?'

His arm tightened round her. His eyes were angry now as well as scared.

'I think it's more a case of what Janie might have to tell me,' I said. He relaxed just a little.

'Let him stay,' she said, tears flooding her face. 'I want him to hear. Whatever's to be told, he's got a right to hear.'

He took the baby from her, settled it gently in a wooden rocking cradle, beautifully carved with ducks and ducklings, and stood rocking the cradle, looking at us.

'That Sunday,' I said, 'the Sunday before Daisy died, Mrs Venn came and went out for a walk with Janie.'

'Yes. She said her head was aching and she was going to Church Coppice to pick leaves to draw and would I like to come with her. She did that sometimes. We were picking some bits of oak twigs with acorns on them. When we heard somebody on the path we didn't think much of it because a lot of people walk in Church Coppice on a Sunday but when we turned round, there was a man.'

'What was he like?'

She hesitated. 'Dark-haired, quite big.'

'What did he say?'

'He asked her if she had a brother named Daniel. No good afternoon or excuse me, just came out with it.'

'What did she do?'

'She said yes.'

'Did she seem scared of the man?'

'Startled, more. Then he said something else.'

'What?'

'He asked if she knew of a girl called Daisy Smith.'

'Did she answer?'

'She just looked at him for a while, then she asked me to excuse her and took him off down the path. A few minutes later back she came without him.'

'Did you ask what had happened?'

'I didn't like to ask, but she said something like her brother-in-law met some very odd people when he was out collecting songs.'

'Except you knew it was more than that, didn't you? You recognised the man.'

Walter's fists were clenched and the cradle had stopped rocking.

Janie covered her face with her hands, nodded her head. Walter stared at her, eyes even more miserable than when she'd been missing.

'He came from your part of the world, didn't he? That Saturday in the workshop we all thought you were scared because of the cabinet. But it was something that Daniel Venn said. He told everybody he'd been collecting songs near Ogbourne. That's where the man Fardel came from and it scared you. I think you recognised the man in the copse because you came from there too.'

Another nod, hands still clasped over her face.

I asked as gently as I could, 'A relative?'

'Uncle.'

It came out as a retching sound.

'Then Daisy Smith was . . . ?'

'My sister . . . my half-sister, that is. I hadn't seen her for five years, since I ran away from him.'

'From Fardel? Your uncle?'

'Yes.'

'And you didn't know he and Daisy were both here until you met him with Mrs Venn?'

'No.'

'Did he recognise you?'

'No. I kept my face turned away. I thought . . . God forgive me . . . I thought let him go after poor Daisy if that's what he's come for, only leave me alone. I'd got away from him, made a life for myself here with Walter and the baby and now . . . here he was. I could have killed him.'

Walter made a move towards her, probably to stop her saying anything else, setting the cradle lurching.

'It's all right,' I told him. 'Janie didn't kill anybody. Janie's done nothing wrong at all.'

'I have, though. I could have gone to her, couldn't I? Gone to my sister?'

'But you didn't.'

'No, I didn't. I didn't want anything to do with any of them – not even Daisy. We weren't so close. She was only a kid when I went away. He was looking for Daisy and if I went looking for her too he'd have found me and dragged me back. And I was ashamed . . . ashamed of having anything to do with a man like that. I wanted to forget I ever knew him.'

I watched Walter's face and thought there were things I might have to tell him, for Janie's sake, about why she'd needed so much to get away from Fardel but that would have to wait until I got him alone. 'But you did tell somebody,' I said. 'You told Mrs Venn.'

'I had to. She could see anyway. When she came back from talking to him I was shivering so much I could hardly stand up. So she asked me what was wrong. I told her. Then I begged her not to tell him or Daisy I was there, almost went down on my knees and begged her.'

'What did she say?'

'She was so kind. She knelt down and put her arm round me and said she wouldn't tell anybody. Then she said she'd make him and Daisy go away and it would be all right.'

'You're sure she said that – she'd make him and Daisy go away?'

'Yes.'

'Did she say how?'

'No.'

'But you didn't think she could do it. You still ran away.'

'I thought she would. Then, on the Monday morning . . .' She took a deep breath. 'They were moving that cabinet and I heard his voice down in the workshop here, helping them move it out to the cart. There he was, inside our own house. She hadn't made him go away after all. So I had to go. I took the baby and went.'

'Without seeing Daisy?'

'I never saw Daisy.'

'What happened to her wasn't your fault. None of this was your fault.'

Which was as near true as it needed to be. In all the various neglects and betrayals of Daisy, her sister's had been the most excusable. The two of them needed time together, so I said I must go. Walter Sutton came down the stairs after me. The workshop was empty. Through the window we could see the craftsman and apprentices out in the yard. I expected Walter to show me out but he led the way to the dark back of the workroom.

'How did she die?'

'Her throat was cut. She was by the pond. I think she must have gone to meet him.'

His big body sagged. He let himself sink down on a low table like something melting.

'Why didn't she come to me?'

The mirror frame he'd carved so carefully was standing on the top of a chest of drawers between us and the light, the beautiful cupped hands in silhouette. I thought of how they'd held the reflection of Carol's face and the way he'd looked at her. Pride in his own craftsmanship, I'd thought. Now I guessed it had been a lot more than that.

'You loved her?'

'Yes.' It came out as a groan, but he couldn't stop himself glancing upstairs to where Janie and the baby were. 'She doesn't know. We wouldn't have hurt her, neither of us, not for the world.'

'And Carol loved you?'

A nod. 'Yes. I couldn't believe it. She'd done so much for us, done everything. She was so good to us, so beautiful, I just couldn't believe it. There was one day – we were working on a piece together and our hands touched and . . . it wasn't taking anything from Janie, not anything. It was just different, that's all.'

'Upstairs just now, you thought I was going to tell Janie.'

He nodded.

'I'm not going to. I hope she never knows.'

'Where did it happen? Where did he kill her?'

'By the pool at the bottom of the coppice. I think she'd arranged to meet him there in the middle of the night. She took your best knife to protect herself. She picked it up from your bench, the night she came in and took her own money. Did you guess that?'

'Not till now, no. I can see now. I can see it all now.'

'I think she needed the money because Fardel was blackmailing her. Why? Had he seen the two of you together?'

'It was worse than that. It was a lot worse than that.'

Silence. The sweet smell of wood was all round us, from upstairs the sound of the wooden cradle rocking.

'Will you look after Janie and the baby?' he said. 'Somebody's got to look after them.'

'But why? You're not going away, are you? She needn't know about you and Mrs Venn.'

'When I'm in prison, I mean.'

'You won't go to prison. It's not a legal offence to love another man's wife.'

'I don't mean that. I mean they'll say I killed Daisy.'

'No. Carol Venn did. You've known that all along, haven't you?'

'That Sunday, when she brought Janie back, she told me what had happened. I wanted Fardel to go back where he came from and stop scaring Janie. She wanted Daisy to go back where she came from because of all the trouble she was causing in the family. So she said if he'd come to get Daisy he could take her and go, best thing for everybody all round. The only thing was bringing the two of them together, but Carol had an idea about that.'

She would, of course, Carol the cool solver of everybody's problems.

'What was the idea?'

'She got a message to Daisy at the camp saying her sister was here and wanted to meet her in the wood by the church. She wouldn't be, of course. Janie didn't know anything about it. Then she said she'd find out where Fardel was and let him know to be there at the same time so that he could come across Daisy there and take her back. As it turned out, she didn't have far to look for him because Bestley went and hired him to help take the cabinet up.'

'She did see him that morning, then?'

'Of course she did. It went well enough, at first. Daisy came to the coppice and Carol kept her talking, waiting for him. We'd arranged I'd be there watching from behind a tree in case he caused any trouble.'

'Did you know she'd brought a gun with her?'

'Never in the world.'

'So then what happened?'

'When Fardel arrived, Daisy screamed and tried to get away. Fardel grabbed her and was getting rough with her and Carol tried to stop him. Once she saw how scared Daisy was of him and how she didn't want to go back with him, she changed her mind. She got the gun out and shouted to him to let Daisy go. I was running out, trying to help her, then the gun went off. Carol was only trying to scare him, but he twisted round and it was Daisy who got shot.'

'What did you do?'

'We were scared, all of us. We hoped she was just hurt, but she was dead. It was Fardel's idea to bury her under a lot of leaves in the old quarry, then when we'd done it, he ran off. We thought . . . Carol thought when she was missed people would just think she'd wandered off back home.'

Such a small hole in the world Daisy made, no wonder Carol thought it.

'We went away, but he must have had another thought about it and come back and put Daisy's body in the cabinet deliberately to scare Mrs Venn, put the blame on her.'

Or his way of claiming his twenty pounds. Goods returned, payment expected.

'Did you know he was blackmailing her?'

'No. I wish she'd come to me. But by then I was so worried about Janie going I suppose she didn't like to. I knew the sort of man he was, you see. I really thought he'd killed Janie.'

Footsteps and voices sounded from outside: the craftsman and apprentices on their way back in.

'What shall I do?' he said. 'Shall I go to the police and tell them?'

'Not yet.' Not ever, if I can help it. 'For now, go to Janie and the baby.' I watched him going back up the stairs as the men came in.

'All right now, then?' a craftsman asked me cheerfully.

I don't know what I answered, if anything, because I'd turned again to look at the love gift of clasped hands. There was a little corner of paper sticking out from under the base and I pulled at it, thinking: She's left him a letter. If so, I'd have to find a time to let him know when Janie wasn't there. It was an envelope, with neat italic handwriting that might well be Carol's and a name, only the name wasn't Walter Sutton's, it was her husband's.

Beside the road up to the Venns' house a farmer had already started ploughing, two great horses, one grey and one bay, drawing a gleaming line through silver-yellow stubble, a few seagulls following as if they expected herring to leap out of the furrow. The windows of the house were blank and dark, the sun not on them.

Rounding the curve in the drive I found three vehicles parked outside the front door, two gigs and the police motor car. The door was ajar. I knocked, got no answer and walked in. Part of my mind that still hadn't caught up with things still expected to hear Carol's steps on the stairs and see her looking over the banister at me. No sign or sound of anybody. I walked slowly towards the studio, pushed open the door. Adam was sitting on the sofa, staring at the woman in the tapestry.

'She left you a note,' I said.

I gave it to him and watched while he read. He blinked, put it in his pocket.

'Where was it?'

'In the workshop. I think if things had gone differently she'd have gone back and taken it.'

'So you were right, then,' he said, not looking at me. 'He was out there all the time. He killed Carol.'

'Yes. But not Daisy.'

'They'll hang him in any case when they find him, so does it matter?'

'Did you know she was going out last night to try to buy him off?'

'No, I'd have stopped her.'

'She had to steal her own money back from the workshop because Fardel was blackmailing her for anything he could get. She took the knife from there too. Up to the end, she might have been wondering whether to use it on herself or Fardel. Don't you think so?'

'She wouldn't have killed herself. She promised me she wouldn't kill herself.'

'Did you know he was blackmailing her?'

He shook his head.

'But the rest . . . ?'

'Yes . . . afterwards. On the Tuesday morning after . . .'

'After we found Daisy's body in the cabinet. No wonder she broke down. So she confessed to you that she killed Daisy?'

'She didn't mean to. She was trying to protect Daisy.'

Which fitted with Walter's story, but I didn't tell him so.

'Poor Daisy,' I said. 'We thought she was too timid to go anywhere on her own. But can you imagine how pleased she must have felt when Carol went to her and said her half-sister was in the village and wanted to meet her. So she left the other girls and went to the coppice and instead of her sister there was the man she never wanted to see again.'

The cruelty of it still amazed me.

'She was trying to do her best for all of us,' Adam said.

303

'So she brought the gun back and hid it in the summer-house. Did Felicia really just find that as she said?'

'Yes.'

And I was the one who jumped to the wrong conclusions, making both Daniel and Felicia suspects. I wasn't pleased with myself and I couldn't be angry with Adam any more. He'd had to sit there and see both his brother and his mistress coming close to a murder charge, facing an intolerable choice.

'Felicia thought you'd killed Daisy,' I told him.

'I know.'

'And you said nothing when the police arrested Daniel?'

'It's the hardest decision anybody could have to make. I wouldn't have let him go to trial. Neither of us would. We just hoped . . . I suppose hoped something would happen.'

'That I'd find Fardel? Pin the whole blame on him?'

'The blame should be on him. He's a monster.'

I said nothing, noting that he hadn't mentioned that Sutton was there when Daisy was killed. Carol hadn't told him. Sutton was the person she'd been trying to protect all along. It was as if even after her death she'd passed that responsibility on to me – still posthumously arranging things.

'You hate us all, don't you?' he said. 'You blame us all.'

'Is that the point now? The question is, what we're going to do. When the police catch Fardel, it will all come out anyway.'

'They won't believe anything he says.'

'So he'll be charged with two murders when he only committed one?'

A constable put his head round the door. Inspector Bull would be grateful for another word with Mr Venn. Also, the inspector had noticed me coming up the drive and would I please see him before I left. While I was waiting on my own I heard the sound of wheels on gravel, then Daniel's and Galway's voices in the hall sounding subdued, asking Annie where Adam was. Probably Galway had managed to arrange bail on compassionate grounds, but the charge against Daniel would soon be dropped in any case. He'd have to know why, but this time I wouldn't be the one who had to break the news. Every time I looked up, the woman who was so much like Carol was staring at me from the tapestry. It was almost a relief when the constable came back to say Inspector Bull was ready for me.

Our last meeting took place in the same upstairs room as the first one, with a different constable. It took a long time to get my statement down, from Fardel coming out of the carrier's cart to finding Carol's body. At the end of it he looked at me.

'Well, what are you hiding this time?'

'She killed Daisy. She didn't mean to and I didn't know until this morning.'

It had been another decision. If they never caught Fardel, if Adam had decided to say nothing about the note, nobody need ever know. Daisy would be tidied out of all our lives. It was only after I'd made the decision and spoken that I noticed the corner of Carol's envelope sticking out from under the inspector's papers. Perhaps he'd meant me to see it. He was nodding.

'Did Mr Adam Venn tell you that?'

'Yes,' I said. 'Just now.'

Not a lie, as it happened, and it meant I could leave out Sutton. I asked him if they were still looking for Luke Fardel.

'Oh, didn't I tell you? He was arrested on the road to Moreton-in-Marsh a couple of hours ago. Apparently he had a collision with a young lady on a horse.'

'Bobbie Fieldfare.' I was certain of it. 'Was she hurt?'

'I don't know the young lady's name, but there were no reports of any injuries. Not to her at any rate.'

It was the best news I'd had in weeks. I signed the statement and went downstairs and out. As I walked down the drive I saw two people in the garden. Daniel and Felicia walking slowly, heads down, a little distance between them. I guessed she was telling him about Adam and hoped for both their sakes that Carol had been right about her walking out of earthquakes.

Chapter Twenty-Four

I FOUND BOBBIE SITTING ON MRS Penny's doorstep in her brown check riding habit, with Mrs Penny peering round the curtains from inside as if under siege from some exotic and alarming animal.

'Don't you ever do what you're told?' I said.

'But I did. You told me to look out for him. I'd have had him yesterday only he got away with the hook, when I tried to reel him in.'

'I said you were on no account to try and do anything, just let me know if you found him.'

'I did try, but you weren't there. So I rode back and found him where I'd left him, asleep under a tree. He jumped up and tried to run away, so I reached out and got my riding crop hooked over his collar, only he twisted and got away, crop and all.'

'I found that crop.'

'Oh good. Can you let me have it back? It belongs to the friend I'm staying with.'

'I found it in the wagon where he was living. I thought he'd killed you. I nearly went mad worrying about you.'

'Anyway, I wasn't going to give up. I borrowed my friend's horse again and came across him in broad daylight, running along a road. He looked pretty well done in. He tried to dive into a ditch when he saw me but we went after him and skittled him over and then these two policemen came along in a dogcart and said they were looking for him. They spooked the mare and she bolted, but she's probably home by now, so that's all right.'

'Nothing's all right, nothing at all.'

She gave me a critical glance. 'You do look a bit tucked up. What's wrong? Is it true he's killed another woman?'

'Yes. Only he didn't kill the first one.'

'Did you know her?'

'Yes.'

There were things I didn't intend to explain to anybody, least of all Bobbie. Luckily, her butterfly mind didn't stay with any subject long enough to be curious. If her riding crop had held in Fardel's collar she might have been dead by now, or Carol Venn might have been alive and facing a murder charge on his evidence. Bobbie Fieldfare as an agent of the fates. I nudged her aside to make room on the step and sat down beside her, legs weak and shaky. Perhaps – against all previous evidence – she was thinking, because she went quiet for a while. Then:

'There are police all over the place, aren't there?'

Two constables visible from where we were sitting, standing outside the Crown looking thirsty. Half the police in the county must have been drafted in to look for Fardel, when it was too late.

'Yes, a lot of police.'

'So I suppose that means we can't do it today. I'll go back to my friend's and meet you here tomorrow when it's getting dark and—'

'What are you talking about?'

She looked at me, wide-eyed. 'Bessie Broadbeam. I know we had some bad luck last time but . . .'

In terms that even Bobbie could understand I told her what I thought of her, of myself, of pictures and the love of money.

'But if it's for the cause . . .'

'The cause doesn't need her. We're better off without her. I hope I never set eyes on her again.'

Pure, simple causes were what I longed for, nothing to do with love or money or all the mixed motives in between. You never get them, of course.

'It does seem a pity,' Bobbie said. Then, after another silence, 'I'm pretty sure I broke his collarbone, but if they're going to hang him anyway, I don't suppose it matters.'

Luke Fardel was hanged at Oxford several months later for the murder of Carol Venn. He still had Sutton's knife in his pocket when the constables dragged him out of the ditch where Bobbie had toppled him, blood all over him, down to his underclothes. At the trial Fardel claimed that Mrs Venn had lured him to the pool and tried to attack him. The sheer unlikelihood of that made the jurors grin and murmur, particularly since the judge cut short various other mutterings from the dock against the late Mrs Venn. He said Fardel was doing himself no good by trying to blacken a lady's reputation. I think it was in his mind that the prisoner was claiming some unlikely romantic liaison with Mrs Venn. I didn't attend the trial but when I heard about that my conscience pricked me into going to Oxford and speaking to Fardel's barrister. Without telling him the whole story I said that there could even be some truth in what his client had claimed and it might be worth speaking to Mrs Venn's husband. The barrister was elderly and cynical from a career of representing hopeless cases.

'Just suppose we were to take this seriously enough to subpoena the grieving widower for the defence and suggest that a frail and artistic young woman for some reason chose to make an assignation with a man like Fardel and attack him. Can you imagine the effect that would have on the jury?

I appreciate your concern, Miss Bray, but I really think that would be all we needed to make quite certain of the black cap.'

So that was that. Even if I'd wanted to do more – and he had killed her, after all – nobody signed clemency petitions for the likes of Luke Fardel. The murder of Daisy Smith remains on police files officially unsolved. Inspector Bull knows, but perhaps there was pressure from higher up to have him moved on to other things back at Oxford head-quarters. Harry Hawthorne wrote another trenchant paragraph about it in the *Wrecker*, then, like the rest of the world, moved on to other things.

As for our Odalisque, I had to see her again whether I wanted to or not. The lawyers went to work on the tangles of the Venn estate and Philomena's various trusts. Adam Venn some-how avoided prosecution and bankruptcy, the house was sold and, on a grey January day, the genuine version of the picture came up for auction at Christie's at last. As far as Emmeline was concerned, she was still my responsibility and I had to be there. It may have been in her mind that Oliver Venn would even at this point manage some last-minute substitu-tion, though he was comfortably tucked up by then as a permanent resident in a private hotel in Torquay. There was drizzle in the air, the umbrella stands at Christie's were crammed with damp black umbrellas, the hush of the crowded auction room disturbed by sniffs and muffled coughs. And yet, when the two white-gloved porters carried her in and settled her lovingly on the easel, it was like the sun coming out. The coughs stopped and a little sigh of pleasure flut-tered round the room. She sprawled on her cushions, pink and peachy, and the lazy mocking look in her eyes, chal-lenging anybody to put a price on her, did half the auction-eer's work for him. I can't pretend I followed the bidding because after a little hanging back it went so fast, but I did catch the resentful whisper of 'Americans' from a man behind me and the stir of excitement in the room. She was knocked down in the end for a very satisfactory sum of guineas.

As the porters took her off the easel to begin her long journey across the Atlantic there was a moment when her eyes seemed to be looking straight into mine, laughing. I thought how she, Bobbie and I had shuffled along the dark corridor, crammed into the broom cupboard among the mops and bedpans. I'd taken her to places where she wouldn't have wanted to go and she'd certainly done the same for me. She looked better on it than I did. I waved her goodbye and went back to Clement's Inn trying to be as pleased as everybody else would about the money.

Walter Sutton didn't have to go back to Swindon and the railway carriages after all. Some other lover of craftsmanship appreciated his work so much that he set up a new studio for him near Chipping Campden. He and Janie had another baby and last I heard were prospering. And Daniel and Felicia got married. He teaches music at a girls' school in London and in their spare time they run folk-dancing classes for children in the London docks. I happened to drop in on one of them recently and saw him leading the dancing with almost as much bounce as ever and her playing the piano, children's voices chanting *Here we come up the green grass, This fine day.* Not much green grass in the docklands. No place for a girl playing her violin in the firelight, insubstantial as a flame. But then those were wild times and she belonged in a different song.